Praise for Sherry Thomas

"Sherry Thomas dazzles with her intelligent, compelling story and memorable characters. This well-crafted romance places her among the very finest of the next generation of authors." —*Romantic Times* (Top Pick!) on *Delicious*

"Ravishingly sinful, intelligent and addictive." —Eloisa James, *New York Times* bestselling author, on *Private Arrangements*

"Sherry Thomas neatly blends subtly nuanced characters, a stylishly detailed late Victorian setting, and a sublime, fairy-tale-inspired romance into an irresistible literary treat." —*Chicago Tribune* on *Delicious*

"Sherry Thomas breathes new life into the historical genre with her rich, sensual tale. . . . You'll not want to be interrupted once you start." —Jane Litte, DearAuthor.com, on *Private Arrangements*

"Deft plotting and sparkling characters . . . Steamy and smart." —*Publishers Weekly* (starred review) on *Private Arrangements*

"A love story of remarkable depth . . . Entrancing from start to finish." —Mary Balogh, *New York Times* bestselling author, on *Private Arrangements*

"If you've worried (as I have) about the future of historical romance, just remember two words: Sherry Thomas. Readers, don't miss this one. It's a keeper and be very thankful that historical romance has a new, shining star."
—TheRomanceReader.c̶o̶m̶ ... *Private Arrangements*

D1014130

Also by Sherry Thomas
Published by Bantam Books

PRIVATE ARRANGEMENTS

DELICIOUS

Not Quite a Husband

SHERRY THOMAS

BANTAM BOOKS

A Bantam Books Mass Market Original

Published in the United States by Bantam Books, an imprint
of The Random House Publishing Group, a division of
Random House, Inc., New York.

BANTAM BOOKS and the rooster colophon are registered
trademarks of Random House, Inc.

ISBN 978-0-553-59243-6

Cover design: Yook Louie
Cover art: Alan Ayers

Printed in the United States of America

www.bantamdell.com

OPM 9 8 7 6 5 4 3 2 1

Getting a finished draft out of me takes
a good editor.
Making me cheerfully commit to start-over-from-
scratch revisions takes a great editor.
Getting a revised book out of me twice as good as
what I started with takes an extraordinary editor.

This book is dedicated to Caitlin Alexander,
my extraordinary editor.

Acknowledgments

My readers, for their encouragement.

Kristin Nelson and Sara Megibow of Nelson Literary Agency, who are not just fabulous agents, but all-around fabulous people.

My friend Vikram Jakkamsetti, M.D., Ph.D., for calmly and patiently answering all my questions about malaria. Sally Driscoll-Renta and Dr. Rainer Engel, for reassuring me that indeed surgeons still dug out bullets at the end of the nineteenth century.

Google Books, the best research tool I've ever had.

Courtney Milan, for unstintingly sharing her legal expertise.

Janine, for kind words, good advice, and pure friendship.

ACKNOWLEDGMENTS

Meredith Duran, whose superb globe scene in her debut book, *The Duke of Shadows*, inspired me to write my own globe scene—only without any globes, of course.

My wonderful husband, for capably shouldering the preponderance of household responsibilities when I'm buried under a deadline. My mother, for all the good food she cooked for me when I spent this past Christmas on my own, madly scribbling away.

And as always, if you are reading this, thank you. Thank you for everything.

Prologue

In the course of her long and illustrious career, Bryony Asquith was the subject of numerous newspaper and magazine articles, almost all of which described her appearance as *distinguished* and *unique*, and unfailingly commented upon the dramatic streak of white in her midnight dark hair.

The more inquisitive reporters often demanded to know how the white streak came about. She always smiled and briefly recounted a period of criminal overwork in her twenties. "It was the result of not sleeping for days on end. My poor maid, she was quite shocked."

Bryony Asquith had indeed been in her late twenties when it happened. She had indeed been working too much. And her maid had indeed been quite shocked. But as with any substantial lie, there was an important omission: in this case, a man.

His name was Quentin Leonidas Marsden. She'd known him all her life but never gave him a thought before he arrived in London in the spring of 1893. Within weeks of meeting him again, she proposed. Another month and they were married.

From the very beginning they were considered an unlikely pair. He was the handsomest, most popular, and most accomplished of the five handsome, popular, and accomplished sons of the seventh Earl of Wyden. By the time of their wedding, he, at age twenty-four, had had numerous papers read at the London Mathematical Society, a play staged at St. James's Theatre, and a Greenland expedition under his belt.

He was witty, he was in constant demand, he was universally admired. She, on the other hand, spoke very little, was not in demand, and was admired only in very limited circles. In fact, most of Society disapproved of her occupation—and the fact that she had an occupation at all. For a gentleman's daughter to pursue a medical training and then to go to work every day—*every day,* as if she were some common clerk—was it really necessary?

There were other unlikely marriages that defied all naysayers and prospered. Theirs, however, failed miserably. For her, that was; she'd been the miserable one. He had another paper read at the mathematical society; he published an acclaimed account of his adventures in Greenland; he was more lauded than ever.

By their first anniversary things had quite deteriorated. She'd barred the door to her bedchamber and he, well, she did not think he wallowed in celibacy. They no longer dined together. They no longer even spoke when they occasionally came upon each other.

They might have carried on in that state for decades but for something he said—and not to her.

It was a summer evening, some four months after she had first denied him his marital rights. She'd returned home rather earlier than usual, before the stroke of midnight, because she'd been awake for seventy hours—a small-scale outbreak of dysentery and a spate of strange rashes had her at her microscope in the laboratory when she wasn't seeing to patients.

She paid the cabbie and stood for a moment outside her house, head up, the palm of her free hand held out to feel for raindrops. The night air smelled of the tang of electricity. Already thunder rumbled. The periphery of the sky lit every few seconds, truant angels playing with lucifer matches.

When she lowered her face Leo was there, regarding her coolly.

He took her breath away in the most literal sense: She was too asphyxiated for her lungs to expand and contract properly. He aroused every last ounce of covetousness in her—and there was so much of it, hidden in the tenebrous recesses of her heart.

Had they been alone they'd have nodded and walked past each other without a word. But Leo had a friend with him, a loquacious chap named Wessex who liked to practice gallantry on Bryony, even though gallantry had about as much effect on her as vaccine injections on a cement block.

They'd been having excellent luck at the tables, Wessex informed her, while Leo smoothed every finger of his gloves with the fastidiousness of a deranged valet. She stared at his hands, her insides leaden, her heart ruined.

". . . awfully clever, the way you phrased it. How exactly did you say it, Marsden?" asked Wessex.

"I said a good gambler approaches the table with a plan," answered Leo, his voice impatient. "And an inferior gambler with a desperate prayer and much blind hope."

It was as if she'd been dropped from a great height. Suddenly she understood her own action all too well. She'd been gambling. And their marriage was the bet upon which she'd staked everything. Because if he loved her, it would make her as beautiful, desirable, and adored as he. And it would prove everyone who never loved her definitively wrong.

"Precisely!" Wessex exclaimed. "Precisely."

"We should leave Mrs. Marsden to her repose now, Wessex," said Leo. "No doubt she is exhausted after a long day at her noble calling."

She glanced sharply at him. He looked up from his gloves. Even in such poor soggy light, he remained the epitome of magnetism and glamour. The spell he cast over her was complete and unbreakable.

When he'd come to London, everyone and her maid had been in love with him. He should have had the decency to laugh at Bryony, and tell her that an old-maid physician, no matter the size of her inheritance, had no business proposing to Apollo himself. He should not have given her that half smile and said, "Go on. I'm listening."

"Good night, Mr. Wessex," she said. "Good night, Mr. Marsden."

Two hours later, as the storm shook the shutters, she lay in her bed shivering—she'd sat in her bath too long, until the water had chilled to the temperature of the night.

Leo, she thought, as she did every night. *Leo. Leo. Leo.*

She bolted upright. She'd never realized it before, but this recitation of his name was her desperate prayer, her blind hopes condensed into a single word. When had mere covetousness descended into obsession? When had he become her opium, her morphia?

There were many things she could tolerate—the world was full of scorned wives who went about with their heads held high. But she could not tolerate such pitiable needs in herself. She would not be as those wretches she'd witnessed at work, wild for the love of their poison, tenderly fueling their addiction even as it robbed them of every last dignity.

He was her poison. For him she'd abandoned sense and judgment. For the lack of him she could neither eat nor sleep. Even now her mind reached toward those few moments of all-encompassing happiness she'd known with him, as if they still mattered, as if they still shone untarnished amid the rubble heaps of her marriage.

But how could she free herself from him? They were married—only a year ago, in a lavish affair for which she'd spared no expense, because she wanted the whole world to know that *she* was the one he'd chosen, above all others.

Thunder boomed as if an artillery battle raged in the streets outside. Inside the house everything was silent and still. Not a single creak came from the stairs or the chamber that adjoined hers—she never heard any sounds from him anymore.

The darkness smothered her.

She shook her head. If she didn't think about it— if she worked until she was exhausted every day—she could pretend that her marriage wasn't a complete disaster.

But it was. A complete disaster, as cold as Greenland itself, and about as nourishing.

The solution came with the next flash of lightning. It was really quite simple. She had enough funds for enough lawyers to manufacture some sort of after-the-fact invalidity with the wedding ceremony. That plus one small lie—*This marriage has never been consummated*—would void the marriage altogether.

Then she could walk away from him, from the wreckage of the greatest and only gamble of her life. Then she could forget that she'd been stabbed in the heart, that all she'd ever known with him was a festering disappointment as unwholesome as any malarial swamp on the Subcontinent. Then she could breathe again.

No, she couldn't. She could never leave him. When he smiled at her, she walked on rose petals. The few times she'd allowed him to kiss her, for hours afterward everything had tasted of milk and honey.

If she asked for and received an annulment, he would marry someone else, and *she* would be his wife, give him the children Bryony knew she could not.

She did not want him to forget her. She would endure anything to hold on to him.

She could not stand this desperate, sniveling creature she'd become.

She loved him.

She hated both him and herself.

She hugged her shoulders tight, rocked back and forth, and stared into shadows that would not dispel.

வ§

She was still sitting up in bed, her arms wrapped around her knees, when her maid came in the morning. Molly went about the room, opening curtains and shutters, letting in the day.

She poured Bryony's tea, approached the bed, and dropped the tray. Something shattered loudly.

"Oh, missus. Your hair. Your hair!"

Bryony looked up dumbly. Molly rushed about the room and returned with a hand mirror. "Look, missus. Look."

Bryony thought she looked almost tolerable for

someone who hadn't slept in more than three days. Then she saw the streak in her hair, two inches wide and white as washing soda.

The mirror fell from her hand.

"I'll get some nitrate of silver and make a dye," Molly said. "No one will even notice."

"No, no nitrate of silver," Bryony said mechanically. "It's harmful."

"Some sulphate of iron then. Or I could mix henna with some ammonia, but I don't know if that will be—"

"Yes, you may go prepare it," said Bryony.

When Molly was gone she picked up the mirror again. She looked strange and strangely vulnerable— the desolation she'd kept carefully hidden made manifest by the translucent fragility of her white hair. And she had no one else to blame. She'd done this to herself, with her relentless need, her delusions, her willingness to risk it all for a mythical fulfillment conjured by her fevered mind.

She set aside the mirror, wrapped her arms about her knees, and resumed her rocking. She had a few minutes before Molly rushed back with the hair dye, before she must arrange a meeting with him to calmly and rationally discuss the dissolution of their marriage.

But before that, she would permit herself one last indulgence.

Leo, she thought. *Leo. Leo. Leo. It wasn't supposed to end this way.*

It wasn't supposed to end this way.

Chapter One

In the bright afternoon sun, the white streak was a gash of barrenness against the deep rich black of her hair. It started at the edge of her forehead, just to the right of center, swept straight down the back of her head, and twisted through her chignon in a striking—and eerie—arabesque.

It invoked an odd reaction in him. Not pity; he would no more pity her than he would pity the lone Himalayan wolf. And not affection; she'd put an end to that with her frigidity, in heart and body. An echo of some sort then, memories of old hopes from more innocent days.

In a white shirtwaist and a dark blue skirt, she sat between two fishing rods set ten feet apart, a bucket by her side, a twig in her hand, tracing random patterns in the swift-flowing, aquamarine water.

Across the stream, fields glinted a thick, bright gold in the narrow alluvial plain—winter wheat ready for harvest. Small, rectangular houses of wood and stacked stone piled one on top of another along the rising slope, like a collection of weathered playing blocks. Beyond the village, the ground elevated more rapidly, a brief stratum of walnut and apricot trees before the bones of the hills revealed themselves, austere crags that supported only dots of shrubs and an intrepid deodar or two.

"Bryony," he said. His head hurt, but he must speak to her.

She went still. The twig washed downstream, caught in a rock, then spun and floated free again. Still facing the stream, she wrapped her arms about her knees. "Mr. Marsden, how unexpected. What brings you to this part of the world?"

"Your father is ill. Your sister sent several cables to Leh, and when she received no response from you, she asked me to find you."

"What's the matter with my father?"

"I don't know the specifics. Callista only said that the doctors are not hopeful and that he wishes to see you."

She rose and turned around at last.

At first glance, her face gave the impression of great tranquillity and sweetness. Then one noticed the bleakness behind her green eyes, as if she were a nun on the verge of losing her faith. When she spoke, however, all illusions of meek melancholy fled, for she had the most leave-me-be voice he'd ever heard, not strident but stridently self-sufficient, and little concerned with anything that did not involve diseased flesh.

But she was silent this moment and reminded him of a churchyard stone angel that watched over the departed with a gentle, steady compassion.

"You believe Callista?" she asked, destroying the semblance.

"I shouldn't?"

"Unless you were dying in the autumn of ninety-five."

"I beg your pardon?"

"She claimed you were. She said you were somewhere in the wastes of America, dying, and desperately wanted to see me one last time."

"I see," he said. "Does she make a habit of it?"

"Are you engaged to be married?"

"No." Though he should be. He knew a number of beautiful, affectionate young women, any one of whom would make him a suitable spouse.

"According to her you are. And would gladly jilt the poor girl if I but give the command." She did not look at him as she said this last, her eyes on the ground. "I'm sorry that she dragged you into her schemes. And I'm much obliged to you for coming out this far—"

"But you'd rather I turned around and went back right away?"

Silence. "No, of course not. You'll need to rest and reprovision."

"And if I didn't need to rest or reprovision?"

She did not answer, but turned away from him. Then she bent down, retrieved a fishing rod, and reeled in something that was struggling to escape.

Weeks upon weeks of trekking across some of the most inhospitable terrains on Earth, sleeping on cold, hard ground, eating what he could shoot and the occasional handful of wild berries so he wouldn't be weighed down by a train of coolies carrying the usual necessities deemed indispensable for a *sahib*'s travels—and this was her response.

One should never expect anything else from her.

"Even the boy who cried wolf was right about the

wolf once," he said. "Your father is sixty-three years old. Is it so unlikely for a man of his age to ail?"

With a deft turn of her wrist, she unhooked the fish and dropped it into the bucket. "It is a six-week journey to England, on the off chance that Callista might be telling the truth."

"And if she is, you will regret not having gone."

"I'm not so certain about that."

Her ambivalence toward most of Creation had once fascinated him. He'd thought her complicated and extraordinary. But no, she was merely cold and unfeeling.

"The journey need not take six weeks," he said. "It can be done in four."

She looked back at him, her expression unyielding. "No, thank you."

It was 370 miles from Gilgit, where he'd been peacefully minding his own business, to Leh, that much again back to Gilgit, then 220 miles from Gilgit to Chitral. For most of the way he'd done three marches a day, sometimes four. He'd lost a full stone in weight. And he hadn't been this tired since Greenland.

Fuck you.

"Very well then." He bowed slightly. "I bid you a good day, madam."

❧

"Wait," she said—and hesitated.

He turned around halfway.

When she'd fallen in love with him, he'd been that magical man-child, with the beauty of a dark-haired Adonis and the playfulness of a young Dionysus. She couldn't think of anyone else who'd have gotten away with that song about a cold-blooded duchess and her very hot teapot, which had a three-inch spout that could nevertheless "fill all the right cups, be they shallow or deep, and then to patiently, lovingly steep."

Toward the end of their marriage, he'd already lost some of that deceptively cherubic sweetness to his looks. Now his profile had become angular and precipitous, like the bleak heights that concealed the Kalash Valleys.

"Are you leaving *now*?" she asked. She was conflicted about it, but it would be churlish to not at least offer him tea.

"No. I have promised to take tea with your friends, Mr. and Mrs. Braeburn."

"You met them already?"

"They were the ones who directed me to you," he answered, his tone matter-of-fact, but with an edge of impatience.

Suddenly she was alarmed. "And what did you tell them about us?"

Surely he would not have given the Braeburns an account of their short, infelicitous history.

"I didn't tell them anything. I showed them a photograph of you and asked if I might be able to find you here."

She blinked. He had a photograph of her? "What photograph?"

He reached inside his jacket, pulled out a squarish envelope, and held it out toward her. Beyond weariness, his expression gave away nothing. After a moment of wavering she wiped her hands with a handkerchief, walked to him, and took the envelope from his hand.

She opened the unsealed flap of the envelope and pulled out the photograph. Her retinas immediately burned. It was her wedding photograph. *Their* wedding photograph.

"Where did you get this?"

He'd moved out of their house in Belgravia the day after she'd asked for an annulment, leaving behind his copy of their wedding photograph on his nightstand, which she'd fed to the grate along with her copy.

"Charlie gave it to me when I passed through Delhi." Charles Marsden was Leo's second eldest brother, formerly political officer at Gilgit, another forward station on the Indian frontier, currently personal aide to Lord Elgin, Viceroy and Governor-General of India. "I suppose he didn't get the hint when I didn't take it with me, because he sent it again by post."

"What did the Braeburns say after you showed them the photograph?"

"That I'd find you fishing upstream by the water mill."

"Did they—did they recognize you?"

"I believe they did," he said coolly.

Surely, none of this was real. The man who had once been her husband was not standing before her, smelling of horse and road dust and speaking with a voice scratchy with fatigue. He did not mean for her to travel with him. And he had not exposed her as a sham to the kind and decent Braeburns.

"And what will you tell them now, when you sit down to tea?"

He smiled, not a very nice smile. "That will depend entirely on you. Were we to start our journey immediately after tea, I would compose a lovely tale of forced separation, heart-wrenching mutual longing, and a joyful reunion here in this most inaccessible of locales. Otherwise, I'll tell them we are divorced."

"We are *not* divorced."

"Let's not split hairs. It was a divorce in everything but name."

"They will not believe you."

"And they will believe *you* who, until a quarter hour ago, was a widow?"

She took a deep breath and turned her head. "It cannot be helped. To me, you no longer exist."

From time to time she would be at the most incidental activity—lacing her boots or reading an article on the adhesion of the intestine to the stump after an ovariotomy—and a physical memory would barrel out of nowhere and mow her down like a runaway carriage.

The boutonnière he'd worn the evening he first kissed her, a single stephanotis blossom, pure white, as tiny and lovely as a snowflake.

The sensation of raindrops on warm wool as she placed her hand on his sleeve—he'd come personally to the curb to see her into her carriage—and the wonderful stillness of her world as he said, smiling, through the still-open carriage door, "Well, why not? It should be no hardship to be married to you."

The almost prismatic glint of sunlight on the fob of his enameled watch—which she'd given to him as an engagement present. He held it suspended in midair, staring at its pendulum swing, while she asked for his cooperation in obtaining an annulment.

But mostly those upsurges of memory were

nothing but ghost pains, nervous misfires from limbs that had been long since amputated.

To me, you no longer exist.

He moved as if in recoil. As if he flinched. When he spoke, however, his voice was wholly serene. "Divorced it is then."

Chapter Two

M r. and Mrs. Braeburn were originally from Edinburgh. Mr. Braeburn was a Presbyterian minister and an avid scholar of the lands and peoples between the frontier of Russia and the frontier of India. Mrs. Braeburn said, laughing, that she'd married Mr. Braeburn thinking she'd be arranging flowers for the church and taking soup to sick parishioners, only to spend most of their married life tramping all over the Himalayas. For the past ten months they'd lived in Rumbur Valley, studying the cosmology of the Kalasha, the last unconverted people of the Hindu Kush—an island of paganism in a sea of Islam.

Because the stacked stone Kalasha house the Braeburns occupied was not much larger than a postbox, tea was held alfresco. The Commander, the

Braeburns' small Portuguese cook, had managed to make a fresh cake in the time since Leo's arrival. With eggs, Mrs. Braeburn informed him, smuggled in two days before from the nearest Muslim village, since the Kalasha's religion frowned upon both chicken and eggs in the diet.

Leo managed a grin at this account of The Commander's ingenuity. Mrs. Braeburn returned a nervous smile. She was waiting, Leo realized, for Bryony to join them. And then The Questions would finally be asked.

When Bryony did appear, conversation stopped. She carried the fishing rods in her right hand, the bucket in her left. She'd fished often when she was fifteen, spending the whole day by herself, with a basket of sandwiches and a canteen. His eleven-year-old self used to watch her from the opposite bank of the stream, wishing he knew what to say to the silent, intense girl from the neighboring estate.

To me, you no longer exist.

To her, he'd never existed, except those few wonderful weeks before their wedding that distant spring of 1893.

He watched her wend her way past women in vibrantly embroidered black robes guiding water into the irrigation canals that supplied the fields of wheat, women in vibrantly embroidered black robes shaking ripe mulberries from trees onto blankets, women in vibrantly embroidered black robes cutting hay to make winter fodder.

Mrs. Braeburn said something about the Kalasha men being away at summer high pasture. Leo nodded, barely registering her words. Bryony handed the bucket and the fishing rods to The Commander, who was chopping carrots on the veranda of the house, with a soft "Only one, I'm afraid." And then she approached the table at last.

He rose. His joints ached with the movement—all the traveling had taken its toll on him. The fever that had ragged at him since he set out from Chitral in the morning was beginning to subside, the chills largely gone, but his headache still lingered. He wished he'd thought to take some more phenacetin in Ayun.

"Mrs. Marsden," he murmured as he pulled out her chair.

The corners of her lips tightened. She glanced at him, then at the Braeburns, as if trying to gauge how much truth had been irreversibly spilled.

"Oh good, now we are all here," said Mrs. Braeburn, her cheer rather overbright.

She poured tea for Bryony, who accepted the teacup, but set it down in the same motion. "Do you still have your special whiskey, Mr. Braeburn?"

Mr. Braeburn cleared his throat. "Why, yes."

"Would you mind serving us a few drops of it?"

So whatever she'd decided needed the help of strong liquor.

"Of course not," said Mr. Braeburn, somewhat puzzled. "I was going to serve it at dinner, but I suppose now is as good a time as any."

He gestured at The Commander. The Commander ducked into the house and promptly returned with a bottle of whiskey and four small glasses.

Mr. Braeburn poured. "What shall we drink to?"

"To fond memories," said Bryony, raising her glass. "Mr. Marsden and I are leaving as soon as my belongings can be packed. I wish to take this moment to thank you both for your excellent and admirable friendship."

"So soon?" gasped Mrs. Braeburn. "But why?"

Bryony gave Leo a hard stare. "Mr. Marsden can tell it far better than I."

Across the table she sat rigidly, as tightly wound as the mainspring of a newly cranked clock. He still remembered a time when the tension she carried within her had been unbearably erotic to him, when he'd believed that all she needed was some proper lovemaking to turn her limp, relaxed, and happy.

Life had its way of beating humbleness into a man.

Bryony felt it in her stomach, the keen pitch of interest around the table, including her own—she had no idea what he could possibly say. But he was in no hurry to gratify the collective curiosity. With great leisure, he finished the remainder of the cake on his plate.

He reached for his glass of whiskey. Instead of lifting it, however, he only turned it a few degrees by its base. For the first time, she noticed the condition of his hands. When they'd been married, he'd had very fine, gentlemanly hands. Today his fingers were rough and chapped, with faint cuts and bruises along his knuckles.

But then he smiled at his audience and she forgot all about his hands, for it was a smile that conquered, as sweet as it was merciless. With that smile came a light in his eyes, an irresistible light: This was the Leo who had taken London by storm.

"It's a long story," he said, taking a sip of Mr. Braeburn's whiskey, "so I will tell only a very condensed version of it.

"Mrs. Marsden and I grew up on adjacent properties in the Cotswold. But the Cotswold, as fair as it is, plays almost no part in this tale. Because it was not in the green, unpolluted countryside that we fell in love, but in gray, sooty London. Love at first sight, of course, a hunger of the soul that could not be denied."

Bryony trembled somewhere inside. This was not their story, but *her* story, the determined spinster felled by the magnificence and charm of the gorgeous young thing.

He glanced at her. "You were the moon of my existence; your moods dictated the tides of my heart."

The tides of her own heart surged at his words, even though his words were nothing but lies.

"I don't believe I had moods," she said severely.

"No, of course not. 'Thou art more lovely and more temperate'—and the tides of my heart only rose ever higher to crash against the levee of my self-possession. For I loved you most intemperately, my dear Mrs. Marsden."

Beside her Mrs. Braeburn blushed, her eyes bright. Bryony was furious at Leo, for his facile words, and even more so at herself, for the painful pleasure that trickled into her drop by drop.

"Our wedding was the happiest hour of my life, that we would belong to each other always. The church was filled with hyacinths and camellias, and the crowd overflowed to the steps, for the whole world wanted to see who had at last captured your lofty heart.

"But alas, I had not truly captured your lofty

heart, had I? I but held it for a moment. And soon there was trouble in Paradise. One day, you said to me, 'My hair has turned white. It is a sign I must wander far and away. Find me then, if you can. Then and only then will I be yours again.'"

Her heart pounded again. How did he know that she had indeed taken her hair turning white as a sign that the time had come for her to leave? No, he did not know. He'd made it up out of whole cloth. But even Mr. Braeburn was spellbound by this ridiculous tale. She had forgotten how hypnotic Leo could be, when he wished to beguile a crowd.

"And so I have searched. From the poles to the tropics, from the shores of China to the shores of Nova Scotia. Our wedding photograph in hand, I have asked crowds pale, red, brown, and black, 'I seek an English lady doctor, my lost beloved. Have you seen her?'"

He looked into her eyes, and she could not look away, as mesmerized as the hapless Braeburns.

"And now I have found you at last." He raised his glass. "To the beginning of the rest of our lives."

❧

Leo had not come alone—he'd hired the necessary personnel in Chitral to ensure a comfortable journey for Mrs. Marsden, he'd explained to the Braeburns.

The coolies he'd brought with him began taking down Bryony's tent shortly after tea.

The tent, rugged and waterproof, was open and cool in summer. In winter it manfully bore a foot of snow and, with the help of her heaviest overcoat and two paraffin burners, kept her blood from congealing in her sleep.

Bryony experienced a moment of sharp distress as the tent came apart. Or perhaps it was fear: She was afraid to go with him.

The collapsing of the tent exposed its paltry contents: a camp bed, two steamer trunks, a folding table, and a folding chair. The table held a collection of old medical journals and her medical bag. One steamer trunk had a few toiletry items on top; the other her straw hat, a shawl, and two pairs of gloves.

Casually, he picked up her hat and turned it in his roughened hand. The knuckles of his other hand grazed across the brim. She swallowed. The gesture was intensely intimate, almost as if he were touching her hair. Her skin.

He set the hat down, went to his horse, and came back with another hat. "I took the liberty of buying you this. You can get sunburned easily in the lower altitudes if you are not careful."

The hat he presented her was practically a helmet, with a rolled-up flap in the back that released to shield the nape, and a veil of netting in the front, in case the sun became too harsh for the eyes.

His presumption galled her: He'd known precisely how he'd bend her to his will, long before he ever set foot in Rumbur Valley.

She returned the hat to him: "I cannot accept articles of clothing from a gentleman."

It was a convenient excuse. He was not related to her—or married to her. And therefore had no business buying such things for her.

He glanced down at the rejected hat. "That rule, if I'm not mistaken, does not apply to a gentleman who has fucked you."

At the last two words, he lifted his eyelashes. Such a current of heat jolted through her that she was unable to slap him as he richly deserved.

"You, sir, are no gentleman," she said. "And no, thank you. I will not wear that hideous thing."

He looked at her a minute, his gray eyes the color of morning mist, and she could not tell whether his expression was disgust, amusement, or something too dark and raw for easy labeling.

"Suit yourself," he said. "Let's have your things packed."

Everything she had went on her person, on a coolie, or on a mule. Scarcely an hour after tea, they were shaking the Braeburns' hands, saying their farewells and promising to write regularly.

After one last embrace with Mrs. Braeburn, Bryony mounted the spare horse that Leo had brought for her. He handed her the reins.

"I hope you are happy," she said quietly, for his ears alone.

He gave her a lopsided smile that was at once intimate and distant. "Oh, intemperately so."

Chapter Three

The afternoon was cool, the sky cloudless. Rumbur Valley, squeezed between two high ridges, lowered rapidly toward the southeast. They followed the descent of the river, blue with churns of white foam where it came to sudden drops and angles, and passed village after village—Grom, Maldesh, Batet, Kalashgram, Parakal.

Birds sang in rhododendron bushes that would have been wild with flamingo pink blooms in spring. Water wheels creaked productively. Kalasha women in their elaborate shell headdresses and deep-piled bead necklaces prepared dinner around fire pits on the verandas of their tiny houses.

The valley was not precisely a lost Eden—Kalasha children fetched high prices on the Chitrali slave market for their beauty and docility, Kalasha herds were subject to raids and poaching from their more aggressive neighbors—but for this day it was peaceful, shining, and idyllic.

Then the walls of the valley closed in. Fields, houses, and goat stables became scarcer, and then disappeared altogether. They exited Rumbur Valley where the Bumboret River and the Rumbur River joined, and entered a narrow gorge where no trees or grass grew. The river rushed impatiently far below; red and gray cliff walls blocked out the sun. Their path hung from the cliffs, twisting and turning with the whimsy of nature.

At dusk the defile gave onto the wide alluvial plains of the Chitral Valley. The town of Ayun, draped in paddy fields, lay before them, its architecture strikingly different from the openness Bryony had become used to among the Kalasha. Here the houses all had high mud walls to protect their female inhabitants from the eyes of strangers. Only boys and men walked abroad.

"I left the other coolies waiting for us on the outskirts," said Leo. "We have no need to go into town."

She was relieved and irked at the same time. "You've planned this well, haven't you?"

"It never hurts to be prepared," he answered smoothly.

He'd sent ahead their guide, a leathery man

named Imran, to inform the coolies of their arrival. By the time they rode into camp, an ayah had a hot towel on hand for Bryony to wipe away the dust of travel from her face. As she took her tea, buckets of steaming water were poured into the tub already set up in the bathing tent. And when she'd washed and dressed, she was given a plate of hot *pakoras,* vegetables dipped in gram flour batter and deep fried, to snack on while Leo bathed and the cooks prepared dinner.

They sat down to dinner at almost the exact time she would have sat down to dine with the Braeburns. Mrs. Braeburn enjoyed this time of the day, the wisps of wood smoke rising in the cooling air, the streaks of twilight in the sky, the first pinpricks of fireflies.

Dinner was mulligatawny soup, chicken cutlet, and curried lamb over rice. Bryony ate with her eyes on her food, cutting a trench around herself with her demeanor. But he did not take the hint.

"What were you thinking?" he asked, in the same dulcet tone he'd used to compare her to a summer's day. *Thou art more lovely and more temperate.* "Leaving Leh without a word to your family? And why were you in Leh to begin with—is nobody in need of doctors anymore in all of Delhi?"

She considered simply ignoring him. "Delhi was too hot," she said finally.

The heat had indeed been traumatic. Mere heat, however, she could have endured. But with Leo's brother in town, everyone seemed to know not only who she was but that her marriage had ended badly. She had not traveled thousands of miles to have a duplicate of London society thrust upon her.

"When the Moravian missionaries in Leh called for a temporary replacement for their resident doctor on home leave, I thought the climate would suit me better."

And the solitude.

Leh was the capital of Ladakh, a high, arid plateau to the east of Kashmir, otherwise known as Little Tibet. Bryony had thought Leh would be a sleepy hamlet long past its days of glory. Instead, Leh was still a bustling city, playing host to caravans from as far as Chinese Turkestan. Within sight of the abandoned palace from whose rafters still fluttered long strings of prayer flags, merchants from Yarkand and Srinagar traded with their counterparts from Lahore and Amritsar.

It was the Moravian mission house, as humble as a cowshed, that had been quiet and somnolent. There a handful of brave, naïve Christian do-gooders converted perhaps one Ladaki a year and slowly forgot their homelands.

Bryony had not planned to stay at the mission beyond the return of the resident doctor. She also had not looked forward to returning to Delhi. When a team of German alpinists coming back from a climb had passed through Leh on their way to Rawal Pindi, she'd bought a tent from them for no reason other than that the tent, a symbol of nomadic life, had appealed to the restlessness inside her. A week later, the Braeburns stopped by the dispensary. And when they told her they'd be most glad of the company of a physician on their westward journey, she'd said yes without another thought, ready to move again, her new tent in tow.

"But the climate of Leh didn't suit you any better, did it? And once you had enough of Leh, you bribed the missionaries to not reveal your destination to anyone."

She shrugged. "Don't you ever get tired of letters from Callista?"

Callista had missed her calling as a novelist. Her letters, when it came to Leo, were full of cheerful fabrications, little asides on his illnesses, disappointments, and courtships that were certain to upend Bryony with concern, helplessness, and jealousy.

When Bryony left Leh, she'd decided to do herself

a favor and sever all contact with Callista for a year. To that end, she'd scribbled enough short, uninformative letters for the good missionaries to post weekly and requested that they not give out her whereabouts to anyone—even Christian do-gooders could be tempted by the promise of five hundred pounds to keep a few harmless secrets.

"Letters are written on paper. You could have thrown them into the fire."

"I did."

But each time she burned a letter from Callista unread, it was a fresh reminder that she still cared—and cared too much. A far worse feeling than if she never received those letters in the first place.

He pulled out a silver flask from his coat pocket, took a swallow—Mr. Braeburn had insisted that Leo help himself to some of his special whiskey—and said nothing.

She was uncomfortably reminded that he was here because of her ruse. A coolie cleared away their dinner plates and set down a slice of mulberry tart before her. She poked at it. "I hope you didn't come all the way to India just because Callista asked you to find me."

"No, in fact, I was already in Gilgit."

"What were you doing in Gilgit?" She was astonished. Of all the places in the world he could be when Callista needed someone to find her, Gilgit, in the foothills of the Korakoram, somewhere halfway between Leh and Chitral, could not be a more convenient departing point.

"A friend of mine organized a ballooning expedition to reconnoiter the upper slopes of the Nanga Parbat. They decided on Gilgit as their base camp. Since Charlie had been the political officer at Gilgit before he went on to greener pastures in New Delhi, my friend invited me along to expedite matters, so to speak."

She tried to contemplate the mind-boggling coincidence of it and gave up.

"And how did you find me in the end?"

"You mean how did I pry your current location out of the missionaries?"

"No. I mean—did you show them the photograph too?"

It would have been the biggest scandal at the drowsy mission in years—the widowed physician's husband materializing out of nowhere. She did not care if people thought of her as cold or unapproachable, but she did not want to be remembered as deceitful.

He rolled his eyes. "I wish I could have. The photograph arrived in Gilgit only after I'd left to look for you in Leh."

She frowned. "Then how did you get the missionaries to tell you where I was? They were supposed to keep it a secret."

He took another swallow from the flask. She realized that he had not eaten much at all, had waved away the mulberry tart untouched.

"I pretended to be your very angry brother and threatened to burn down the place," he said.

"You did not."

He screwed the cap on the flask and pocketed it. "I did pretend to be one of your stepbrothers; I didn't have to pretend to be very angry. And no, I didn't threaten violence. I merely pointed out, very reasonably, that it would be terrible for it to be known that an English lady of means had disappeared from the mission—people would instantly construe that she'd been done in for her money. That prospect frightened our missionaries quite a bit, though by that time they'd hemmed and hawed for so long that I was more than half ready for arson."

She chewed slowly on a forkful of tart, then patted the corners of her lips with a napkin. "It was not my intention to inconvenience you. I only wanted to get away."

He did not ask her from what she was trying to

get away. She'd left England as soon as the annulment was granted, spent the rest of '94 in Germany, most of '95 in America, and arrived in India early in '96. But the past, it seemed, had a way of catching up no matter how far she traveled.

"Get some rest," he said. "Tomorrow we start south."

He was the one who needed rest. The more she looked at him, the more he looked not just abruptly lean, but malnourished.

"How long have you been on the road?"

His brows furrowed. "I've lost track. Six and a half weeks. Seven. Something like that."

From Gilgit east to Leh, then from Leh back through Gilgit to Chitral and the Kalash Valleys: It must be close to a thousand miles. A thousand miles over a roadless land that was full of teeth and serrated spine, where even the flat stretches were fragmented and disjointed. She did not know it was possible to make this trek in under fifty days.

And he would have had to be minimally equipped, with probably only a guide to show him the way, for it was definitely not possible to achieve such speed with coolies, cooks, tents, and beds.

"How?" she asked, in sheer puzzlement. And then, more important, "Why? Why did you do it?"

"Why did I do it?" he echoed her question, as if surprised by it.

"Yes. Why not tell Callista to go to the Devil?"

He chortled, a sound that contained more scorn than mirth. "Callista knows how to pick her fools, apparently."

❧

Their paths would never have crossed again had Bryony's stepmother not invited Leo for dinner.

After she graduated from medical school in Zurich, Bryony had obtained her practical and clinical training at the Royal Free Hospital and then accepted a resident post at the New Hospital for Women, both situated in London. For convenience, she lived at the Asquith town house with her father, sister, stepmother, and stepbrothers but she participated only minimally in either familial or social functions.

On that particular day, she'd had half a mind to take her dinner in her room. She'd worked a long shift and she was never in the mood for company even on the best of days. But they'd have been thirteen at the table, so she'd reluctantly dressed and presented herself in the drawing room.

And then he'd arrived and smiled at her. And she'd spent the evening in a haze, not knowing what she ate or said, aware only of him, the spark in his gray eyes when he spoke, the shape of his lips as he smiled.

From that day hence she lived in search of him. She

accepted invitations to anything that might include him. She went to his heavily attended lecture on Greenland at the Royal Geographical Society. She even braved many a surprised look to listen to him read a paper at the mathematical society, though beyond the first minute she understood not a thing.

Curiously enough, she had no aspirations at all concerning him. A drunk did not expect the bottle to love him back; and she only wished to drink him in whenever she could.

That was, until he kissed her.

It was at the house of his eldest brother, the Earl of Wyden. Specifically, in the library, while a musical soiree raged in the drawing room. She had been quite dejected by his absence—she'd been sure he'd be there, since he was temporarily lodging with the Wydens. But she couldn't leave yet, as Callista, who'd wanted no human contact as a child, had somehow developed as an adult a great fondness of large gatherings of Homo sapiens.

So she'd sought solace in an encyclopedia. Incunabula. Indazoles. Indene. Index Librorum Prohibitorum.

Abruptly she became aware that she was no longer alone in the library. He stood just inside, his back against the door.

"Mr. Marsden!" How long had he been there, watching her?

"Miss Asquith."

His regard was unsmiling. She was not used to this seriousness from him, he who was always in the merriest of moods. Then he did smile, one of his dazzling smiles that restored sight to the blind and instilled music in the deaf. But even that smile had an undercurrent to it that made her heart do medically worrisome things.

"I wouldn't read at that desk if I were you," he said.

"Oh?"

"Both Charlie and Will lost their virginity on that desk."

Her hand went to her bare throat. The pulse under her thumb hammered. "Goodness," she managed. It was better than an outright squeak, but not by much.

"Why don't you come away?" he said with a deceptive gentleness.

She would dearly love to, but for some reason, her legs were quite rubbery. "Surely, my virtue should be quite safe in this house."

He left the door, came to the edge of the desk, and smiled again, a smile beatific enough to bring about peace on Earth. "Has anyone ever made an effort to rid you of your virtue, Miss Asquith?"

She couldn't remember ever having such a startlingly inappropriate conversation. Yet she did not want him to stop. His words had a darkly pleasurable effect on her, like very fine liqueur mixed with very fine chocolate.

"Nobody is interested in my virtue. Or the riddance of it."

"That can't be true."

"It is."

"All right, if you insist. But one can sin a great deal with a woman of intact virtue."

Good gracious. She swallowed. "I'm sure one can. But I assure you, sir, my sins, whatever they are, are not of the carnal variety."

"Mine are," he murmured. "Whatever else they are, they are also of the carnal variety."

"Well, how very . . . diverting for you."

He moved even closer, next to the chair in which she sat. "I must confess, Miss Asquith, I feel an urgent need to make up for the attention the masculine species owes you."

"I'm—I'm quite certain that the masculine species owes me nothing."

He leaned forward and placed his hand on the armrest of the chair. "I disagree strongly."

She pushed her body against the back of the chair. "And how will you rectify things?"

"Make love to you, of course, thoroughly and tirelessly."

So much of her melted that she was surprised she did not slide under the table. "Here?!"

This time, it was a squeak, quivering and breathless.

"Did I not warn you about this desk and the iniquity it inspires? You should have left when you could. It's too late now."

He whispered those last words almost directly against her lips. Her heart slammed, like an unsecured shutter in a windstorm. Far away in the drawing room someone more ambitious than talented launched into the opening bars of Beethoven's Fifth Symphony. Here in a corner of the library she understood for the first time that yes, it was exactly this that she sought from him, this proximity, this great disequilibrium.

He laughed then, a burst of mirth, as if he'd been keeping a straight face a long time and finally could no more. "I'm sorry. You looked so studious when I came in, I couldn't help myself."

It took her perhaps a dozen heartbeats to understand that he'd been teasing her. That none of it had meant anything.

"Come." He offered her his arm. "Your sister was looking for you. I told her I'd locate you and take you back."

She rose and pushed past him. "It was not funny."

"I apologize. I didn't mean to take it as far as I did. But you were so delectably innocent—"

"I am not. What's making love but a penis penetrating a vagina, discharging semen in the process?"

He was taken aback. Then he smiled lopsidedly. "That is most edifying. And here I thought it was all about valentines and sonnets."

"Well, I'm glad one of us is amused," she said huffily.

She made for the door, but he reached it before she did.

"You are angry. Was I truly reprehensible?"

"Yes, you were." Here she was, following in the wake of this beautiful young man like a devoted dog, while for him *she was but an elderly virgin—almost twenty-eight, oh the horror—and any thoughts of intimacy with her must begin and end in farce. "I will have you know I do not lack for masculine admiration. And I know exactly how to sin to keep my virtue intact. There is frottage. There is manual manipulation. There is oral stimulation. Not to mention good old bugg—"*

He kissed her. She had no idea how it happened. One moment she was in the middle of her irate speech and he had his back against the door. The next moment her back was against the door, he was kissing her, and she was frozen in shock.

He pulled back slightly. "My God," he murmured. "Did I just do that?"

The door seemed to vibrate behind her back; the Gs and Fs and D flats from the drawing room sent hot little pings along her vertebrae. Leo Marsden kissed her. She didn't know what it meant. Did young people kiss for amusement nowadays? Should she demand an apology? Did women still slap men for such unauthorized incursions?

"You had me convinced for a moment . . ." His voice trailed off.

Of course she meant to convince him. She wanted him to think that beneath her elderly virgin exterior was a Messalina who hosted wild orgies at dispensaries across the city. But what did that have to do with anything?

"I might as well kiss you properly now," he murmured.

"I suppose you might as well," she heard herself answer, still indignant.

His lips came very close to hers. "What kind of soap do you use?"

"I don't know. The strongest."

"You don't smell like any other woman I know."

"What do they smell like?"

"Flowers. Spice. Musk, sometimes. You, on the other hand, make me think of industrial-strength solvents."

She stared at his mouth. "Do you like industrial-strength solvents?"

His lips curved a little. And then he kissed her again, a curious but unhurried kiss, as light as a butterfly's landing, as patient as the tides. A kiss almost innocent enough for public viewing—he touched her nowhere else, except for his fingers under her chin. A kiss that felt oddly like falling, and oddly like flying.

So this was why people did it, she thought faintly, despite the act of kissing being one of the surest vectors of disease transmittal. How strangely pleasurable it was. And breathtaking. And electrifying—currents must have been generated by the locking of their lips, because every nerve in her sizzled, every cell sang.

She wasn't sure when the kiss ended. She emerged from a daze and had to blink for everything around her to come back into focus.

"Promise me you won't kiss me again," he said. "Or you will ruin me for all other women."

Likely he delivered the same line to every woman he'd ever kissed—it was too perfect to be spontaneous. But it made her dizzy all the same. She nodded slowly.

"Good. Because I would never forgive you, were you to break my heart." He smiled, the very image of gilded youth, beloved of the gods. "Now shall we go before Callista comes looking for us?"

Chapter Four

Over breakfast, Bryony feigned a steady interest in the blood-and-gold sunrise over the jagged peaks that formed the eastern wall of Chitral Valley. But out of the corner of her eye, she followed Leo's movements around the camp. He supervised the dismantling and packing of the tents, checked the load on each mule, conferred with the guides, and even spoke to a few of the coolies and the ayah in some native tongue.

This last did not reassure her, for she had seen *sahibs* and *memsahibs* go at their native attendants in a mixture of English and what they believed to be Hindi and then simmer in frustration when the attendants returned with a sheaf of betel leaves instead of a glass of water.

But she was in his hands now.

The Chitral region was the pinnacle of the Hindu Kush, containing its tallest peaks and greatest glaciers. From Gilgit, Leo had come via the 12,000-foot Shandur Pass. To return to the plains of India, they would scale the 10,500-foot Lowari Pass, cross into still-mountainous Dir, and proceed south.

Mountain travel was one of Bryony's least favorite pastimes. Her trip from Kashmir to Leh, with a trio of English tourists, had been marred by squabbling coolies, bad food, and incessant complaints on the part of the English tourists about the laziness and untrustworthiness of all Kashmiris. The trek from Leh to Chitral, while without quite the bad blood, had suffered from chronic disorganization, the cooks falling far behind while the travelers starved, cake for tea saturated in fishy oil because it had been packed next to an open tin of sardines, and the Braeburns' galvanized iron bath unusable for much of the trip, as a result of having had three holes knocked in it from careless handling.

"You said we can be in Peshawar in one week?" she asked when he came to tell her that they were ready to depart.

"Peshawar is out of our way. Nowshera is closer."

"We can be in Nowshera in one week?"

"I can in four days. Whether *we* can in a week depends on how hardy a traveler you are."

She was hardy enough. But *he* had shadows under his eyes. He was thin almost to the point of gauntness. And despite the tan of his skin, his face had a pallor to it.

An unwilling concern tugged at her. The constant travel of the past so many weeks had worn him down. He must be close to a state of exhaustion. To attempt to reach Nowshera in four days—or even a week—would probably send him into a breakdown.

"Have you had breakfast?" she asked.

He'd already started to walk away. He stopped. "I had something earlier."

"What did you have?"

He frowned, as if irritated by her detailed questioning. "Some porridge or such."

That was scarcely enough nutrition for an already underfed man who had a strenuous trip ahead. She examined him again, looking for some visual clue to his state of less-than-robust health.

"Are you suffering from a suppressed appetite?"

"I would have thought that to be a natural result of seeing you," he said, in perfectly polite viciousness.

She bit her lower lip. "Is that a yes or a no?"

"That is an 'I don't need a doctor so leave me be.'" He pivoted on his heels, then turned back toward her. "And even if I did need a doctor, you are the last doctor I would choose."

Are you quite certain you haven't developed some dreadful condition that will lead to much bleeding, vomiting, and putrefaction? Will had asked—only half jokingly—when Leo had relayed the news of his betrothal. *I've never known Bryony Asquith to display the least interest in a healthy man.*

You are feeling inadequate because she never displayed the least interest in you, Leo had replied, laughing, on top of the world, gloriously young and gloriously stupid.

He raised his hand for an ironic tip of the hat toward her, but she reached forward and caught his wrist. Her fingers were cool, her grip firm but not tight: impersonal. And her hair, her beautiful hair, ruined, like a bolt of silk slashed by a careless knife.

"You may not have a choice of doctor," she said calmly. "The next nearest trained physician is at the garrison in Drosh. Beyond that, none until Malakand."

After fifteen seconds or so, she released his wrist and placed her palm against his forehead.

He didn't want to be so close to her. And he emphatically did not want her to touch him. "I'm not running a fever," he said impatiently.

Though he might, tomorrow. It had started almost a week ago, with dizziness and body ache. But he was well the next day, so he'd chalked it up to fatigue. Then the day after that, he'd run a low fever with chills. And so it went, one day relatively better, next day not so well. With every cycle, however, the fever got worse, as did the chills. Yesterday he'd even shivered when he'd passed through the sunless defile on his way to Rumbur Valley.

She withdrew her hand and regarded him with some puzzlement. "No, there is no fever. Do you have any rashes or spots? Localized pain? Generalized pain? Dizziness? Shivering?"

Will had been right. She was only ever interested in a man's physical malfunctions.

"No, nothing. I already told you, I don't need a doctor. Let's stop wasting time. We've a long way to go."

"Not today," she said.

"I beg your pardon?"

"I'm not used to being in a saddle anymore—I need a few days to get accustomed. I don't wish to ride too long today."

He would have much preferred to get them through Lowari Pass by the end of the day—if the fever returned again tomorrow, more severe than the previous time, he didn't know if he could handle either the trek up to the pass or the descent.

Her request vexed him. Perhaps if she were a more

delicate sort of woman . . . but when they'd been married she'd worked appalling hours. Despite her insubstantial frame, she was the last thing from delicate.

"All right," he said grudgingly. "I'll make sure we don't ride for too long today."

"Thank you," she said. "Most kind of you."

She inclined her head and walked away toward her waiting horse. Only then did the strangeness of her request make itself felt. This was not at all like her. The Bryony he knew would rather have her haunches rubbed raw by the saddle than admit anything was the matter, the way she'd suffered through his love-making with clenched fists and rigid thighs.

Sometimes people change, said a voice inside him.

And sometimes they don't.

❧

They crossed the river at Drosh, where Leo took the trouble to telegraph Callista from the British garrison to let her know that he'd found Bryony and that they would cable again when they had reached Nowshera. Afterward they had a light tiffin and continued on their journey—which, surprisingly enough, was smooth and without any memorable incidents whatsoever.

They stopped for the day at the edge of an orchard

and waited for the coolies to catch up so they could strike camp. Bryony sat atop a waist-high retaining wall, fanning herself with her straw hat. He stood with his back against the same wall, facing the slender blue river below.

The river looped half a circle here, near the tapered southern end of Chitral Valley. The arable land on either side of the sinuous bend was terraced to cultivate tiers upon tiers of rice, maize, and fruit trees. But the scale of human occupation was dwarfed by enormous crags that jutted skyward on three sides.

"You still don't speak to your father?" he asked.

The question snapped her out of her determined contemplation of the river. "I've never *not* spoken to my father," she said.

He looked up from the pear he was peeling with a pocketknife. Again she noticed his hard-worn hands. But their motion was still elegant: The peel of the pear fell in one long, unbroken curl.

He'd bought the fruit from the owner of the orchard. Bryony liked pears very much. But she was damned if she would ask him for any. Perhaps later, when he was busy supervising the setting up of the tents, she'd slip away and buy a few for herself.

"You don't care whether your father lives or dies," he pointed out.

His hat sat at a careless angle on his head. His clothes could surely use a thorough ironing. And he seemed far too fatigued to be awake, let alone standing—she was very glad she'd chosen to limit his exertion by refusing to ride more than twenty miles. But she could not stop looking at him, standing there, peeling his pear, his jacket hanging loosely about his frame. And she could not help feeling for him something close to tenderness, as if he were a weary, lost traveler Fate had cast at her doorstep.

"Geoffrey Asquith is a stranger to me."

"Fathers shouldn't be strangers."

She shrugged. "Sometimes they are."

"Like husbands?" he said, not looking at her, smiling oddly.

But apparently he did not expect her to answer that question, for he handed her a slice of pear. She hesitated, then stripped off one glove and accepted. The pear was cool and juicy, sweet with a trace of that faint bitterness particular to pears.

She'd never imagined they'd be strangers. Sometimes she wished Miss Jones had never fallen prey to food poisoning. Then she would never have been called upon to perform the caesarean section in Miss Jones's stead at that house on Upper Berkley Street. Then her illusion would have remained intact.

And they might still be married, and today she might still be ignorantly content.

She put her hat back on and tied the ribbons firmly under her chin. "So how was my father when you saw him last?"

Unlike her, Leo had always been on the best of terms with everyone in her family. He seemed to find something to like about each one of them; and they admired him ardently in return.

He raised one straight brow. "My, and here I thought you were completely heartless."

She stiffened. "Maybe I am. Maybe this is merely a pretense to converse."

He snorted. "You don't know how to converse. Sometimes I think the spaces between the stars are filled with your silence."

"That's not true. I talk."

"When you are forced to." He offered her another piece of the pear. She had half a mind to decline, but the pear was very fresh and just the perfect ripeness.

"When I dined with your family at the beginning of the year, your father seemed hale enough. Before I left, he presented me with a copy of his new book on Milton. I read it crossing the Red Sea." He glanced at her. "You've never read any of his books, have you?"

She shook her head. She'd never read them, but she'd burned some copies when she was eight or nine, when she still cared that Geoffrey Asquith had all the time in the world for his books but none for his daughter.

"It was an excellent book, with much insightful analysis."

"I am sure it was. How was Callista?"

"Same as always, full of quirks and oddities of her own. And still not married."

"She takes after me then. Everyone else?"

"Your stepmother looked somewhat frail. She'd fractured her wrist the previous winter and hadn't gone out in public for a while. Paul was the same. Angus was nursing a broken heart over having his marriage proposal rejected by Lady Barnaby." He offered her yet another slice of pear. "But you don't really care about them, do you?"

He didn't know her at all. And yet sometimes he knew her so well it frightened her.

"How is your family?"

He gave her a bemused look, but answered. "Well enough. Will and Lizzy have moved back to London. Matthew is commanding astronomical sums for his portraits. Charlie has decided he will marry any living, breathing woman willing to become a stepmother to his vast brood. And Jeremy is just busy being the earl."

His siblings all adored him, their baby brother.

And both of his late parents had been devoted to him. The favorite, the beloved, who knew nothing of neglect and desperate loneliness.

"And Sir Robert, is he well?"

He is the finest young man I know, and you without question, the stupidest woman, Leo's godfather had coldly informed Bryony on the eve of the granting of the annulment.

"Quite well. It's a good time to be a banker with all the gold wealth pouring in from South Africa."

She nodded. In time, a good chunk of that wealth would go to Leo. Would she still have had the courage to propose to him had she known of his place in his godfather's will, known that he didn't really need the money she'd bring to the marriage? Yes, probably. Once he'd kissed her, all she could think about was kissing him again and again—and doing everything else that had, until then, seemed ridiculous on paper, acts that ought to cause civilized people to die of embarrassment.

"You should have saved a few of your questions," he said, biting into the stump of the pear. "We will have nothing to say to each other for the rest of the trip."

She looked at him, looked at her now-empty hands, and realized that he'd given all the good pieces of the pear to her, that he himself hadn't eaten any until now.

And she suddenly had one more question—because it was far easier to tell him that he no longer existed for her than to actually make it so. Because the tides of her heart demanded it.

"And how have *you* been?"

He tossed away the core of the pear. "What do you care?"

She compressed her lips. And shrugged.

"Ah, I forgot, you are but conversing," he said, with a tilt of his lips that wasn't a smile. "I would say I have done exceptionally well. I have traveled the world, met interesting men and beautiful women, and been feted and toasted wherever I went."

She could very well believe that: a simple return to his glamorous bachelor life.

He wiped his hands with a handkerchief. Stowing the handkerchief back in his pocket, he braced his hands on either side of him. The hand closest to her rested in the shadow cast by his own person. Out of the direct reach of the light, the cuts and bruises on his knuckles weren't so prominent, only the elegant shape of his fingers.

During their extremely brief engagement, he'd called on her every Sunday afternoon. And whenever they were left alone in her father's drawing room, he would set those long, tapered fingers upon her person. She'd let him hold her hand, but his fingers always stole further north. On his last Sunday call, he'd managed to not only unbutton her sleeve, but kiss her on the tender inside of her elbow. And she, trembling with newly awakened desire, had not been able to sleep a wink that night.

"And you, how have *you* been?" he asked, as if it were an afterthought.

Outwardly, other than her hair, she had not changed much. She was still more or less the same cool, aloof woman who garnered more respect than affection. On the inside, however, it had been impossible to return to the person she used to be.

She'd been content. She had not wanted to marry. Nor had she much interest in the largely empty rituals of Society. Medicine was a demanding god and she a busy acolyte in its vast temple.

Then he had come into her life. And it was as if she'd been struck by lightning. Or a team of archaeologists had dug up the familiar scenes of her mind to reveal a large, ancient warren of unmet hunger and frustrated hope.

It took her some time, after leaving him, to realize that she could never go back to the staid, narrow obliviousness that had characterized much of her twenties, when she'd been blithely unaware of all the secrets and upheavals just beneath the surface of her heart.

But except for a curious restlessness that had her pack her bags and move to the opposite end of the globe every year or so, she'd coped—if she hadn't been at peace, then at least she wasn't at war with herself.

Until he'd abruptly reappeared in her life.

"I don't know," she said at last. "I suppose—I suppose I have survived."

❧

Leo had lied. The happiest hour of his life was not his wedding. The week before the wedding he'd been away, giving a series of lectures at the Académie de Paris. And when he'd returned and they'd exchanged their vows, it had been the first time Bryony wore that expression he would later name The Castle, wooden and emotionless. Until the moment the Bishop of London had pronounced them man and wife, he'd had a lump of fear in his throat that she would suddenly jilt him.

No, the happiest hour of his life had been when she proposed.

He'd last seen her when he was fifteen. He never thought that eight years later, when he met her again, it would be as if no time had passed at all, that he'd still be as enthralled with her as he'd been as a boy.

More, if anything.

For she had become even more beautiful than he remembered. Cool and self-possessed. Capable and accomplished.

He wasn't so shabby himself. London celebrated him as a new kind of Renaissance man at the dawn of a new age. But he feared that he'd become too frivolous, that he was a little too tainted with the glitter and gloss of Society for her lofty soul.

But at least she'd come to hear him speak at both the mathematical society and the geographical society. And had watched him with such grave attentiveness that he'd nearly lost his place in the lecture both times.

He was completely enamored of the severely cut jacket-and-skirt suits she wore, so serious and put together—his lady knight, in her armor of crisp silk, ready to do battle with London's microbes and infirmities. He adored the tarry-sweet whiff of carbolic acid, the great antiseptic beloved by her profession, that always clung to her hair—not that he often got close enough to smell her. And her quiet, so composed and assured, intrigued him far more than the endless babble the other young ladies were so fond of unleashing.

At night he lay awake and thought of her prim little hats, her utilitarian walking boots, and the buttons that strained just slightly at the rise of her breasts. Thought of her unkissed lips, unlicked nipples, unpenetrated thighs.

Then his lust had gotten away from him at the soirée musicale. He'd kissed her, not once, but twice, where any one of a hundred guests could have walked in on them.

He had no idea what to do next. Should he call on her

and apologize? Should he call on her and not apologize? And it wasn't a simple matter to call on her, since she worked and kept no at-home days.

So here he was, on an overcast, drizzling London morning, too cold and dismal to be called spring, pacing his brother's library in a strange agitation, flipping the card she'd given him between his fingers. Miss Bryony Asquith. Internist. Anesthesiologist. Senior House Surgeon— New Hospital for Women. Lecturer—London School of Medicine for Women.

Someone knocked. "Sir, Miss Asquith would like to know if you are home," said Jeremy's butler.

"Which Miss Asquith?" It was a stupid question to ask. Only the eldest daughter of the family was referred to solely by her surname.

He tried to think why she'd come to see him. Probably to berate him, which he deserved, of course, but he'd rather that she not be displeased with him. Perhaps she had a lecture of her own to give somewhere and wished to invite him to attend. But then again that could have been easily done with a note.

He gave up and told the butler to show her in.

She was so pretty. Raven hair, porcelain complexion, a natural blush of the palest rose on her cheeks. His heart had taken to beating faster when he was around her. And he was all too aware of the indent of her upper lip, the richness of her lower lip, the whole shape and curve and softness of her mouth.

They spent a minute or so standing in the drawing room, exchanging platitudes. He offered her a seat; she thanked him but made no move. He offered her tea; she turned it down outright.

He gave her a mock severe look. "You don't want a seat and you don't want tea. Is there anything you do want, Miss Asquith?"

She cleared her throat. "Well, I was rather hoping I could offer you something that you would want."

"Indeed?" He had no idea what that could be but he smiled all the same. At least she wasn't unhappy with him. "Well, go on, I'm listening."

She launched into an analysis of their finances, logistics, and temperaments. It took him at least three minutes to understand that she was speaking in the context of marriage. She believed their differing dispositions would complement each other, her quiet a natural foil to his brio. Their schedules would align nicely, as she was sure he needed plenty of time for his work, which he could do while she was at the hospital. And she would bring with her Thornwood Manor—which, having once been part of her mother's dowry and stipulated in the marriage contract to go to the first Mrs. Asquith's offspring, actually belonged to her—along with considerable monetary assets.

In his daze, it was some time before he realized that she'd stopped speaking.

"Have I shocked you very much?" she murmured.

"Yes, rather," he said slowly.

She sat down at last, in a Louis XV chair before the fireplace. "Not too horribly, I hope."

"No, not too horribly."

"Is it something you could consider then?"

It was definitely something he could consider. But marriage had been only a glimmer in his eye. He was three weeks short of twenty-four. And he'd thought it would take at least another year for the two of them to get to know each other properly.

"I will consider it most earnestly—you know I've nothing but the greatest esteem for you."

She bit her lip. "Here's something else you should take into consideration then. It is highly unlikely that I could have children."

He was stunned. "Are you sure?"

"Unfortunately." She looked away from him. "Do you like children?"

"Yes." He did like children, very much. He spoiled his nieces and nephews rotten as often as he could.

Her eyes dimmed. "Then you should probably say no right now. Otherwise, it would be a hardship for you."

How ironic that upon being presented with his heart's desire, he was also presented with one of the starker choices a man could face. "May I have some time to think about it?"

She gave a wan smile. "Of course."

He walked her out of the house to her waiting carriage

and handed her inside. She settled herself into the tufted seat and lifted a hand to smooth back a strand of hair that had escaped her coiffure. Perhaps it was the watery day, or the lugubrious light of the English not-quite-spring, but she looked forlorn, desolate.

The rain that had sprinkled on and off the whole morning suddenly became a downpour, falling coldly upon his bare head. And he had an epiphany.

He belonged to her.

He'd loved her since he was four feet high. Children would be lovely, of course, but children were not essential. She was essential. She had been alone her entire life. He would see to it that she was never alone again.

"Well, why not?" he said, smiling at his beloved. "It should be no hardship to be married to you."

❧

Perhaps she had survived their marriage, but he had not.

He'd lived a charmed life. He was widely hailed as the greatest mathematical prodigy in a generation. Magazines begged to publish his accounts of his jaunts abroad with his godfather. Even the play, which he'd written in a week, on a dare to be as naughty as possible without the censors coming after him, had turned out to be a resounding success: He was told that his portrayal of three Cambridge students gambling at love had become a favorite production to mount in drawing rooms and parlors and wherever else young men and women gathered and desired to exchange innocent-seeming double entendres right under the noses of their chaperons.

He'd come to his wedding this blessed youth, this boy wonder on whom the world doted. And it had been the beginning of the end.

Oh, she'd let him have her, but only as a slave tolerated her loathsome master, her teeth clenched tight, her throat making noises so distressed that on some nights he wondered if she ran to the water closet the moment he left her.

Every time he went to her had been a rejection. A rejection of his touch, his lovemaking, his body. Of him. And he'd smiled and chatted in a hundred drawing rooms, all the while carrying this enormous, shameful secret.

He'd gone into their marriage determined that she would never be alone again. In the end, she'd made him as alone in the world as she.

Chapter Five

Leo awoke with a high fever and a splitting headache. He forced himself out of bed, checked on the mules, then stopped by the cook, who was already at work preparing breakfast, and asked for a cup of black tea.

The cook, a man named Saif Khan, glanced at him balefully. Even though Leo had hired him only three days ago in Chitral—he'd hired the entire entourage that had accompanied the family of an officer to the Chitral garrison—he knew that he'd already proved a severe trial to Saif Khan, who was accustomed to Britishers with proper stomachs, who polished off plates of fried fish, omelettes, dal and rice, and scones and jam before they set out for the day.

When Leo had gone shooting with his godfather

in Kashmir—goodness, was that eleven years ago?—he'd had just that sort of appetite. He'd eaten prodigiously, making the cooks teary-eyed with happiness.

And God knew when he'd been traveling alone with the Gilgiti guide and not eating nearly enough, the sight of one of Saif Khan's breakfast spreads would have had him vertiginous with gluttony. But his appetite had simply disappeared in the past week.

He managed some porridge. The tea had cooled enough. He counted out three phenacetin pills and washed them down with a large swig.

"What are those?"

He looked up. He hadn't heard her approach. She had on a precisely tailored, sandstone-colored jacket and skirt set. Always so neat and put-together, Bryony Asquith, even in the middle of nowhere.

"What are which?" he asked, rising from the folding chair on which he'd been sitting.

"Those tablets you just took."

"Hair pills."

"I beg your pardon?"

"They are Will's hair pills. You remember Will, my brother? Everyone is always asking Will what he does to make his hair so beautiful. Well, these pills *are* his secret."

She looked suspicious. "What do *you* need hair pills for? Your hair is perfectly fine."

"To prevent balding, of course."

His glibness exasperated her. "Nothing prevents balding. You are better off using those pills to reinforce your levee of self-possession against the rising tides of your heart."

He laughed. She always did away with his more fanciful flights of words.

They could have been happy together.

"What's the matter?" she asked, her tone subdued.

"Nothing," he said softly. "I forgot that you could make me laugh, that's all."

Her reaction was a slow, downward sweep of her lashes. When she raised her eyes again, her face had assumed a plasterlike smoothness.

The Castle. He'd seen this expression far too many times during their marriage. The Castle was Bryony drawing up the gates and retreating deep into the inner keep. And he'd always hated it. Marriage meant that you shared your goddamn castle. You didn't leave your poor knight of a husband circling the walls trying to find a way in.

Perhaps it was his pounding headache, perhaps it was his rising temperature—the phenacetin had yet to have an effect on either—or perhaps his fatigue had impaired his judgment at last. He threw down the metal tea mug, gripped the front of her jacket, and, before she could summon a cry of outrage, kissed her.

A Vikings-at-the-gate, loot-and-plunder, barbarians-dragging-away-the-lady-of-the-keep kiss. Her mouth was cool and moist. She tasted of tooth powder. His physiology changed. Ever since he understood what sex was he'd wanted it with her, the girl who kept everything inside, who ached and yearned and mourned in complete solitude.

She shoved him away, hard. They stared at each other. She was panting. After a moment, he realized that so was he.

She opened her mouth and closed it. When she did speak again, it was only, "You are feverish. You are burning."

"Yes," he said. "I've always wanted to burn down your castle."

It would have been a good moment to depart, upon those triumphant words. But a debilitating dizziness came upon him. He saw things he shouldn't, strange patches of yellow and green floating before his eyes.

"What's the matter, Leo?" she cried, as if from very far away.

He stumbled. She caught him, her arms amazingly strong.

He began to shiver violently.

❧

He was at Princeton and it was freezing—the central boiler that normally supplied hot water to the radiators in the lecture hall threw one hell of a tantrum. Before him, in neat rows and full of that particularly American enthusiasm, his students, wrapped in scarves and overcoats, waited for him to begin. They'd been working the whole term toward this day, when they would tackle absolute differential calculus and redefine everything they'd ever learned about scalars, matrices, and vectors.

He talked. And derived equations on the board, the chalk in his gloved hand delineating the sinuous symbols of higher mathematics. But it was rote motion. She would be leaving the States after the New Year, this time headed for India—the Zenana Missions were always looking for women doctors to minister to those who could not leave the *purdah*.

He didn't know why people thought it was necessary to inform him of her movements. If he wanted to keep track of her, he would have forbidden the annulment.

God, so cold. His hands were shaking. He couldn't read what he'd written. Was that an "$\int$" or an "α" and how could he confuse the two?

No, he wasn't cold. He was burning. And he was not in America, but in the dunes of Tunisia, waiting for the mercury-melting day to pass, lying across the Bedouin tent from his Cambridge classmate, whose father happened to be the French proconsul of these parts. "Why geometry? Of course geometry. How else will man discover the shape of the universe?"

"What if we never discover the shape of the universe?"

"It's still not wasted. There is nothing like higher mathematics to impress an overly serious woman," he said, grinning.

But even in the desert he'd never been quite so parched. And so hot, as if he'd been left outside to broil in the sun. He moaned. His head hurt like one of Nero's hangovers.

Now he knew when he was. He was ten and suffering from delirium as the result of a snake bite. Because he'd been unaccountably fascinated by the scalpel-wielding girl who lived on the next estate. Because he'd been perched in a tree for three consecutive afternoons, watching her dissect a grouse, a pheasant, and a trout. The fourth day she didn't come. And when he climbed down from the tree, he'd stepped on the viper.

Too hot. Too hot. Someone lifted his head and pressed something cool against his lips. He had no idea what he was supposed to do.

"Drink," the person said.

He still didn't understand.

A minute later water trickled into his mouth—he was being spoon-fed. He half expected any liquid to evaporate upon coming into contact with him, but the water pooled pleasantly at the back of his mouth.

"You'd better swallow that."

So he did.

But the next thing that came into his mouth, a pill as bitter as injustice, did not please him at all. He spat it out.

"Leo, you blockhead. If you'd been honest about the state of your health I'd have put you on quinine already. You are running a temperature of a hundred and five. You'd better take it fast."

Bloody hell. Not malaria. He hated quinine with a passion. He'd stopped his prophylactic doses after his first week in India, because they wreaked havoc with him.

"Leo, don't be a ninny." She tapped the tablet against his teeth.

If ever there existed a cure worse than the disease, quinine must be it. He refused to budge. She tried to pry open his teeth and grunted at the futility of it.

"If you don't cooperate, I'll have to administer the drug rectally."

He laughed. "Bugger me," he said.

Or at least in his mind he spoke.

"Don't think I won't," she threatened.

He was serenely unconcerned. He wouldn't have to taste it if the quinine came up his behind.

She sighed in frustration. "You need to take the quinine, Leo."

He ignored her. The coolies talked among themselves somewhere in the distance. Pots and pans jangled as Saif Khan packed away his implements. A breeze snapped some external flap on the tent.

And then he was twenty-four again. It was his wedding night. And he was with her for the very first time, dying to come, and dying a little inside.

He could tell at the ceremony and the subsequent wedding breakfast that she was having doubts. He understood cold feet. He'd had a case of it before he left for France, the sudden realization that he was about to make the commitment of a lifetime, to Bryony Asquith no less, a decision that everyone except him regarded as insane.

In his bout of confusion, he'd done something

stupid. But at least that incidence of stupidity had cleared his thinking: For him it was Bryony, it had always been—and the hell with what everyone else thought.

He would reassure her that she'd made the right choice, that *they*'d made the right choice. He would seduce her slowly and properly, the way he'd want to be pampered and cherished if he were a woman lying with a man for the first time. And he would hold her in her sleep, afterward, quietly rejoicing in his good fortune, in holding his heart's desire in his arms.

But he never imagined she'd lie beneath him like this—stiff as a log, her teeth ground together, her face turned so far to the side that the tendons of her neck trembled with the strain.

He did everything he could think of to ease the discomfort of her first time, to give her pleasure. But nothing he did pleased her.

The climax of his own body stole upon him. He ejaculated into her. But the pleasure of it was eclipsed by his growing dismay. He withdrew from her and held her beside him, seeking some sort of assurance from the warmth and closeness of their bodies pressed together, even if she still had on her nightgown and he his nightshirt—she'd asked him not to disrobe them entirely, and he'd agreed because it was her first time and he would take things slowly.

"I would like to sleep now," she said.

It took him a minute to understand that she'd asked him to leave, to go to his own room.

"Is something the matter, Bryony?"

"Nothing," she said curtly. "Nothing's the matter. I just want to sleep now."

He tried to kiss her before he left, but she only blocked her lips with her fingers. "Remember what I said? I've a summer cold. I wouldn't want to give it to you."

He did his best to calm himself. It was her first time. Newlywed jitters. Nothing to it. She needed a few days to get used to everything, that was all.

But as he slumped out of her room, he could only think, *What if that isn't all? What if it will always be like this?*

✍

"If I kiss you, will you take your medicine?"

The question jolted him out of his near unconsciousness. "What?" he mumbled weakly, unable to open his eyes.

"If I kiss you, will you take your medicine?"

He was twenty-eight, in the grips of a full malarial attack, in a tent one march northwest of the Lowari

Pass. And the woman who'd once been his wife wanted to know if she could get him to save himself with the bribe of a kiss.

"Make it good," he said.

He wasn't swallowing God's turd—as he'd privately come to think of quinine—for some sisterly peck.

Her hands cupped his face. She breathed against him, uneven, tooth-powder-scented exhalations. The kiss grazed around his lips, as innocent as Easter bunnies gamboling on a meadow.

All of a sudden, her tongue was in his mouth. He reacted with equal abruptness. In the space of a heartbeat he had her under him. She tasted sweet, so sweet, pure and delicious. And her body—how he coveted her, an unholy lust, like burning in hell.

She trembled, his little piece of heaven. So cold, so distant, beloved and despised. He would worship her if she but let him. But she would never let him, would she? She would always remain out of reach, on her icy perch, indifferent to the struggles of mere mortals such as he.

She set her hands on his shoulders. He expected her to push him away, but she didn't. Instead, she rubbed her palm across his cheek. And he was lost.

He shoved her skirts aside, freed himself from his trousers, and sank into her with one push. The sensation—God, the sensation blinded and deafened him. He could not see, hear, or speak; he could only feel. Yes, she was heaven, his heaven. He had never felt pleasure but this knife-sharp pleasure, never known solace but this heart-crushing solace. He shuddered into her, a fanatical release, a hot dark surge that drained everything from him and some more.

Utter exhaustion came over him. He could barely breathe, let alone move. And he was only dimly aware of her leaving him.

She slipped the quinine tablet between his lips. "You promised," she said, her voice shaking.

He swallowed the quinine, drank the water she gave him, and fell back onto his pillow.

He was twenty-eight, his marriage three years annulled, and he'd just taken possession of Bryony.

❧

She was in shock.

He'd been hallucinating, mumbling about obscure mathematical concepts. She'd been furious and anxious, and truly ready to shove the quinine up his posterior should he continue to resist treatment.

And then he'd called *her* name, over and over again. *Bryony. Bryony, sweetheart. What's the matter, Bryony?* Once she realized that he was still only barely conscious and not responding to her answers, the repetition of her name on his tongue became a painfully sweet music, an ode, an incantation.

It had seemed a very logical thing to offer him a kiss, since he'd kissed her just before the malarial attack got the better of him. She could not have predicted that it would lead him to such a fevered concupiscence. One moment she was braced on her arms over him, the next moment she was under him, and the moment after that he was inside her to the hilt, his breaths harsh with pleasure.

That was not what shocked her—that he'd been able to perform in his condition. But that she'd let him—and that she'd derived such a fierce, if incomplete pleasure from that brief, intense joining.

And that she wanted more.

Chapter Six

Quinine made Leo wretchedly sick: He was either fighting a violent nausea or being soundly defeated by it. The rest of the time he was so weak he could scarcely lift a finger. She did not leave his side. With a heroic calm, she dealt with his vomitus that profoundedly disgusted him.

"How do you stand it?" he asked her once.

"I've seen worse," she answered. And that was that.

When he could not bear the taste on his own tongue, she made a solution of menthol and thymol for him to use as a mouth rinse. She gave him honey water for nutrition, brushed his teeth, and changed his clothes.

"Why are you so nice to me?" he asked her another time, too tired to open his eyes, as she rubbed salve on his hands, rope-burned and rock-scraped from crossing the awful terrain between Gilgit and Chitral, the slippery warmth of her hand melting the sweet-smelling beeswax salve into his knuckles, his calluses, the creases between his fingers.

"You are ill. I'm a doctor."

The answer he wanted to hear, of course, was that her meticulous care was motivated by something beyond medical obligation. Even though he already knew better.

In the last month of their marriage, he had found a crumpled letter in the wastepaper basket of the study when he'd gone to look for a page of equations he'd thrown away in a fit of agitation. The letter, from a young woman who owed her life and the life of her child to a successful caesarean section performed by Bryony, had been one of the most moving pieces of English prose he had ever read.

He never doubted that Bryony was a first-rate physician. He never doubted her professional devotion. And he'd always understood that her essential interest was in diseases, not patients, her drive less compassion than the desire to triumph over nature's more pernicious agents.

During the afternoon he spent standing over the letter, however, its large, painstaking, almost childish handwriting slowly burning into his mind's eye, he finally had to accept that his wife's reserve was less aloofness than wholesale apathy: Only a person allergic to human proximity of any kind, physical or emotional, could disdain such heartfelt gratitude.

"I'm sorry," he said.

"As well you should be." The pad of her thumb massaged circles on the back of his hand, his palm, and even two inches up his wrist. He did not want her to stop. "What were you thinking, concealing your symptoms from a doctor?"

"That's not what I meant."

Let me have you again. Let me make love to you properly. Let me give you the kind of pleasure that you gave me, delicious, terrible pleasure.

"I know what you meant." She let go of his hands. "Let's not speak of it again."

❧

The second day after the malarial attack, a mule train made its way down from Lowari Pass.

Where Leo and Bryony had stopped at the end of their first day of travel—and where they'd stayed ever since—was the precise spot where their path would diverge from the Chitral River and head up again into the mountains. Since many of the mountain passes surrounding the Chitral Valley were impassible in winter, the bulk of the regional trade was conducted during the more clement months.

Bryony poked her head out of Leo's tent long enough to see that the mule train was just a merchant caravan, before she returned inside. Imran and his son, Hamid, offered the traders tea. The men chatted for a while before the traders headed north, presumably to the bazaars at Chitral.

"I need to speak to Imran," Leo said.

She looked at him in surprise. She'd thought him asleep. Besides, he'd asked to see Imran already, earlier in the day. They'd spoken about the provisions, and Leo had issued the necessary rupees for the coolies' per diem. "Is there anything I can get for you?"

"No, thank you. I need to know what news the travelers brought," he said, his eyes still closed.

She fetched Imran and returned with him to the tent.

"What news from Swat?" Leo asked directly.

"They do not come from Swat, but Dir. In Dir they say a great fakir has arrived in Upper Swat Valley. A miracle man. And he will drive out the English." The guide shook his head. "Always these miracle men."

Leo nodded, thanked the guide, and dismissed him.

"How did you know there was news from Swat?"

Bryony asked, half amazed. "What language were they speaking?"

"Pashto, which I don't understand, but Swat is still Swat."

Most Chitralis belonged to the Khow tribe and spoke Khowar. South of Chitral, however, the population of the North-West Frontier was largely Pathan, or Pashtons, as they were called by some.

She was even more amazed. "Then how did you know the news from Swat mattered to us? They could have been talking about the crops."

"They mentioned 'fakir' repeatedly, and also 'sirkar' several times. Since 'sirkar' almost invariably refers to the government of India, I wanted to at least ask."

She nodded. The North-West Frontier was an uneasy place. In '95 there had been pitched battles at Chitral, when various unhappy factions in a nastier-than-usual succession struggle for the princely seat of Chitral had laid siege to a 400-man British garrison sent to settle the dispute.

And in June of this year, there had been an attack on a British political officer and his convoy in broad daylight in Tochi Valley. It was far enough away—hundreds of miles southwest of Peshawar in the unruly uplands of Waziristan, where no foreign power had ever breathed easy—that neither the Braeburns nor Bryony had been alarmed for their own safety. But still it had been a reminder that the peace they enjoyed was easily ruptured.

Bryony took the map from Leo's saddlebag and spread it open on her knees. Their course was marked in red. As soon as they crested Lowari Pass, they would be in Dir. A short distance out of Dir Town, which was some twelve, fifteen miles from the pass—distances were difficult to judge on the map— they'd encounter the Panjkora River. From there, their road would follow the Panjkora River until a village marked Sado, where they'd turn away from the river, strike southeast, and make for Chakdarra, on the bank of the Swat River.

The Swat River was one of the most important rivers in the region, and Swat Valley one of its greatest population centers. At Chakdarra, the Swat Valley ran roughly east-west, while their route turned directly south. Once they crossed the river, they would be done with Swat Valley almost immediately.

"Swat Valley is how far from here? A hundred fifty miles?"

"Thereabout. And where we will cross the Swat River is the Lower Swat Valley. Upper Swat Valley is further away upstream, beyond the Amandara Pass."

She folded the map and put it back into his saddlebag. That was too far to worry about for now.

Besides, on the frontier, the religious profession was and had always been solidly opposed to any outside power. Fire-breathing clerics weren't exactly new. Most of them failed to inspire anything other than wishful thinking in their followers. The itinerant fakir in Upper Swat Valley was likely merely another fist-shaking imam whose following had been greatly exaggerated in the telling.

She wasn't wholly without sympathy for the local population's desire to be free of the British. After all, the English themselves idolized Boadicea, the great queen who fought against the Romans. But she simply didn't think this particular imam was the man to accomplish the task.

"Do you think you can eat anything?" she asked Leo.

He shook his head, looking green at even the mention of food.

"Then sleep some more," she said.

He closed his eyes. She sat down on her stool by the bed and watched him. After a while, when he seemed asleep, she touched her palm to his cheek. He'd become so thin it hurt to look at him, yet she could not stop looking. Could not stop longing.

Her thumb skimmed lightly across the tips of his eyelashes. Her index and middle fingers caught his ear between them and felt its cool softness—his fever had come down with the first dose of quinine. Her little finger traced its way to his jugular, and pressed against it to feel the rhythm of his blood.

It had begun to register on her that his heart was beating too fast when he caught her hand and brought it to his lips. She pulled back, but not before his kiss had left an imprint in the center of her palm.

An imprint that burned long after he had truly fallen asleep again.

෴

On the fifth day after the malarial attack, Leo awoke from a shallow sleep in the afternoon. The quinine had been vicious, but also effective. He was still weak, but all his symptoms were gone. He was recovering and recovering well.

She sat on a stool by his camp bed, holding a half-eaten biscuit in her hand. That hand rested against a deep green wool skirt in which was tucked a white-and-green striped blouse that buttoned all the way up to her chin.

She had a sweet chin, perfect really; he used to kiss her there, patiently, with hope, when she would not allow him to kiss her on the mouth. Her chin, her jaw, he'd followed the contour of her face to nibble on the delicate folds of her ears. But those too were soon forbidden to him. And the next night she'd asked that he not release her hair from its plait—it would be too much trouble to untangle in the morning, she'd said, and she must be at the hospital on time.

Today her hair was parted in the middle and pulled back, smooth as glass, glossy as lacquer. She leaned to her left to reach for a canteen on the floor of the tent. He caught a glimpse of white. Her hair—he was shocked anew.

Her hair turned white because of you.

Or so Callista had claimed.

You believe Callista?

Their eyes met. Heat jolted through him. He'd been deep inside her and she had not protested.

She turned her head away abruptly. "I've your lunch here," she said. "Mutton broth and chicken *biryani*. Saif Khan also made a convalescent pudding for you."

He sat up to eat. She'd anticipated his needs quite accurately. The five-day course of quinine had concluded the day before. His stomach had ceased its treasonous ways. And he was hungry.

She watched him; he felt her gaze on him, something with a weight and a touch of its own. Whenever he lifted his head from his plate, she looked elsewhere. But her eyes always came back to him.

Straight on or sideways, she studied him, stealthily, surreptitiously, in bits and snatches.

"Your boots, they have an imprint on the soles," at length she spoke again. "They were made in Berlin."

Once upon a time, he'd been quite fastidious in his appearance. Good quality wasn't enough. Every piece of apparel he owned had to be a work of art—or at least a work of impeccable craftsmanship. But after the annulment, he didn't care half as much. When he needed a new pair of boots while he was in Berlin, instead of writing his London bootmaker, he bought a pair ready-made, something that would have dismayed his old self.

"What were you doing in Berlin?" She offered him a second bowl of mutton broth.

He accepted the broth. "Thank you. I lectured at the university."

She added another heap of biryani to his plate. "Callista said you were in Munich. She said you were going to buy a vineyard somewhere in Bavaria and retire to it."

"I was twenty-five, a bit early to retire to a place as old-fashioned as Bavaria."

"She also said that you changed your mind after a while and went to America, to Wyoming, to take up cattle ranching."

"Not an unlikely scenario for a younger son. But I

was in America to corrupt its youth—at Princeton University, in New Jersey, a few thousand miles east of Wyoming."

She cleared her throat. "I was in Germany, at the University of Breslau, for advanced surgical training. And America too—I taught at the Women's Medical College in Pennsylvania."

"Yes, I know."

He'd moved to Cambridge after the annulment. He'd always loved Cambridge. He'd always meant to become the Lucasian Professor of Mathematics at the university, a chair once occupied by the illustrious Sir Isaac Newton. The incumbent professor had been at his position nearly fifty years. The timing could not have been better for Leo, his genius hailed left and right in those days, to be appointed the next holder of the professorship.

But by autumn he was in Berlin. A year later he was at Princeton. And three terms after that, India.

An annulment, as it turned out, wasn't quite enough to stop him from caring. Did it bother no one else that she was alone in a foreign country? That she left home further and further behind with each move? That, God forbid, should something happen, her family was thousands of miles away?

He scorned himself for giving a damn, when she didn't give a damn about him. But it didn't matter.

He had choices, and each time he chose to accept the one invitation that placed him in the same country as her, so that help, should she need it, didn't have to be summoned across oceans.

"You thought I was in Leh when you agreed to the ballooning expedition in Gilgit?"

He took a drink of water and nodded. Their eyes met again.

You were the moon of my existence; your moods dictated the tides of my heart.

It might have been hyperbole, but it wasn't fiction.

❧

After lunch, they spoke briefly of their itinerary. He wanted to get back on the road the immediate next day, but she insisted that after the end of quinine treatment he must allow himself at least two days of rest and warned darkly of consequences were he to ignore a physician's directive on the matter.

To help him pass the rest of the afternoon, she gave him the old copy of *Cornhill* magazine he'd picked up when he stayed overnight at the Chitral garrison, told him she was going for a walk, and denied him permission to do anything more strenuous than reading in bed.

"Take Imran with you," he said.

She looked puzzled for a moment, as if she'd forgotten that she was in a place where women rarely left their houses, and certainly never unaccompanied— the Chitral region was particularly conservative that way. "Right, of course."

When he estimated she'd gone off far enough, he got up, went out of the tent, and got a pair of coolies to erect the folding table for him and bring him a folding chair. He was still in his unadorned white cotton *kurta* pyjama, the native tunic-and-trouser set he wore to sleep. But just being outside the tent, unsupported, made him feel more himself already.

The air had that pellucid mountain clarity that made shapes sharper and colors truer. The green of the paddy fields wasn't just green, but a lusty green, full of hunger for sunlight and moisture. And the slopes weren't mere hulks of rock, but the ribs of the valley, protecting the delicate strip of fertile soil from the worst of the harsh elements.

With the westerly sun on his face and a breeze ruffling his hair, he sat down and opened his notebook.

After the annulment, he'd produced no original work for almost two years. He taught, and checked the work of other mathematicians with whom he maintained scholarly correspondences, but his own mind had been resolutely barren. Even when he did start to work on new postulates, he managed only derivative scribbles, timid echoes of his earlier output.

It was almost as humbling an experience as his marriage to realize that he could not take his youthful brilliance for granted. That he might never duplicate the grace and ease with which he'd dashed out his first papers, between mountain climbing jaunts, safaris, and the assorted other adventures of a young man who liked fun as much as he liked glory.

After an hour he put away the notebook and brought out a travel chess set, something else he'd acquired from the garrison at Chitral. He played a game against himself, a game that, predictably enough, came to a draw. He reset the pieces.

White king pawn, black king pawn, white king bishop pawn—the classic king's gambit opening. The last game he'd declined the gambit. This time he took out the white king bishop pawn with the black king pawn. King's gambit accepted.

He set down an elbow on the table, rested his chin in the valley between his thumb and index finger, and considered his next move.

"Disobeying the doctor's order already?" The sun had dropped behind the mountains, but he could still see that Bryony was rosy-cheeked from her exercise. "No, don't stand up."

"It's not much more strenuous to sit in a chair than sit up in bed," he cajoled. And motioned a nearby coolie to bring her a chair.

"Well, you'd better defeat yourself soon. I've asked Saif Khan for an early dinner. You still need your rest."

"It's hard to defeat myself."

"Well, then, I'll defeat you," she said casually, sitting down.

He laughed, even though he didn't mean to.

"You think you are invulnerable at chess?"

He turned up his hands. It wasn't whether he thought so, but that he hadn't been bested since he was eleven.

"If you think you are so strong, I'll take white."

White moved first; it was the smallest concession she could have asked of him. Usually he had to give up significant pieces before anyone would play with him. She continued the game he'd started, her choice of maneuver the white king knight. King's knight gambit.

He responded with his king knight pawn. "I didn't know you played."

She advanced her king rook pawn. "There are probably a great many things you don't know about me."

He set his king knight pawn one step forward. "Then you should tell me. I can't know otherwise."

Her king knight leaped over the four pawns that had neatly lined up in e4, f4, g4, and h4. His king knight joined the battle. Her king knight dashed back and took out his king knight pawn. He removed her king pawn.

"You are not going to tell me anything, are you?"

"I don't know what you don't know."

They jockeyed for control of the center of the board—she was a far superior player than he'd supposed. He deployed his king knight deep into her territory and took out her king rook.

"I do know, for example, that my godfather called on you after our petition for annulment had been lodged with the ecclesiastical courts," he began. "And I assume he offered you a bribe if you remained married to me. But I don't know what precisely he dangled before you."

She marched both her king knight and her queen bishop to his door. "A new wing for the hospital. Land and facility for the medical school too."

He disposed of her queen bishop with his king and said nothing. Even with such enticements, even with the guilt she must have felt at turning down the gifts for the hospital and the school, she'd left him all the same.

She repositioned her king knight. "Your move."

He narrowed his eyes. Her king knight was in place to demolish either his king or his queen. How had he been so careless? There was no choice but to protect his king. He retrenched.

She took his queen. "He is your natural father, isn't he, your godfather?"

He glanced up from the board. Her eyes were the deep green of the underlayer of a glacier, her skin as clear as a snow-fed lake.

"Yes," he said. Very few people knew. But then, very few people cared about the paternity of a fifth son. "Do you mind?"

"Not particularly. Do *you*?"

"When I first learned, I did. Not anymore."

"When did you learn?"

She had eyes only for the board, but he felt her curiosity. It was such an odd thing, coming from her, because it was normal. It was what a man and a woman sitting down to chess did under unclouded circumstances: talk about themselves, about the people and things that mattered to them.

"My mother told me when I was fourteen."

"That's a bit young."

"I'm not sure there is a right age for this sort of thing."

"And how did you take it?"

"Not too well. I was thoroughly embarrassed at the thought of my own mother having had an affair with a man, any man. I nearly died from mortification when she further informed me that the affair was still ongoing. My father's passion was mathematics. I felt that hers should have been something similarly sexless, botany or Shakespearean tragedies, not something that would, my God, shag her regularly."

Her lips twitched. "Did your father know?"

"He did. I felt wronged on his behalf, even though my mother reassured me that they were all very good friends, that they all knew, and that nothing would change just because I now knew too. Which only made me feel like a dupe since I was the only one who didn't know."

She looked up at him now, with an expression that was almost a smile. "And then what happened?"

"And then something wonderful happened. I went home that summer and found out that indeed, nothing had changed. My father was thrilled to see me. We cloistered ourselves in the library for hours every day, read the latest papers, debated the insufficiencies of Euclidean geometry, and developed our own list of axioms as a foundation for a new approach to geometry."

When Leo finally plucked up the courage to ask the earl whether it bothered the latter in any way that he had under his roof someone who was not of his own flesh and blood, Lord Wyden had only smiled and said, "All you need to know is that you are the son I've always wanted."

Later, on the fjords of Norway with his godfather, with whom he was no longer angry, Leo had related the conversation with the earl. Sir Robert had sighed wistfully—the closest to sentimentality the ever-practical man ever came—and said, "I will always envy Lord Wyden for that. That you are his son—and not mine—in the eyes of the world."

In the end, there had been more than enough affection and esteem to go around. He grew closer to both Sir Robert and his father. He became so close to his father, in fact, that when the earl disowned Matthew for a youthful infraction, then disowned Will for standing up for Matthew, for the longest time Leo had refused to believe that the severity of Lord Wyden's action might not have been entirely justified.

Bryony sighed. "He knew and he loved you all the same."

His bishop took out her knight that had knocked off his queen. "Is that why you don't speak to your father, because he doesn't love you enough?"

She moved not a single muscle, yet he sensed her tremor. Her response was to summon her queen to lay waste to his king knight.

He took out her queen knight pawn. After she'd ransacked his queen, he'd moved aggressively to endanger her king. But she'd been equally fearless in coming after him.

She used her queen to check his king. "Watch out."

He whisked his king out of harm's way. "Watch out for what?"

She menaced his king bishop. "Imminent defeat."

He sacked her queen knight. "Yours?"

"No, yours." She sailed her queen across the width of the board. "Checkmate."

He didn't understand immediately. He surveyed the board with the laborious incomprehension of a middling student forced to master calculus. Then, shock. It was a true checkmate, with no escape for his embattled king that he hadn't even realized was embattled.

Her lips twitched again. She rose. "I will go tell Saif Khan he may serve dinner whenever it is ready."

He watched her go. "Now why did we never play chess?" he murmured.

The question was addressed more to the river and the sky than to her. But she stopped, her head turned, her profile perfectly limned, for a moment, against the purple shadow of the mountain. A strand of hair fluttered against her lips. Then she went on, without offering any answers.

❧

"Who taught you to play?" he asked later that evening over apricot pudding, an English preparation except for the addition of rosewater and cardamom. Until then he'd been too busy eating, his recovering appetite ravenous for innumerable helpings of food.

"Callista's mother," she said.

Day had faded. The lantern light cast copper gleams upon her cheeks and her hair. He no longer reeled back in renewed shock each time he saw the white in her hair, but he would never get used to it, the destruction of perfection.

"Toddy?" Callista's mother, the second Mrs. Geoffrey Asquith, had been born Lady Emma Todd, according to her tombstone—she'd died giving birth to Callista. But among the Marsden brothers, she'd always been referred to as Toddy.

She looked up from the pudding, surprised. "You remember her? You were only three when she died."

"I remember her funeral. It was one of my earliest memories—everyone in black, all my brothers crying."

It was also his earliest memory of Bryony, a starkly etched remembrance against the fog of time.

She'd been the only child who did not cry—even he'd wept out of confusion.

"Is that all you remember of her?"

He could not tell whether she sounded relieved or disappointed.

"That's all *I* remember, but my brothers remember more. They used to tell me about this fancy dress party she threw for the children. They all went as the Knights of the Round Table. Except me: I was the Holy Grail in a bassinet."

As the youngest of five boys, he'd been the butt of all sorts of jokes during his infancy.

"I remember that party," she said.

Her voice was different: not so self-isolating. Her expression had turned softer, more wistful. He'd never seen her wistful.

"What do you remember?"

She thought for a moment. "A white velvet dress, a pointy hat, and a belt with bells on it—I was a princess, I think."

"Did the Knights of the Round Table pay court to you?"

"Yes, but only because I had a basket of sweetmeats and prizes to hand out." The corners of her lips curved slightly. "The Knights of the Round Table had me well surrounded."

It was strange to hear her talk of a time before his

earliest memories of her. It was strange, in and of it-self, to hear her speak of her nursery days. When he'd been a boy, she'd seemed so much older than he, as if she'd sprung into life nearly full grown, or at least well above and beyond the clumsiness and vul-nerability of childhood.

She poked at her pudding. "What else do they re-member about Toddy?" she asked, almost hungrily.

"That she organized terrific picnics. Though the one they remember best was a disaster, apparently. Will fell into the stream and then ripped off his wet clothes and ran around naked. I believe he was later soundly caned for it."

"That was my sixth birthday," she said. "It wasn't a disaster at all. Your mother did choke on a piece of chicken when Will sprinted about without a stitch on, but the rest of us thought it was hysterical. And then, after Will was spirited away, we played games for the rest of the afternoon."

He felt as if he were up in a dusty, cobwebbed at-tic, opening creaky, ancient trunks, only to find in-side perfectly bright, undiminished jewels.

"Did they tell you about anything else from those days?" She *was* hungry for it. Her tone reminded him of the way he used to ask obliquely about her— *And Callista's sister, is she still cutting people open?*

There had been another story. And he had taken

an unbelievable amount of ribbing for it when he'd announced their engagement to his brothers. Matthew had cabled from Paris and Charlie all the way from Gilgit to say the same thing: *Lord Almighty, she was Mary and you were Baby Jesus*.

"The first Nativity play Toddy put on," he said.

"Hmm. I remember more the last Nativity play she put on. She got a camel on loan from somewhere. But the camel didn't care for what our groom fed it. It—it fertilized the entire chapel and the smell made the ladies swoon. Do you not remember that?"

"No." He had no personal recollection of Toddy.

"Now that was a proper disaster. My father was quite angry at her for that bit of foolishness. But then, later, after the two of us finished crying about it, we laughed so hard that we cried again."

He stared at her, amazed. When they'd lived together as man and wife, there had not been a single memento of Toddy among her possessions. It had seemed reasonable enough to assume that she had stayed as distant from Toddy as she had from her current stepmother—an assumption in keeping with her dry-eyed stoniness at Toddy's funeral.

A drop of tear tumbled down her cheek. Shock paralyzed him—he hadn't even known she was capable of tears.

She was as flabbergasted as he. "I'm sorry." She

fumbled for her napkin. "I'm sorry. I don't know what's the matter with me."

He handed her his handkerchief. Clumsily she dabbed at her eyes. But her tears did not stop. For a long minute, he did not move. Then he stood up, thinking to give her some privacy. Instead, he rounded the table and pulled her to her feet.

He'd embraced her before, toward the beginning of their marriage. Her rigid unresponsiveness had put an end to that. He took a deep breath and drew her into his arms.

She stiffened. He almost stepped away by instinct. Instead he hugged her tighter.

"It's all right," he whispered in her ear. "It's all right. You can cry. Sometimes God makes perfect people. Why shouldn't you be devastated?"

"I don't cry," she said, her words muffled. "I never cry."

"Yes, I know," he said. "It's fine. You can cry as much or as little as you want."

As if he'd given her the permission she needed, her quiet tears turned into trembling sobs. She was slight in his arms—she'd become thinner, a wisp of a woman. He stroked her back and kissed her hair, as if she were a niece who'd skinned her knee. After a while, she relaxed into him—her body surprisingly supple, surprisingly soft—and her sobs subsided into hiccupy exhalations.

"There is something I never told you," he said. "When we were still married, I paid a call to one of my mother's old friends. Her sister happened to visit her on that day and it turned out that the sister and Toddy had gone to finishing school together. When she learned who I was married to, she said to let you know that Toddy had thought you the most wonderful child who ever lived."

They'd been still married, but her bedroom door had already been barred. And he'd been in no mood to pass on such compliments. In fact, he'd thought Toddy sadly deceived, given how little Bryony remembered *her*.

She raised her head. "She did?"

"Those were Lady Griswold's precise words. When we get out of the mountains, I'll cable her and see if she can find some of Toddy's old letters to give to you."

She lowered her face again. "You don't have to go to so much trouble for me."

He let her go. "It's no trouble."

She stood in that spot for a long moment. Then she leaned in and kissed him on the cheek, a quick brush that barely touched his skin. "Thank you. Good night."

"Good night," he said to the darkness beyond the reach of the lamplight, as her footsteps faded behind him.

❧

Before Toddy, Bryony's memories had consisted of dim, gray impressions of Thornwood Manor's cavernous rooms. Her mother, disappointed to bear only a girl after years of infertility, had died of acute pneumonia before Bryony turned two. Her father, preferring to be a widower in town, but believing children were better off in the country, had been overwhelmingly absent.

But with Toddy's arrival, her world burst into color. According to all accounts, they'd been instant friends, the lively twenty-year-old new Mrs. Asquith and her shy, reserved four-year-old stepdaughter. And from that moment on, for the entire three short years that remained to Toddy, they were never apart.

They traipsed over the estate and the nearby hills, collecting leaves, petals, and seeds to help Toddy document the local flora. They organized picnics and children's parties and scavenger hunts. And when the weather did not allow for walking or riding, they drank hot cider, played chess, and stuffed their minds with obscure bits of knowledge by opening the encyclopedia to random pages.

They'd had so many plans, she and Toddy. The arrival of the baby was to be such a celebration. But then Toddy had died in childbirth—smiling, vibrant Toddy who'd been full of life and energy and curiosity and kindness.

It had been the end of the world.

Three months after Toddy's funeral, Bryony's nanny died. Six months to the day after Toddy's death, Bryony's father married again. But between the engagement and the wedding, misfortune befell the third Mrs. Geoffrey Asquith: one of her sons was struck by poliomyelitis, the other tuberculosis.

Immediately after the wedding, she came up to the estate and deposited a governess to take command of her stepchildren, the wet nurse, and the new nanny that the housekeeper had hired. Then Bryony did not see her again for five years, as she shuttled between the sanatorium in Germany and a hospital in London.

The governess she hired, Miss Branson, was better suited to manage a half-dozen criminally inclined boys than two orphan girls. Miss Branson instituted a reign of fanatical order and discipline, until she married the vicar and left to tyrannize the vicarage instead.

The governess who followed, a Miss Roundtree, was a great improvement, an absentminded old dear. Bryony's father, her stepmother, and her two still-sickly stepbrothers came to live part of the year in the country. The family was together at last.

Callista took to her suddenly enlarged family like a fish to water. But for Bryony it was too late. By that time she'd already turned resolutely inward. Humans, herself included, held no interest for her except as living machines, mind-bogglingly intricate, beautiful systems that somehow housed individuals not quite worthy of the miracle of their physical bodies. In due time, she left home without a backward glance, studied with the single-minded focus of those who cared for little else, and practiced with a cool, impersonal dedication.

And forgot that she'd once wanted pageantry, companionship, and love.

Chapter Seven

Leo asked for a bath the next day—he'd come to be in a rather medieval state of hygiene. The tub was set up for him in the bathing tent. He undressed, set himself down in the steaming water, and closed his eyes in the enjoyment of it. Several minutes later, someone entered the tent behind him. He first thought it was a coolie, bringing in more buckets of water. But he did not hear anything being set down.

He turned halfway around. It was Bryony, standing just inside the tent flaps, holding a cloth bag in one hand and a stool in the other.

"Why are you here?"

"To help wash you," she said.

He looked at her with more than a little disbelief. Their ayah was Hindu, not Muslim, and could therefore, presumably, be persuaded to help him with the bath. Failing the ayah, they had no shortage of other lackeys, any one of whom could be prevailed upon to scrub a back, pour some water, and hand him a towel. There was no need for her to trouble herself.

"I'm unclothed," he said.

Not that she hadn't seen him plenty in the past few days, changing his clothes regularly so that they could be laundered.

"I imagine you are since you are in a bathtub."

She unbuttoned one sleeve and rolled it up, in neat, creased folds, exposing her arm inch by inch and stopping only well past her elbow. Then she did the same with her other sleeve.

He was not easily moved by the sight of a woman undressing. But with her, everything was different. The sight of her removing her gloves used to make his heart beat faster. And in the library of the Wyden town house, he, no stranger to the female anatomy, had been wholly seduced by what on any other woman would have been a most prim neckline—he'd never seen her shoulders, let alone the swell of her breasts, which she'd traced absentmindedly with one thumb as she flipped the pages of the encyclopedia, as if she were unfamiliar with the topography of her own body.

"Lean your head back," she said.

He did. She poured warm water over his hair and washed it with a bar of Castile soap, her fingernails scraping his scalp gently. When she was done, she poured more water over his hair. The water collected in a bucket she'd set under the edge of the tub.

She toweled his hair before sitting down on her stool by the side of the tub. From the cloth bag she'd brought she took out a piece of sea sponge, briefly submerged it underwater to moisten it, then soaped it with the meticulousness of a surgeon preparing for an operation.

Her hands were wet. Her forearms too glistened. Lovely, smooth, wet skin. His breaths came in a little shallower. She started at his left shoulder and washed him down to his fingertips. Then she changed sides and did the same to his right arm, her gaze staying well away from the center of the tub, where the water, though turning slightly opaque with suds, hardly disguised his reaction.

The tent was warm and dimly misty with the steam from the bath. Her face was dewy and flushed. He licked the back of his teeth. He wanted to lick *her* teeth: There was a slight chip to her front tooth that he'd wanted to lick since he sat down to dinner that first night at her father's town house.

He lifted his hand and undid the top button of

her blouse. She rose immediately, knocking over the stool.

"Please don't do that."

She rounded behind him, sponged and rinsed his back. Then she returned to his side and tapped on his kneecap, which was above the water, to indicate that he should raise his foot to the rim of the tub.

From where she now stood it was impossible for anyone not three-quarters blind to miss what had happened to him below his waist. And did she really think that she of all people could bathe him without provoking this very reaction?

The sponge made its way up the length of his leg. It was soft and just slightly grainy against his skin. She was efficient about it—swift, firm strokes, no teasing, no dawdling.

And yet his arousal only burgeoned. The sponge brushed his erection. He hissed. As if she hadn't heard, she moved to the other side of him and tapped on his other knee. Again she washed him to almost the top of his thigh.

He considered defining cock-teaser for her and decided he was being much too harsh. This was Bryony, who was probably doing her best to give him a proper bath while ignoring his rampant erection.

She scrubbed his torso and his abdomen. He thought they were done, but she rolled her sleeves further up and knelt down. She reached underwater to his midsection. He sucked in air. The sponge lapped at his scrotum. And below and to the sides of it, light, smooth strokes on skin that was extraordinarily susceptible to touch. He swallowed. And swallowed again.

The sponge climbed. It moved up the trunk of his erection, skimmed around the head, slid down, then up again. The sensations of it . . . as if she were an electrical source. Or a wildfire.

Then it was no longer the sponge touching him, but her bare hand. A skimmer, almost like the brush of a fishtail. But it was still too much after nearly three and a half long, starved years. He came, his hips tilting, his facing contorting, his throat working sounds of hopeless pleasure.

When he opened his eyes, she stood a few steps away by the foot of the tub, her arms held stiffly at her sides. The sea sponge floated just beneath the surface of the water.

"I assume you lost the sponge and were feeling around for it," he said. He could not imagine that it could have been anything *but* an accident.

She made no response for a long moment. And then, "Shall I rinse you?"

There was nothing else for it. He rose to his feet. Her gaze swept him. Then she looked away and hurried to the buckets of water that had been brought earlier just for this purpose.

Warm water sluiced over him. When all the soap residue had been rinsed from him, she held out the towel for him.

"I'll let you dress now."

After having seen him in the altogether and brought him to orgasm, however accidental?

"Are you sure you are the same person who refused to let me remove my nightshirt when we were married?"

"If God wanted men to go to bed unclothed, he would not have made nightshirts," she said, already outside the tent. "And besides, you removed your nightshirt anyway on certain occasions."

❦

When their conjugal relations had become more awkward, not less, with time, he'd stopped coming to her at bedtime. Instead, he'd come in the witching hours of morning, when she was fast asleep, and made love to her then.

For several days things seemed to thaw inexplicably between them. He smiled more often. Spoke more at dinner. And looked at her in ways that made her breath catch and her face burn.

And for those several days she thought she'd had frightfully vivid erotic dreams. Until one night she woke up to find herself naked and impaled, her ankles on his shoulders.

She couldn't stop—not him, not herself. She could only whimper and pant and moan helplessly.

The next day she'd asked him to desist. She could not live like that, so thoroughly in his power. But of course she did not say that to him. She only listed how important it was for her to get her night's sleep and that he was welcome to exercise his conjugal rights at any other time, but not when she was asleep.

He'd listened very quietly as she'd delivered her speech. Then he left without giving any response. That night she'd awakened screaming with a climax brought on by his lips and tongue. And of course she could only shudder futilely as he entered her, whispering in her ear that one day she would return the favor.

The next day she spoke to him again, this time in sharper tones. For her trouble, she found herself bent over the edge of the bed, her feet on the floor, her legs pulled wide apart, trembling too close to the edge of pleasure to wield any mastery over the situation.

Her requests to halt these nocturnal jaunts were met with stares more and more hostile—and pleasures more and more addictive. She feared the pleasures. She feared him, especially when he promised her that one day she would beg him to fuck her. Because she might.

And on it went. Until she couldn't go to sleep for fear of

*what he would do to her that night. What he would make
her do. Until she almost killed a patient because she was so
under-rested and distraught.*

*That evening she went home, bolted all the doors to her
chamber, and never let him into her bed again for as long as
they lived under the same roof.*

❧

*He'd gone to her in her sleep because he was tired of playing
the lion to her martyr. He wanted a chance to hold her and
touch her without being made to feel that he somehow de-
filed her.*

*He hadn't meant to go further than that, but as he'd lain
next to her, she'd turned and fitted herself to him. Her body,
always so rigid, had been as pliant as a belly dancer's. He
had not been able to help himself. He'd disrobed them both
and made love to her. And she'd put her arms about him
and clutched him tight to her for the very first time—asleep,
but whispering his name.*

*Leo, she'd said. Leo. Leo. Leo. And he'd emptied into
her like a dam breaking.*

*It frightened him, the hold she had over him, that in one
moment of crushing pleasure he would forget all his resent-
ment and hopelessness. But the sweetness of it, he could not
get enough of it—he could not get enough of her, his wife of
the witching hours.*

Perhaps this could be a new beginning for them. He

could woo her with lovemaking, something as sweet and artful as spun sugar, a meringue of sensations, a froth of kisses and caresses to float her to the clouds.

He wanted it, how he'd wanted it, that newlywed idyll they never had, that halcyon of mad corporeal infatuation. If he had it, a year, a month, or even a solid week of it, he could change her, repair the misalignment of their temperaments, and remold their marriage into something lovely and worthwhile.

Instead she banished him altogether. They grew further and further apart. And their marriage dissolved like a pearl in vinegar.

❦

The summer night sky over the Hindu Kush, domed by the Milky Way's mage light, was infinitely splendid. Strewn against this craggy luminosity, millions of tiny stars shone, a diamond heist gone awry.

Bryony left the flaps of her tent open, the next best thing to sleeping under the stars. If only she could sleep, that was. But the otherwise inoffensive camp bed felt like a heap of rocks against her back. And she was hot in the frustratingly still air—Chitral Valley was a good two thousand five hundred feet lower than the village of Balanguru in Rumbur Valley, and noticeably warmer in climate. The collar of her nightgown chafed her throat. Within the long flannel sleeves, her arms sweltered.

She wanted what she should not want, what she could not have.

She wanted *him*.

The bath had been her way of scratching her itch, to touch him under a semi-legitimate guise. The weight he'd lost and the illness had not been enough to diminish what months of strenuous daily exertion had done for him. His body was efficient and compact, his shoulders strong, his abdomen ridged, his legs long-thewed and shapely.

And his skin, so very wonderful to the touch. When she'd brought the sponge down to his forearm and her wrist had slid over the hair on his skin, she'd almost jerked her hand away in surprise. She'd forgotten how different a man felt.

Or perhaps she never truly knew.

I assume you lost the sponge and were feeling around for it.

No, she'd let go of the sponge to touch him. But she'd been too timid to grab him along his length—it seemed an awfully rude thing to do. She'd only barely brushed him, in the end. And his response had been truly out of all proportion to her hardly-at-all caress.

But it had shaken her and aroused her. And the memories of it had continued to arouse her for the remainder of the day, though she'd taken pains to avoid him around the camp. And now the lack of him was a physical torment. Her skin was oversensitive for the want of his touch. Her head, already aching from her inadequate rest during his illness, throbbed with frustration. Certain other parts of her throbbed too, biological imperative exerting itself at the worst possible moment.

She raised herself to a sitting position and shoved her fingers into her hair, digging her nails at her scalp. After a few minutes she got up and ducked out of the tent.

Overhead the sky was so saturated that it was a wonder it did not rain stars, the way an over-festooned ball gown shed seed pearls and crystal drops deep into a waltz. The mountains were massive shadows. The silence was unearthly, the eerie quiet of the deepest night, when birds dozed and nocturnal creatures slunk soundlessly on their unseen hunt.

She walked the thirty feet or so that separated their tents and slipped into his tent to check on him. He slept, his breaths quiet and steady. She knelt down, took his pulse—normal—and his temperature—also normal. He was young and hard-wearing; by morning he would be back to his old self.

She tucked in the sheet more snugly about him. There, all done. Now she would go back to her tent and try again to sleep.

Except she didn't move. She remained as she was and listened to his hypnotically easy breaths. Then she touched him again.

Her hand landed on his shoulder. She followed its outline to his throat, then his chin. He'd shaved before the bath, but already the beginning of stubble scraped her palm. Her hand shook—the rest of her shook too—but whatever it was that drew her toward him was more powerful than her much-justified, tremor-inducing fear.

She leaned down and kissed him, his neck, his cheek, his ear. He smelled still of her Castile soap, of oil of olive from faraway Iberia. It made her light-headed, the feel of him, the scent of him, the madness of what she was about to do.

She unbuttoned her nightgown at the throat and pulled it over her head. It had affected her strangely to know that he'd been in the same countries she had, as if they'd been fellow refugees, fleeing from the same wreckage. That did not diminish the stupidity of what she was about to do. But stupid things had a gravity and a momentum of their own; they crushed good thinking and resistance as colonists with guns and cannons overcame spear-throwing natives.

Her heart hurt. But her skin felt delicious, freedom after an eon of oppression. "Leo," she said softly, more to herself than to him. *Why must it always be you, Leo?*

She pulled off the sheet she'd just carefully tucked in around him. He wore nothing to cover his torso. His chest was smooth and taut. She drew a finger down the center of it, from the base of his throat to his navel, then she pressed her lips to his skin and kissed the trail she'd drawn.

Her hand traveled further down the center of him. She was not surprised to find him hot and hard. It seemed almost . . . inevitable.

He slumbered on, even as she climbed onto the camp bed, straddling him, careful to keep her weight on her own hands and knees. Even as she grazed her nipples against his torso. Even as she took him inside her.

The slip and slide of her hair on her own skin was an unfamiliar, decadent feeling. Where his sheets had shifted, her knees sank into the raw canvas of the camp bed. The smallest movements on her part brought her floods of sensation. She heard herself murmur, little prayers at the altar of Eros. What did she want? Surely not this terrible loneliness, this complete isolation in the midst of the most physically intimate act possible?

Then her prayers were answered and a long chain of climaxes began. She shuddered and cried out in desperate gratitude. "Leo. Leo," she breathed. "Leo."

Suddenly he joined her in it. His hands clamped over her thighs, his pelvis raised, his breaths tumbled out in gasps. He was rough and massive against her. She couldn't help coming again, her entire body seizing with the violence of her pleasure.

And then her mind seized in dismay. For he touched her, tracing a line down the center of her torso as she had done with him.

"Bryony," he murmured. "Bryony."

Chapter Eight

On the day Bryony asked for an annulment, Leo had bought her a present: a W. Watson & Sons microscope. An imposing piece of equipment, with a rotating slide holder, two substage condensers, a camera lucida attachment, and a magnificent finish of polished brass that gleamed like Cupid's golden arrow.

Why the present? He had not a single reason. He didn't even know whether she needed a new microscope. But sometimes the males of the species brought home shiny, beautiful things, with hope burning in their hearts.

The microscope and its numerous accessories had come in a handsome mahogany case. He laid the case on the desk of the study, then crossed the room to pour himself a drop of brandy.

"Do you have a moment? I need to speak to you."

He turned around in astonishment. She stood at the door

of the study, dressed in a jacket-and-skirt set of blue silk, her usual uniform for heading to the hospital. Except it was the middle of the afternoon—he hadn't seen her home during the day in God knew how long.

"Certainly," he said. "Could I get you something to drink?"

She declined and took a chair in front of the desk. "Would you like to have a seat also?"

He sat down behind the desk, across from her. She sat stiffly, her face wan, her lips pinched, her eyes deeply shadowed. And she smelled of some strange chemical substance, not carbolic acid, but the offensive pungency of ammonium. Yet he'd never been so glad to be near her, to be on speaking terms again.

She placed her hands on the desk, her fingers interlaced, and began to address him.

Beyond the first sentence, her words washed through his hearing like a random sampling of the Oxford English Dictionary. He stared at the movement of her mouth, the shaping and reshaping of her lips, and felt the vibration of her speech against his eardrums, but understood nothing beyond that she meant to push him off a cliff.

At some point he left the desk and opened his watch by the window. Some barmy part of himself wanted to keep track of time, to see how long it took her to make the case that they should end their marriage in a pack of lies. But he could no more read time than he could read Etruscan. So *he only stared at his watch, a watch she'd given to him as an engagement present, a watch that had the words "Love is patient. Love is kind." inscribed on the inside of the lid.*

He felt neither patient nor kind. When she finished speaking, he was going to drag her upstairs. And she could tell the bedpost what she thought of his barbarity.

And then she did finish speaking. He looked back at her. She gazed at him expectantly. "May I count on your assistance in this matter?"

She'd stood up. One of her hands rested on the surface of the desk, the other on the case that contained the microscope.

He walked back to the desk, pulled out the case from under her hand, opened the clasp, and assembled the microscope as she watched. When it was done, he took a step back. Yes, it was very fine-looking indeed, and he'd been promised that it would last a lifetime.

Across the table she cast a blank look at the microscope and raised her eyes to him, eyes that were the green of a wet summer. "Well, may I count on your assistance in this matter?"

And he came to a startling realization: She was not worth it. She was not worth the microscope. She was not worth the effort he'd expend to fuck her quiescent. She was not worth the dignity and solemnity of a marriage.

"Of course," he said. "You may be assured of my every cooperation."

❧

If he stared hard enough, he could make out the shape of a shoulder, the flow of an arm. She sat above him, frozen, as naked as a beached mermaid, her skin a smooth dusky expanse that glimmered faintly blue in the starlight. Her hair, like a rising tide, concealed the curvature of her breasts and half of her face.

He'd never seen so much of her, even though he could hardly see anything of her except shadow and shimmer. In her sleep, in the cool, shuttered darkness of her bedchamber in Belgravia, he'd mapped every inch of her body. He knew her by geography (the ascent of a kneecap, the bumps of her spine), by texture (the slight roughness of heels and elbows, the tiny hairs on her forearms and calves), and by taste (the milky sweetness of a nipple, the soft turmeric tang between her legs). But never by sight.

He spread his hand over her abdomen. She was warm and still, like Pygmalion's statue brought to life. He looped his other arm about her, and pulled her torso toward him.

She resisted, but it was a resistance more of form than substance, for he applied only a slight pressure. When he had her close enough he kissed her chin, her jaw. She turned her face away, as if afraid he would kiss her on the mouth. So he kissed her ear, most attentively, and listened to her soft, ragged breaths of pleasure.

Her ear, her shoulder, the top of her arm. His hands pushed their way down her back, and cupped her soft, round bottom. He was hard again inside her. She whimpered. Such a beautiful sound, pure lust, pure pleasure.

Slowly, for the camp bed was narrow, he turned them around so that he was above her. He kissed her throat, her collarbone, her breasts. Her hips moved, flooding him with sensation.

Her fingers encircled his wrists tentatively. For a moment he was petrified with fear, that she would push him away. But her hands traveled up his arms, and finally hooked behind his neck.

His heart slowly fell back into place. His body moved into an appropriately worshipful rhythm. But her concurrence was a powerful aphrodisiac, and soon he was again drunk on desire, helplessly in thrall, holding back only to please her.

And once she clenched about him and quavered—ah, then he could not hold back anymore at all, the long-gathering wave crashing ashore, the fervent worshipper driven into ecstacy.

He thrust into her fiercely, claiming her, marking her, filling her with himself, dominating and submitting, taking and giving.

Her master and her slave.

As soon as she'd gathered her wits together, she left the bed. She picked up her nightgown and hurriedly pulled it over her head.

"Stay with me," he said.

"I'd better not."

"So you were only exploiting me?" There was a hint of smile in his voice. He knew very well that she was not capable of such a thing.

It took her half a minute to find the sleeves of her nightgown and thrust her arms inside, by which time he'd risen from bed and lit a lantern.

"Don't go yet."

"It's late."

"It was already late when you came." He'd worn only a pair of pyjama trousers in bed, but now he'd put on the kurta tunic too. The three buttons at the top of the kurta, however, were all open. The flickering lantern light gilded the exposed skin of his throat and his chest. "Have a seat."

She shook her head.

He rubbed a thumb across her cheek. "Are you going to force me to keep standing in my condition?"

Medically speaking, he was a well man and could stand any number of hours. Not to mention, they were headed up Lowari Pass in the morning. But he was still too thin, and she was still of the belief that he needed far more rest than he allowed himself.

Reluctantly, she sat down at the edge of the bed. He sat down beside her and placed his arm across her shoulders. "I won't bite, you know," he said. "I might lick, but I won't bite."

"I don't want you to lick either."

"I will lick only where you like, how is that?"

"No. This won't happen again."

"Hmm. Then why did it happen at all?" He kissed her lightly on the corner of her eye. "Have you become delirious too?"

Of course she had. A delirium of primal urges and senselessness. "I'm sorry. It won't happen again."

"I want it to happen again," he said, his voice low but fierce.

She shook her head.

"Why not?"

"Because it was a mistake."

"Just as our marriage was a mistake?" His voice lost some of its warmth.

She swallowed. "Precisely."

He rose; the tent was barely tall enough for him to stand straight. "Did your heart turn into stone when you lost Toddy?" he asked, his back to her.

Her not-at-all-stony heart seared in pain. "Please

don't make conjectures on a subject of which you know nothing."

"You are right, I know nothing of your heart, because you've taken great care to ensure that is the case. But you have studied science; you understand that sometimes indirect observation can yield equally powerful evidence."

"What are you talking about?"

"What I have seen. Irrefutable proof of your unfeelingness."

All the excess warmth of the night drained away. Her toes were cold on the ground. "If this is something to do with our annulm—"

"It's not." He shoved his hand through his hair. "You've likely forgotten this already. But a long time ago, you received a letter from a woman named Bettie Young. You had delivered her baby by caesarean section. In that letter, she wrote that one day, when her baby was old enough, she'd tell him that when they needed it the most, God sent an angel in the form of a lady surgeon."

She was suddenly shaking. "I remember that letter."

"I'm surprised, because I found it crumpled and thrown away."

"I don't keep every thank-you letter I receive."

"I would have thought if you kept any at all, that

would be the one you kept." He turned around and faced her. "Or are you so bitter from losing Toddy that you cannot bear to see another child *not* lose his mother?"

She was on her feet. A loud smack reverberated in the tent. Only as she looked down at her smarting hand in shock did she understand that she'd struck him. "Don't you dare say such a thing about me," she said, her voice just short of a growl. "Don't you dare even think it."

He rubbed the back of his fingers against his cheek. But his expression was relentless. "Why shouldn't I think it? Why shouldn't I draw logical conclusions?"

"Because your conclusion is wrong."

His lips flattened in scorn. "Then you explain it, since you know your own reasoning so much better. Why was the letter in the wastebasket?"

❧

Bryony was having an excellent day. Leo had come to see her at the hospital to take his leave—he was traveling to Paris the week before their wedding, to give a series of lectures—and her fellow physicians, many of whom were meeting him for the first time, had been dumbstruck by her charming, beautiful fiancé. She'd floated on a sharp, superior pleasure.

*And now she could add a successful out-patient cae-
sarean section to the accomplishments of her day. The circumstances were somewhat unusual: A lady's maid who'd
left service to marry, only to return to her mistress's employ
six weeks later, after her husband died in an industrial accident. The housekeeper stressed repeatedly that the maid had
been married—that the child was legitimate—as if Bryony
had a special set of shoddier operations she kept in reserve
for the illicit and the illegitimate.*

*The baby had cried loudly and lustfully when she had
pried it from the womb. The attending nurse had already
bathed him and swaddled him and reported that he was doing well. Bryony snipped the ends of the stitches and peeled
off her bloody gloves.*

*She'd brought printed booklets with her on how to care
for the surgical wounds that resulted from a caesarean section. While the surgical assistants cleaned and packed the
surgical implements, Bryony gave a booklet to the housekeeper, went over the most salient points, and reassured the
housekeeper that a nurse from the hospital would also come
to check on Mrs. Young and the baby every day for three
weeks.*

*The surgery had taken place on the table in the servants'
hall in the basement of the house. As the housekeeper studied
the booklet, a cultured female voice drifted down from narrow windows near the ceiling that opened to the small garden between the house and the mews.*

"There you are."

Then Bryony heard his voice. "I thought you said it was the servants' half day. I can see people in the servants' hall."

No, it couldn't be Leo. He was on his way to Paris. And he would not show up at some woman's back door as if he were conducting an affair.

"Really?" said the woman. "The house is quite empty."

"Perhaps this is not such a good idea after all."

But the voice sounded so much like Leo's.

"Oh come, you are here already."

The door closed. Footsteps crossed toward the front of the house. Then up the stairs.

"Miss?" the housekeeper asked.

Bryony turned toward her blindly. "I beg your pardon?"

"I was just asking if you and your ladies would like some tea?"

"For Miss Simpson and Mrs. Murdock, yes. None for me," she said. "And do you have a powder room that I can use?"

The housekeeper gave her the directions to the powder room. Bryony took the steps up from the basement, through the green baize door, and found the main stairs that led up from the front hall. She climbed up with a quietness that belied what she repeated madly to herself: It couldn't be Leo, it couldn't be Leo, it couldn't possibly be Leo.

He would never do anything like that.

Would he?

The bedrooms for the master and the mistress of the house were usually two stories up from the ground floor. She walked ever more softly as she set foot on the landing.

"Still like to have your door open, I see," said the man.

Bryony jumped. The door was almost immediately to her left. And if she were to take two steps closer and look through the opening, she would—

She covered her mouth with her hand. A woman lay on an enormous bed, completely naked.

"And I still undress faster than you," said the woman. She batted her eyelashes.

"With commendable speed," said the man.

She would not think of him as Leo. She would not, even though she shivered every time he spoke.

He moved. His face became visible in a mirror on the far side of the room. Her mouth opened, but no scream would emerge. For a moment the world teetered on edge. Then she descended the stairs with the swiftness and silence of a ghost, shaking every step of the way.

❧

She had never forgotten Toddy. She had never forgotten her three years of incandescent happiness. And she had never, contrary to what she'd made herself believe, reconciled herself to her loss. All along she'd been waiting for another fairy godmother to come along—because that was what Toddy had been, her friend, her faithful companion, her fairy godmother who'd dispelled loneliness and breathed magic into her life.

Leo had possessed that magic. Whenever he arrived at a gathering, excitement reverberated to the rafters. When he spoke, his audience listened hungrily, as the children had done with Toddy. And when he smiled, young ladies literally swooned—two separate instances of it at the first ball he'd attended in London.

But most important, he'd included her in that magic. In those better days, when he looked at her, it had always been with great interest and singular attention, as if she mattered, truly, significantly, not just to him, but to the world at large. And the world at large had noticed. Society, which had never known quite what to do with an odd duck like her, had warmed perceptibly toward her because *he* had seen something in her.

And *she* had seen *him* as the long-awaited successor to Toddy, the new guarantor of her happiness, the one who would banish the dogged monotony from her life, restore laughter and splendor, and usher in a new golden era. And she'd loved him for it, with the uncritical fervor of an adolescent and the faith of a child.

Her Leo, so bright, so beautiful.

And in the end, so catastrophically flawed.

It was bizarre, thinking back, to see that she hadn't been angry. Not that day, and not in the week that followed—her anger had only come when she saw him again, before the altar, on the day of their wedding. Until then she'd known nothing but shame, such shame that she'd gone straight home to bed, to whimper under the cover, such shame that she could not look herself in the mirror, such shame that she was convinced every conversation in every drawing room must be about nothing but her ignorance and her gullibility.

In time anger had superceded shame. And in time misery had superceded anger. But the shame was always there, a dark, sorry thing that infested the subterranean layers of her heart. It kept her close-mouthed about what happened, because she could not face that shame.

Or the pain of reliving his betrayal.

"You are not really interested in a letter from someone you've never met," she said. "You want to know why I no longer wanted to be married to you."

He stared at her, his gray eyes the color of rain. "Fair enough. Why?"

"Because I realized that you were a callow youth, full of yourself, and full of the sort of frivolities that I despised. It shamed me that I'd chosen so poorly.

That of all the men in London who would have made me a suitable spouse, I had to pick a self-centered popinjay."

He was very still, not even breathing, it seemed.

She exhaled. "And there you have it. Good night."

Chapter Nine

Bryony was awake for a full five minutes before she realized that Leo was in the tent with her. She bolted upright. Judging by the light coming in from the gap between the tent flaps, she'd slept well past sunrise.

"There is something you are not telling me," he said quietly.

He sat cross-legged in the far corner of her tent. Even in the relative dimness inside, she could tell that his eyes were bloodshot. In his hand he held a mug of tea, tea without any steam curling above it.

"How long have you been here?"

"I'm not sure. An hour, maybe." He took a swallow of the tea. "I came in to tell you it was time to get up, but I decided to let you sleep some more. I don't imagine you slept very well last night."

"I'll be fine. If you will step out, I'll get ready and we can start."

"I'm not stepping out," he said calmly. "I'm not going anywhere until you tell me what it is you are hiding from me."

"What makes you think there's something I'm hiding from you?"

"Because I wasn't that callow a youth, I wasn't that full of myself, and I wasn't that frivolous. And self-centered or not, I most certainly was not a popinjay."

"You certainly think well of yourself."

"Other than your virulent dislike of me, I have no reason to think that I grate on people particularly. And you were the one who proposed. How did I go from a man you wanted to spend a lifetime with to a man you couldn't stand?"

"Sometimes much can be discovered in the space of a few weeks."

"A few weeks? You refer to the length of our engagement?"

She rubbed her temple. She'd said too much already.

"You were still working," he said. "We saw each other alone only on Sundays, with one dinner with your family during the week, and perhaps one visit with Will to check on the wedding preparations. And I was gone the whole week before the wedding. Even if my character were truly rotten, there was no time for you to discover it."

He frowned. "Was someone feeding you rumors?"

"Do I look like the sort of person people come to with rumors?"

He looked at her steadily. "Then what was it?"

She got off the bed. "Leave me alone."

"I already told you I won't. We can stay here til the end of time, if you like."

"I need to use the facilities."

"Tell me and you may use the facilities as much as you like." He was adamant. "Even our criminals are formally accused and informed of their crimes. You tried, convicted, and sentenced me without ever giving me a chance to defend myself. I deserve better than that from you. I deserve at least the truth. Or am I truly to think of you as heartless and capricious?"

She was angry again, angry enough that her shame faded into the background. Indeed, why should she be the one who was ashamed? She'd done nothing wrong. He was the one who had destroyed any chance they had at happiness.

She clenched her fists. "No. You may not think of me as heartless and capricious."

✍

Suddenly he was afraid, as if he were faced with Pandora's box, the calamities within which, once let loose, could never be put back again.

But it was too late. Now she wanted him to know. Now her eyes burned with anger. Now her voice took on the weight and the inexorability of that of an avenger.

"That letter you were so sure showed every flaw in my character—the woman who wrote it, Bettie Young, she worked for a certain Mrs. Hedley. When I delivered Bettie Young's baby, it was at Mrs. Hedley's house, on a day the servants were supposed to have the afternoon off."

There was a roar in Leo's head.

"You do recollect, I hope? But then again, perhaps you did this sort of thing all over town, and Mrs. Hedley's was but one address among many."

He shook his head mutely. No, he had not done this sort of thing all over town. And he had a fine recollection of what happened that day.

He'd met Mrs. Hedley in Cairo, at the end of a North African journey that took him from Casablanca to the Nile. A young widow, she'd kept house for her brother, who worked at the British Embassy. During Leo's two weeks in Egypt, they'd had an excellent time together.

Several years later, on the day he was to depart for Paris, they'd run into each other quite by accident in London. He hadn't known that she'd returned from Cairo—her brother had at last married and she was happy to get away from the heat of tropics—but she had known about his upcoming marriage.

Three months after that, they'd met one last time, on the elegant suspension bridge in St. James's Park, this time at his instigation.

"I need to know something," he asked Mrs. Hedley, his voice low even though there was no one nearby. "Are you sure you never told anyone about what happened in April?"

"Of course not." Mrs. Hedley scowled at his question, insulted. "I wouldn't get you in trouble that way. Besides, Mr. Abraham and I had already met by then. He started courting me two weeks after that. I certainly will not have him think that I'd done anything with my widowhood except wait for him to come along."

"But your servants—they were there that day."

"They didn't even know who you were. It wasn't as if you left a calling card on your way out. Besides, they were completely preoccupied: My maid had a baby that afternoon in the servants' hall."

He apologized for questioning her discretion, she accepted his apology, he wished her the best of luck with Mr. Abraham, and they parted amicably, she for an excursion to Bond Street, he to his empty house in Belgravia. Months later, when he read the letter from Bettie Young, thanking Bryony for saving herself and her child, he'd made no connection between the letter writer and Genevieve Hedley's maid.

He should have. He should have known all along that *this* was the dark heart of their story.

❧

He was still and silent, his eyes lowered beneath his dark, straight brows, his chiseled features in shadow.

She was shaking again. She felt raw, torn open, and deeply, deeply ashamed—almost as ashamed as she'd been in the hours and days immediately following what she'd witnessed in that house on Upper Berkley Street.

"What did you see?" he finally asked.

"Your face in the mirror."

"In flagrante delicto?"

"Not yet." He'd approached Mrs. Hedley's bed; he'd been not in it but beside it. And he'd still had his shirt on, his braces strapped firmly over his shoulders.

"Why didn't you stop me?"

"*Stop* you?" In all the intervening years, the thought

had never occurred to her that she could have made her presence known. One did not stop a flaming wreck. One ran as fast as one could. "I'm afraid that as my illusions shattered left and right, I did not have that kind of presence of mind."

He passed his hand over his face. When he looked at her again, his eyes were blank. "Why didn't you call off the wedding?"

She blinked. She'd asked that question of herself many times and it was always the point at which the pureness of her righteous indignation began to be adulterated with the complicity of her own frailty in this matter.

She had not called off the wedding because he was the one great prize of her life other women of her social station would forever covet. Because she feared the aftermath of a broken engagement so close to the wedding. Because she'd convinced herself that she was magnanimous enough to forgive him; that she forgiven him already.

Vanity, cowardliness, and delusion—faults in her character that she hadn't even known, precipitated by the crisis.

"I thought I could forgive you," she said. The human mind was capable of infinite self-deception.

Except she'd never forgiven anyone in her entire

life. Her heart was made of glass: It could break, but it could not expand.

"And when did you realize you could not forgive me?" he asked, his voice soft and bleak.

She turned her face aside. Within the first hours of their marriage she'd realized it—that she hadn't forgiven him at all, that her whole body revolted whenever he touched her. But by then they were already married, and it was too late.

❧

Shame. Self-loathing. Frustration. They churned in him, each enough to drown him outright.

She sat back down on her camp bed again, her face pale as bleached bones. "Was she your mistress?"

He shook his head. "No. We were lovers in Cairo for two weeks when I was nineteen. The day I was to go to France, after I left your hospital, I stopped at a stationer's. That was where I ran into her."

"And she proved irresistible. I see."

Mrs. Hedley had congratulated him warmly. And then, once they were outside the stationer's, she'd winked at him in her bubbly way, and asked if he'd like one last tumble before he became a respectably married man.

He'd turned her down. As he'd turned down other women who'd wanted to be his last lay.

"She was far from irresistible."

"You went with her."

The incontrovertible truth. He had gone with Mrs. Hedley in the end.

"I had a case of cold feet."

"About me?"

"About you."

"And that is your excuse?"

"That's not my excuse. That was just what happened."

"Very convenient, don't you think, to have a case of cold feet just when you run into an old lover."

"It was not like that."

"Then what was it like?"

What *had* it been like?

"I suppose—suppose—I—" He took a deep breath. He'd never stammered in his life. "I suppose there were always doubts in the back of my head. That I'd made too hasty a decision. That you and I hardly knew each other. That we might not be as well suited as we both wanted it to be."

She stared at the hem of her nightgown. "And then what?"

"Then I went to say good-bye to you at the hospital. I thought it would be interesting, to see the hospital. But I'd never been in a hospital before and it unsettled me. *You* in that hospital unsettled me."

He'd arrived at a bad time, possibly. There had been some kind of food poisoning going around, patients were vomiting in the lobby of the hospital, faster than the unfortunate cleaners could mop the messes away.

He should have been reassured by her coolness—she'd walked through the lobby as if it were a flower garden in spring—but it had only further heightened his sense that he truly knew nothing of her. The triumphal, proprietary air she took on as she introduced him to her colleagues also bothered him. He would have expected some such from a society miss, but not from her, whom he'd believed to be above such boastfulness.

"What about me that unsettled you?"

"Your aloofness, which I'd always liked before. Your vanity, which I'd never known existed."

She laced her fingers together. "I see."

He wanted to evaporate, to simply cease to exist. His reasons were in every instance pale and stupid—even more mortifying spoken out loud. But he had no choice now. He owed her this much.

"On my walk to the stationer's, I was—I was suddenly swamped with doubt. I questioned whether my decision to marry you wasn't as lunatic as everyone said it was, whether I was really resigned to a life without children of my own, whether we wouldn't end up in a few years with nothing to say to each other."

He stared at his hands. "And the wedding was in a week."

Outside Imran called to a coolie to take more care with the bathtub. The river babbled cheerfully. The ayah softly hummed a tune that seemed to be a temple song.

"I could have drunk myself into a stupor. I could have unburdened myself to Will. But Mrs. Hedley was there, and she wanted a tumble, so she was the distraction I chose."

Ironic, that in what he'd done out of fear that they might be unhappy together lay the cause of the greater part of their unhappiness.

"If it's any consolation to you, I regretted my choice even before I entered her house. Afterward I thought myself a hundred kinds of stupid. I came back from Paris determined to make something beautiful of our life together, because you were the only one I wanted." Suddenly he had to speak past a lump in his throat. "I suppose it was too late."

She said nothing.

"And if it's any further consolation, I haven't been with anyone else since I married you."

She spread her hands open over her knees. "I would like to dress now, if you don't mind."

He rose from the corner. "Certainly. I beg your pardon."

At the tent flap he turned back. "You are right: I was a callow youth. But I never meant to hurt you. I'm sorry that I did—in such a despicable way, no less. Forgive me."

But he already knew that she would not forgive him.

Chapter Ten

It took dozens of one-hundred-eighty-degree turns for the road to zigzag up the steep slope leading toward Lowari Pass, ten thousand feet above sea level, a narrow gap in snow-peaked mountains that towered thousands of feet higher to either side. From the top, looking down at the way she'd come, Bryony thought the dirt path resembled so many hairpins that a careless goddess had dropped. The mountains, like a choppy sea, stretched blue and jagged toward the horizon.

She tugged her coat more tightly about her—Leo had warned her it would be cold at the top, but it was even colder than she'd supposed.

"Here, drink this."

She accepted the hot tea he offered with a murmured "Thank you." She didn't know how he had managed to get the cook up to the top first—so that there was hot tea for everyone—but he seemed very efficient at this sort of thing.

A gust of wind blew. She shivered despite the hot tea in her gloved hands. He took off his coat and draped it over her shoulders. She waited another minute, until she heard his voice much further away, before she turned her head for a glimpse of him without his coat, standing by the mule train, listening to a gesticulating coolie.

She wanted to cry.

In the isolation of her own imagination, what he'd done had seemed so much worse, one example of a large, pernicious pattern: liaisons all over London during their engagement; and after their wedding, adulterous affairs left and right.

When it was nothing of the sort.

What he did was still atrocious and wrong. And she would have been well justified in jilting him. But she hadn't jilted him; she'd married him. Were wedding vows but so much confetti, an ephemeral sparkle in the air, to be swept away as rubbish the next day? Had she not owed him something more than cold shoulders and locked doors?

Would they have been able to patch things together if they'd had this awful but necessary conversation while they were still married?

She didn't know.

And now she would never know.

❧

The face of the ravine was black rock; the downpours of rainy seasons past had stripped all soil and almost all vegetation from the steep slope. The bottom of it, far below, was barren and rock-strewn, without a trace of the water that had so forcefully shaped the landscape.

Their path was a narrow passage scarped into the very cliff itself: on one side, an implacable wall slanting outward, on the other side, an approximately one-hundred-fifty-foot drop straight down, and in between, a roughly gouged trail that promised sprained ankles, if not a plunge right over the edge.

They'd lost a mule not an hour ago. The poor creature had tumbled over and landed, after a fall that seemed to last a whole day, in a splat of exploded flour bags and what sounded like an almost human whimper.

And then, the horror, it was still alive, broken but alive, its limbs convulsing in agony. Bryony stood with her hand over her mouth, helpless.

A gunshot rang out. With almost frightful precision, a spot of blood appeared between the mule's eyes. It jerked once and went slack.

Bryony turned to see Leo extract a spent round from a breech-loading rifle. She'd known, somewhat vaguely, of the sporting exploits of his youth—his godfather, an enthusiastic sportsman with no other sons, had taken Leo everywhere with him. But she had never seen him operate a firearm—and until this moment had paid no attention at all to the two rifles he had with him.

The deadly accuracy of that single shot astonished her. This man had been her husband. Yet she'd only known him as the drawing room favorite who occasionally produced incomprehensible monographs on some arcane finer points of mathematics.

Perhaps the mule's unfortunate demise colored her perception; perhaps the road truly turned more difficult: Once they resumed their progress she'd found the going hair-raising. She tried to remind herself that 16,000 men had marched northward on precisely this same path to relieve the Siege of Chitral two years ago and that messengers regularly traveled this route with mail and dispatch. But with every wobbly step, she thought only of the whimper of the mule as it hit the scabrous ground far below. And the bullet between its eyes.

The path, following the contour of the cliff, turned abruptly. The already meager width of the trail narrowed to no more than eighteen inches at the turn. Worse, the trail, always uneven, now tipped toward the drop at what seemed to her an almost forty-five-degree angle.

She stopped. She needed to scrape the bottom of the barrel for what remained of her courage. Logically she knew that the path continued beyond the jutting rock blocking her way and that Leo and the guides had already safely rounded it. But she could not see that continuation. And she was not such an experienced mountaineer as to not quake at the tilt of the trail—it would be all too easy to slip off the incline into the sharp-teethed maw of the ravine.

Leo reappeared, coming back toward her. "Are you all right?"

Like her, he had opted to cover this stretch of the road on foot. But whereas she felt herself to be tiptoeing on a tightrope, he walked as easily as if he were on a parade ground.

She nodded by habit before slowly shaking her head.

Without another word he extended his hand. She hesitated only a second before gripping it. Instantly her fear halved.

He took her safely past the tilted ledge skirting the outcrop that cut through the cliff face. She did not let go of his hand on the other side, because it was still the same spine-tingling path. Hands held, he guided her until the path became an ordinary goat trail again, one that did not punish a single misstep with an irreversible plummet.

She could have kissed the ground for simply being there. Releasing his hand, she stripped off her gloves and flexed fingers that were almost numb from tension. She looked up to see his gaze on her hands.

Their eyes met.

"I hear the road is much improved in recent years," he said.

"I can tell," she answered.

He laughed softly.

"Thank you," she added.

He smiled briefly, a sweet smile that drove a bead of pain deep into her heart. "It's no hardship to hold your hand."

❦

Upper Dir was an austere place. Small settlements clung to the skirts of mountains. Broken boulders littered the land, torn loose by earthquakes that occasionally convulsed the Hindu Kush, then deposited willy-nilly by the swift torrents of rainy seasons. And yet occasionally, between forbidding crags, they spied small hidden plateaus, almost alpine in their lushness, and once even a whole slope covered in asters, brilliantly purple.

"Things are running much more smoothly now that you are back on your feet," she said, taking a sip of her afternoon tea, her eyes on the carpet of asters, her mind still on the other side of the Hindu Raj, on the events of the night and the revelations of the morning.

"Did anyone give you trouble when I was sick?"

She shook her head. Imran and Hamid had kept a leash on the coolies. But the coolies had pushed back at the guides, and complained, and dawdled. Only then had she appreciated Leo's talent for putting a ragtag collection of coolies happily to work and orchestrating their tasks so that everything was done the right way at the right time.

She glanced at him. He was looking better, but still tired. Despite their late start, they'd done two marches already, and he planned to get one more in before dark. She wanted to cradle his head in her lap and watch him fall asleep.

"How do you manage the coolies?"

It was strange to be talking like this, of ordinary things, when the sky had fallen. But then she was strangely hungry for his company, as if she missed him, even though he was never more than fifty feet away.

He shrugged. "Experience, I suppose. Do you remember my great-uncle Silverton?"

She thought for a moment. "The old soldier at our wedding who had a chest full of medals?"

"He was a colonel of the Royal Bengal Fusiliers. When we clamored for war stories, he'd tell us that an army marched on its stomach—wars were won and lost less on tactics and strategies than on the soundness of the supply chain. So when I went on safaris with my godfather, I always took it upon myself to oversee logistics," he said, smiling a little. "It was quite heady for the youngest of five sons to finally feel in charge of something."

She was struck dumb with a harebrained realization—harebrained because she should have seen it long ago: He had been the one in charge of their household.

She'd known very little of the complex inner workings of a household. During their brief marriage, however, the house had run like a charm. Her clothes and shoes were kept in perfect shape. The carriage pulled up outside the front door every day just as she got ready to go to the hospital. Dinner appeared every night—always with something she liked—without her having ever consulted with the cook, without her even knowing what the cook looked like.

Even after she'd barred him from her bed.

After he left, however, dinners became too rich, the coachman sometimes drove half drunk, the housekeeper complained constantly about the maids and their followers, and piles of correspondence were left for Bryony to deal with. At that time she'd been in a daze and had taken the various ways her household had fallen apart as merely additional symptoms of her own broken life.

When the truth was he'd taken very good care of her during their marriage and she'd never known it or appreciated it.

❧

Her compact, delicious weight atop him. His name on her lips. Her hips, soft and pliant under his bruising grip. His body, straining off the camp bed, emptying into her in desperate pleasure.

Amazing what a man thought of, looking at a fully clothed woman who did nothing more provocative than sipping her tea while gazing thoughtfully into the distance.

For the thousandth time he wished he'd just met her. That they were but two strangers traveling together, that such lovely, filthy thoughts did not break him in two, but were only a pleasant pastime as he slowly fell under the spell of her aloof beauty and her hidden intensity.

There were so many stories he could tell her, so many ways to draw her out of her shell. He would have waited with bated breath for her first smile, for the sound of her first laughter. He would be endlessly curious about her, eager to undress her metaphorically as well as physically.

The first holding of hands. The first kiss. The first time he saw her unclothed. The first time they became one.

The first time they finished each other's sentences.

But no, they'd met long ago, in the furthest years of his childhood. Their chances had come and gone. All they had ahead of them were a tedious road and a final good-bye.

"Who are those?" she asked.

He looked in the direction she indicated: a band of turbaned, musketed men in the distance, coming toward them.

"The Khan of Dir's levies," he said. "They keep peace along the road."

The Khan of Dir was under obligation to the government of India to maintain the road to Chitral, though the regular posting of levies along the road probably also served as a reminder of force, for the khan's chumminess with the British did not endear him to his subjects. In fact, they seemed to despise him altogether for being a puppet of the distant government whose unwanted influence stabbed through the heart of their mountain fastness.

Leo signaled for tea to be offered to the levies. "Ask them about the situation in Swat," he instructed Imran.

When the levies had taken to the road again, Imran came to offer a summary of the news. The miracle man's fame had grown substantially in Dir in the week since Leo had first heard of him. People talked about the imam at breakfast, lunch, and dinner and debated his chances of success at tea.

Leo wasn't convinced that the imam was anything but a charlatan. But most charlatans, or most small-time martyrdom-seekers for that matter, didn't have people avidly talking of their deeds one hundred and fifty miles away in this kind of terrain.

"Should we worry?" Bryony asked him.

"For now, no. We will keep a close eye on the situation. If and when we receive any solid evidence of danger, any solid evidence at all, we will stop and wait out the trouble."

She nodded, and reached for a piece of the tea cake.

He watched her.

Her blue-black hair, spread like the cape of Erebus. Her

skin, as bare as a beggar's coffer, as fresh and soft as that carpet of asters upon which he would love to place her, her mouth warm, her body sweet and yielding. No past. No future. Only that eternal, glorious moment, unstained by shame or regret.

She intercepted his gaze. Color rose in her cheeks. And he was a smoldering heap of ruins.

"Eat." She pushed a piece of tea cake into his hand. "You need to eat more."

Chapter Eleven

"Will you be in India for much longer?" she asked, as she took out his queen rook.

He returned the favor by eliminating her king bishop. "Probably not. I'm going back to Cambridge."

They were at the confluence of the Dir River and the Panjkora River. It had been a long day. But when she'd lingered at the table after dinner, he'd asked her if she wanted a game of chess and she, pleasantly surprised—once defeated, no man had ever come back for another game with her—had readily agreed.

She looked up at him. He was in his shirtsleeves, sprawled on the folding chair, if it was possible for a man to sprawl while maintaining a perfectly straight back. The two of them were enclosed in the intimacy of a lantern's sphere of light, beyond the faded gold edge of which was a darkness as thick as walls. Beyond that, in the night, there was only the sound of the rivers—the dishes had been washed, the mules fed, the coolies put to bed.

"I hear you already have a house in Cambridge."

"My godfather gave it to me years ago, before we were married. I've never lived in it. Will and Lizzy used it while Lizzy studied at Girton. Now that they've moved back to London, the house is empty again."

"What is it like?"

"The house? Smaller than our house in London, but prettier. It has a back lawn that abuts the bank of the Cam and a good number of cherry trees. In spring, when the trees are in bloom, it's a lovely sight."

"You sound glad of it."

"It will be good to be in Cambridge again—I've been away far too long. But I'm not exactly looking forward to equiping another house."

That was something else she had not appreciated, the enormous task of fully outfitting a house. He'd taken care of all of it.

"No more globe-trotting for you?"

"The wanderings of youth must end at some point." He placed a fingertip on top of his queen bishop, considering, but moved his queen knight instead. "When I'm a wizened old professor at

Cambridge, and can barely climb up to the podium to lecture, I will think back to the frontiers of India—and life's strange paths that had led me here—and remember that this was where the wanderings of *my* youth ended."

His eyes were on the game. She allowed herself to stare at him: the way the lamplight danced upon his hair, hair the color of coffee, a deep, dark shade that was black except in the strongest sunlight; the firm ridge of his nose; the fine shape of his mouth.

"Have you always wanted to be a Cambridge professor?" She urged a pawn forward. So many questions, she thought. So many things she did not know about him.

"Not just any professor: the Lucasian Professor of Mathematics." He placed his chin in his palm. "I thought you'd be impressed by it."

Her heart skipped a beat. "So it was a fairly recent aspiration."

"No, since always."

She blinked. "But I thought you said . . ."

The flame of the lantern swayed. Light and shadow chased across his chiseled cheekbones. There was a stillness to him, a resignation almost. Her heart ached.

He smiled slightly. "I've wanted to be the Lucasian

Professor of Mathematics since I was eleven. And I thought at that time that you'd be impressed by it."

She chortled, out of confusion. "When you were eleven, why would you care what *I* thought of what you were going to do when you grew up?"

"I cared. And when I was twelve, thirteen, fourteen, fifteen, sixteen, and maybe even seventeen." He advanced his queen knight some more.

"What do you mean, exactly?"

"Nothing," he said. "Just that I have loved you, even when I was nothing and no one to you, when you didn't know my name and barely knew my face."

She stared at him, not understanding his words at all. He'd loomed so large in her heart and her imagination for so long that it was difficult to grasp that he could ever have been nothing and no one to her.

A lanky boy sitting down on the stone bridge beside her. A tied handkerchief opening to reveal tiny, bright red cherries. The cherries were cool as the morning air and tartly sweet.

"Any fish biting?"

"No."

"Have you ever thought about what if your father doesn't let you study medicine?"

"He will. Or he can go to the Devil."

"You are a strange girl. More cherries?"

"Yes, thank you."

She shook her head. Where had that come from? She recalled so little of her adolescence—long, blurred years of monotony, waiting impatiently for the day when she could leave Thornwood Manor and her family behind.

The day she at last departed for medical school, her carriage stopped halfway to the train station. A young boy came up to the window and gave her a handful of wildflowers.

"Good luck in Zurich."

"Thank you, sir," she'd said, perplexed, not quite sure who he was.

When the carriage started again, she turned to Callista. "Was that the baby Marsden? What a strange child."

What had she done with those flowers? She had no recollection at all.

Music. Bright lights. Lady Wyden's country Yule ball. She was reluctantly home from Zurich and medical school and reluctantly in attendance. He was her partner in the quadrille that opened the ball, fifteen, and already as tall as she.

"Octavius, is it?"

"Quentin."

"Sorry."

"Don't worry about it. You look beautiful, by the way. I think you are the loveliest lady here tonight."

He'd loved her, in those years when she'd thought of him as little more than an embryo.

"You were a child," she said slowly, still in shock. "You were an infant."

"Old enough to despair of ever being grown-up for you."

"It doesn't make what you did with Mrs. Hedley any less reprehensible."

"No," he agreed quietly. "It only makes everything more terrible."

Silence, as the implication of everything she'd lost slowly began to sink in.

"If only you'd told me . . ." she murmured.

She would not have been so quick to abandon their marriage, as if it were a burning ship.

"I could say the same," he replied. "If only *you'd* told *me*."

She had a sudden vision of herself as a wizened old physician, her hands too arthritic to wield a scalpel, her eyes too rheumy to diagnose anything except measles and chicken pox. The wizened old physician would very much like to drink tea next to her wizened old professor, chuckle over the passionate follies of their distant youth, and then go for a walk along the river Cam, holding his paper-dry, liver-spotted hand.

How ironic that when they'd been married, she'd

never thought of growing old with him. Yet now, years after the annulment, she should think of it with the yearning of an exile, for the homeland that had long ago evicted her.

❧

Bryony had imagined the Panjkora Valley to be like the Chitral Valley, wide and flat and well populated. But the Panjkora Valley was, if not precisely a gorge, not much more than a watercourse. The population seemed mostly concentrated in tiny lateral valleys nourished by smaller rivers and streams that fed into the Panjkora.

Still there were villages along the way and in every village they passed, Leo sent the guides to ask about the situation in Swat. Rumors were as plentiful as microbes in a slum. The men the guides talked to all knew of the deeds of the Mad Fakir, as he was admiringly called in these parts.

The Mad Fakir could not be harmed by bullets; the Mad Fakir had legions of heavenly hosts at his disposal, to be called upon once he commenced his glorious and holy battle; the *Inglisi*, all the *Inglisi*, would be swept away before the new moon.

She didn't know quite what to make of all the rumors. Was there some germ of truth to them or were they wholesale fiction? The population of Dir seemed more entertained than fermented, despite all the excitement generated by the supposed miracles of the Mad Fakir and his grandiose promises to drive out the English.

In the end she mostly ignored the rumors. They were too outlandish and too comical, when she already had so much upheaval inside herself.

They were traveling faster now. In no time at all they would reach the Swat River. And then, Nowshera, where the train would carry her to Bombay, to the next P&O steamer out of India.

She did not want to say good-bye to him. She didn't know what she wanted, for the road to go on and on, perhaps, for them to exist outside of their normal lives, in this bubble, removed from both the past and the future.

Not that they weren't already existing outside of their normal lives. Germany, America, India. She had not set foot in England except en route to some place ever further away, to escape what could not be escaped.

She envied him his firm decision to return to Cambridge. She could not go back to the New Hospital for Women and simply resume her former life. She'd sought peace and serenity in her days abroad. She had not come away with either.

As the elevation of the land decreased, the weather

had become warmer, sometimes uncomfortably hot in the afternoon. Leo, correspondingly, had adjusted their pace to include more rest for both men and beasts.

Bryony, for one, was glad to spend a few minutes in the shade of an apple orchard, her much-swaddled person given a chance to cool. Corsets and petticoats were all very well for never-warm England, but here on the Subcontinent they made about as much sense as a five-legged chair.

She fanned herself a few times with her new hat. He'd produced it again in the morning to ask if she would like it, as the sun was certain to become harsher the further south they traveled. And she'd gratefully accepted.

"I thought you were impervious to weather," he said. He was seated under the tree closest to her. Tiny apples hung from the branches overhead, such a pale green they were almost white.

"I thought so too. But as it turned out, I was impervious to weather as long as weather did not exceed seventy degrees. The heat does not bother you?"

"Not so much." He turned his face toward the powder blue sky. "I suppose it's because I'm enjoying my last hurrah in exotic, sunny places before spending the rest of my life in drear old England, where it never stops raining and the mercury never goes above sixty-five."

His traveling clothes were made of *puttoo*, a Kashmiri homespun wool that was perfect for the variable weather in the mountains, but the last thing from fashionable. His hair was imperfectly groomed. His boots had taken quite a punishment. His face showed the cumulative fatigue that came of months of incessant travel, followed by a severe illness, followed again by travel—there were shadows under his eyes, and the beginning of crow's feet at the corners. And even though all about them it was green, voluptuous summer, there was a solemnness to him, a quiet that made her think of snow-blanketed winter.

He'd never been further from the gilded, angel-kissed youth. And never more beautiful.

❦

Across the river, on the opposite edge of the valley, a man herded a flock of goats up a hidden footpath toward a deodar forest at the top of the slope—the hills and ridges here, though still rugged, were nowhere near as lofty or fearsome as those they'd passed earlier in their travels. She watched the goats' bleating progress, until they disappeared around an outcrop.

"Are you returning to Cambridge straightaway?" she asked, without quite looking at him.

"No."

"Oh," she said, still not looking at him. "Why not?"

If he did, they would be travel companions for at least another three weeks. He could not manage it. To look upon her and know that he'd lost her through his own misdeed—love had become a thing of nails and spikes, every breath a re-impaling, every pulse a bright, sharp pain.

"I need to go to Delhi first, to wait for my luggage to arrive from Gilgit. I also want to see Charlie and the children again one more time before I leave India."

For him and Bryony it was good-bye and farewell come Nowshera.

"Well, say hello to Charlie for me. He called on me twice when I was in Delhi but I was never home to him."

Poor, conscientious Charlie.

"Is there any chance you will stay in London for good this time? Or will you be setting out for Shanghai after two weeks?"

She plucked at her skirt, a sturdy, dun-colored garment made especially for riding astride, with buttons and buckles for holding the extra lengths of the skirt on either side up and out of the way when she was not in the saddle.

"Shanghai has a terrible climate. San Francisco is much better. Or New Zealand, perhaps—I hear it is beautiful."

The pain was almost blinding. He had done this to her. Once she had been one of the finest doctors in all of London, now she was a nomad whose life had shrunk to one tent and two steamer trunks.

"It's time to stop, Bryony. Don't keep running away."

"I don't know that I can stop."

"Give it a try. Stay in London for some time. It would make your father happy."

She raised her face, her expression incredulous. "Where did you get that idea? My father is as indifferent to me as I am to him."

"You are not indifferent to him. You are angry at him. And he is not indifferent to you: He has no idea what to do with you."

"He didn't need to do anything with me. He only had to be there. He could have written his books anywhere."

"So he wasn't there. So he was a grieving widower who ran away from the place where he'd once been happy. But don't you see, once he came back, he gave you everything you ever asked of him."

"What do you mean?" She looked at him blankly.

He was beginning to have the impression he was going after an iceberg with a match. "When it became known that he'd agreed to let you go to medical school, all the neighbors thought he was mad. You are the granddaughter of an earl. Granddaughters of earls do not dissect cadavers or touch strange men to whom they haven't been properly introduced."

She dismissed it outright. "He let me go because he knew that if he didn't let me go then, I'd have gone once I came of age and took control of my inheritance."

"You would not have come of age for another four years. Quite frequently people do not want the same thing at twenty-one that they wanted at seventeen. Most fathers would have gladly taken those odds and forbidden you to go. But he gave you permission."

"You are wrong." She was obdurate, her mind firmly closed. "My father does what is most convenient for him, always. He said yes to me because it was the most expedient answer under the circumstances. He could see that I meant it and he didn't want to be pestered again."

He felt strangely like crying. Between himself and Geoffrey Asquith, there existed an unspoken kinship.

They were both men who had failed her, who could not seem to recover from that failure no matter what.

Her good opinion, once lost, was lost forever.

"So you go back, he recovers, and you buy a ticket on the next steamer out of England."

"Probably."

Despite all her strengths, there was a certain brittleness to her. Sometimes she retreated into her keep. Sometimes she ran away. But she did not forgive and she did not forget.

He raised his face to the cloudless sky again. "Rain is coming," he said.

❧

"Is it?"

"As early as this evening, according to Imran. But there is a dak bungalow ahead, so we should be fine."

He did not look at her, but his sorrow was there, in the set of his shoulders, the strain in his jaw. It touched her, in some inexplicable way, that he cared about the chasm between her father and herself. No one else did—even Callista had long ago accepted it and moved on.

But he had tried to bring them closer together from the beginning. Had invited her father and stepmother to dine at their house. Had answered her father's occasional letters from the country, when she could not be bothered to read them.

He had so many qualities, this man, that she'd never noticed. Suddenly she could not bear to look at him, the same way she could not stare directly into the sun.

She wanted that he should always be there to expect better from her than she expected from herself. She wanted to play a thousand more games of chess with him. She wanted them to grow old together, to gaze into each other's clouded eyes and peck each other on the cheeks with lips sunken over toothless gums.

"You are not worried about the trouble in Swat, are you?" he asked, abruptly.

She caressed the hat he had bought for her. "No," she said. "It's the last thing I worry about."

Chapter Twelve

Mountains of black clouds, like something out of the Old Testament, crested over the valley as they reached the dak bungalow. The main monsoon season in Dir was in winter. Leo had hoped not to run into the more unpredictable summer rains, but now the vanguard of the summer rains was upon them.

Trees had become scarce along this stretch of the Panjkora. They still covered the upper slopes, but the lower slopes of the valley were often shoddily clad, brown bare earth amidst a scarcity of greenery that could have been the result of either thin, barren soil or, more likely, deforestation.

After the rain, the condition of the road was certain to deteriorate. But at least tonight, at the dak bungalow, they did not need to worry about tents blowing away, small-scale mudslides, or other such unpleasantness of traveling in inclement weather.

Dak bungalows were simple structures of a few rooms built and maintained as rest stops for the men who labored on behalf of the Empire's mail service. Travelers who wished to avail themselves of rooms in the dak bungalow paid a rupee for each room and extra for meals.

In Kashmir, there were dak bungalows every fourteen miles. Some dak bungalows where Leo had stayed had a chicken coop looked after by a *murghi wallah,* a few cows cared for by a *gowala,* and a *khansama* who cooked for and served the travelers. This particular bungalow had no resident attendants or barnyard animals, but in most other respects, it was very much a standard dak bungalow, a one-story masonry house with a central vestibule and the rest of the space subdivided into bedroom-and-bathroom suites. A wide wraparound veranda provided plenty of space for the coolies to bed down, protected from the elements.

Saif Khan made chicken curry, steamed vegetables, and chapatis. Leo and Bryony dined in the small, white-plastered vestibule that held, besides one table and the rickety chairs on which they sat, nothing else except a stand on which rested a book of register, for travelers to sign their names and offer any remarks they had on the condition of the bungalow.

After dinner she suggested a game of chess. He agreed, even though the sight of a chessboard hit him like a cudgel, to think of all the games they could have played. And everything else he would not have lost if he had not been so stupid.

She played fast. She had a vision of the board that he could only envy, an instinct for the game that made his more deliberate strategizing seem cumbersome and lead-footed.

Tonight she played more sloppily than usual. But then, in their previous game, she'd let him have every piece of importance and then checkmated him with nothing but three pawns.

"You are not guarding your right flank," he said. "Is it a trap or are you not paying attention?"

"Of course it is a trap," she said.

She sat with her chin pressed into the palm of her hand, her long lashes casting mysterious shadows over her eyes. She lifted those lashes, and his heart skipped several beats, for her eyes were full of hunger.

He took her king bishop pawn. "Well, trap or not, you'll pay for it."

She moved her queen rook pawn. "Be my guest. Take everything."

He'd never known her to speak seductively. And indeed she did not here either. But her words, coupled with the way she looked at him, long, intent glances, set siege to him. Within his thin defenses, his desire ran amok.

He abolished her queen rook pawn. "What else have you got?"

She picked up her king rook, set it down, picked up a pawn, set it down, picked up her queen, and set it down. Finally she looked up at him again, some unknown agitation in her eyes. "You said you wanted me to stay in London."

"I think you should have a place to call home again," he answered cautiously.

"Are you willing to offer me some incentives?"

Was *he* willing to offer incentives? "What kind of incentives?"

"Cambridge is only an hour from London. Perhaps we can find a chess club with mixed membership and meet for a game from time to time."

"I don't think so," he said instantly.

His answer seemed to flabbergast her. She must have thought he'd welcome something of the sort.

"What about by correspondence?" she said more tentatively. "It eliminates the inconvenience of meeting in person *and* we can keep a dozen games going at the same time."

It seemed such a little thing to grant, chess games by correspondence. How harmless could they be, a few missives here and there, pieces of paper with nothing on them but algebraic notations of chess moves?

Except between them, it could never be only chess.

He could see himself reaching for the post, discarding everything but the note from her. He'd take it to his study, where he'd have the games set out, and shut the door. Once assured of privacy, he would linger over the boards, savor her every move, and then spend his evening planning counterattacks: here a smooth ramming of a knight, there a bold insertion of a rook, and now and then a naughty thrust from a bishop.

A moment of tremendous satisfaction when he had everything arranged just so, his moves recorded, his reply ready to go. And then, heartbreak, at this absurdity that passed for lovemaking in his life, at the futility of it all.

"No."

She was bewildered. "Why not?"

"I can't."

"You can't write a letter?"

"I cannot be your friend."

She rose abruptly. He came to his feet. "I'm sorry, Bryony."

She shook her head, her teeth clamped over her lower lip. "My mistake. I thought—I thought perhaps you would like a second chance."

She did not give second chances—she had as good as told him that in the afternoon. This was her physical lust speaking. When her ardor cooled, when they hit that inevitable rough patch, she would retrench again deep into herself.

"I would have, at any point during our marriage."

If he'd known what was the matter, he'd have groveled. He'd have atoned. He'd have handed over the scalpel himself if she'd demanded his testes as penitence.

"Isn't it better late than never?"

"Some things are not meant to be. *We* are not meant to be."

She took two steps toward him. Her hand reached out and caught a strand of his hair. He froze. But she did not stop there. Her fingers caressed his ear. Then she cupped his cheek, and rubbed her thumb over his lower lip.

"We *were* not meant to be, perhaps. But people change and grow up."

If their previous conversation taught him anything at all, it was that she *hadn't* changed. That she remained as adamantly unforgiving as ever.

He took her hand and returned it to her.

SHERRY THOMAS

Her reaction was to kiss him, a kiss hot with both lust and confusion. God help him. Arousal came to him as a tidal wave. He was hard and ravenous. He wanted her. He wanted to bury himself in her and forget everything.

He yanked away from her. "Bryony, please. Don't."

Perhaps if she had not made love to him that night, he might have succumbed, believing that surely she could not offer her body without having first forgiven him. But she *had* made love to him while the memory coiled within her like a disease, like the malarial parasite that could conceal itself for years before emerging in a devastating attack.

Her face crumbled. "So all that talk of loving me for years and years, I guess it doesn't matter after all."

The knife in his heart twisted.

"Sometimes love isn't enough," he said. "Look at you and your father."

Except Toddy, everyone she'd once loved she'd eventually shuffled off to the fringes of her life, ignored or banished outright.

"What does my father have to do with anything?"

"If you can't forgive him for neglect, how can you forgive me for having done you active injury?"

She looked away from him to the bare wall. For a minute she said nothing. "What are you trying to convey, precisely?"

— 184 —

"It is not possible for us to build a new life together. You need a saint, Bryony. You need someone like Toddy, someone who has never done and will never do you wrong, who will never anger or alienate you, in whom your faith never needs testing."

She glanced at him, her gaze ice and shadows. "You imply that I am not capable of love."

He hadn't meant to imply that. But the thing was, talk long enough, and one's beliefs manifested themselves one way or another.

"I don't believe you are capable of the kind of love that can withstand the weight of what we bring to it."

He didn't believe either of them was, frankly.

"And you would not give us a chance to prove otherwise?"

"Would you board a train knowing that the rails end over a cliff? Or a steamer that already leaks?"

"I see," she said, her voice bleak. "I'm sorry for wasting your time. Shall we finish the game now?"

❧

The storm broke shortly afterward and raged through the night. The wind eventually died down toward dawn, but the rain continued unabated.

Bryony was not a fidgety person, but that morning she could not remain still. She paced in her room like a caged wolf, opened and closed the shutters with a rhythmless aggression that would have occasioned much note-taking had she been the inmate of an asylum. When she was convinced no one could hear her, she banged the back of her head against the wall—in frustration as well as in misery.

How ironic that had they been rained in one day earlier, she'd have been secretly overjoyed that nature had stepped in to extend their time together. But now she only wanted to finish the rest of their travels *this* minute, to not remain a second longer than necessary in the company of a man who was as determined to remove her from his existence as a dedicated butler going after the tarnish on the silver in his keeping.

The rain finally stopped in the middle of the afternoon. Bryony was ready to depart immediately. But Leo insisted on first sending the guides ahead to check the condition of the road.

"The tree cover on the slope is insufficient. There is a possibility of substantial debris swept down in a storm like this," he explained.

She nodded and turned to go back to her room.

"Bryony."

She stopped, but did not turn around. "Yes?"

He was silent for several seconds. "No, it was nothing. Please don't mind me."

❧

A blistering sun emerged as the clouds dissipated. Faint curls of steam rose from the ground. The guides returned far sooner than Leo had anticipated and brought with them a group of travelers—not Dir levies, but sepoy messengers from the Malakand garrison, carrying sacks of letters and dispatches for the Chitral garrison. Leo offered them tea and probed them for news.

The Malakand garrison, located eight miles southwest of Chakdarra, with a strength of three thousand men, held both the Malakand Pass and the bridge across Swat River at Chakdarra.

In recent days the bazaar at Malakand had been wild with rumors. But as the sepoys were Sikhs, the traditional adversaries of Muslims, their attitude toward the Mad Fakir and his followers was one of disdain rather than fascination.

"Let the Swatis march on Malakand," said the oldest of the sepoys. "The Indian army will destroy them. And then we will have peace for a generation."

"Are the officers aware of the problem?" Leo asked.

They were, the sepoys acknowledged. The political officer at Malakand had issued a warning two days ago on the twenty-third of July. The troops had rehearsed alarm drills. But no one believed anything would really come to pass, and even the warning only stated that an attack was possible, but not probable.

The Swatis invited the English to settle their disputes. They were happy about the services the small civil hospital at Chakdarra provided. And their valley was a green sward of prosperity, everyone's coffer fattened by feeding and otherwise supplying the garrison. Why should they be so foolish as to throw it all away on the advice of someone who was very likely insane?

Leo nodded his head, happy to have the frothing rumors put in such rational and blunt light—even if the Sikh sepoys' opinions were biased, they were still based on information obtained much closer to the source.

And then the sepoys went on to describe just how unconcerned the camps as a whole were about the prospect of an uprising. Apparently, alarm drills aside, the daily routine for the soldiers had not changed at all. Officers from Chakdarra Fort and the Malakand garrison played polo every evening on an open field miles away from the protection of their cantonment, armed with nothing but unloaded pistols.

The sepoys related this last with nods of approval at their British officers' sangfroid, not noticing that the smile had started to fade from Leo's face. They spoke briefly of the condition of the road—which after the storm was something between an inconvenience and an annoyance. Their tea finished, the sepoys thanked Leo and resumed their journey.

The entire conversation had taken place on the veranda outside Bryony's room, so she could hear their discussion via shutters kept ajar. Now her shutters opened fully.

"Shall we get going then?" she said, her impatience barely contained. "The sepoys managed the road without any problem. Surely we can muddle through too."

"It's late in the day, Bryony."

"Nonsense," she retorted. "We can get in a good four hours. That's at least one march."

She rarely spoke in such a strong tone. In fact, he'd never seen her in a fractious mood. But she was now. She had no desire to cooperate with him. She wanted to leave. And she wanted to leave this moment.

In which case, she would *not* like what he was about to say to her.

"I don't think we should go on."

Her eyes narrowed. "What do you mean by that?"

He took a deep breath. "Have you ever read any accounts of the Great Mutiny?"

"Of course. What does that have to do with anything?"

"Because I'm reminded of it. It wasn't that we had no warnings as the mutiny approached; it was that the people in power refused to believe that such a thing could be possible, that those they considered happy lackeys could rise up against their sage masters. As it turned out, the masters weren't so sage and the lackeys not so happy."

"That was forty years ago. There's nothing comparable here," she said.

"There was fighting in Malakand around the time of the Siege of Chitral. The Malakand garrison was established only after that, to hold open the road to Chitral. It is highly improbable that in two years' time, the Swatis would have forgotten their former hostility altogether."

"So you are criticizing the professional opinions of the officers at Malakand and Chakdarra?" she asked pointedly.

"I know it sounds presumptuous, but I think their daily polo games send a signal not of confidence, but of complacency. Were I a native with rebellion in my heart, I would be encouraged that my enemy is asleep at the post."

She was silent. He pushed on. "Let's stay here, where it's safe and more or less comfortable, and wait until the next set of messengers come up from Malakand with news."

"But that could easily mean we'd be stuck here a whole week."

"A week isn't so much delay when you consider that we are facing an unknown danger that could easily escalate out of control."

"No." Her hand gripped the edge of a shutter, her knuckles white. "I cannot disagree more. If there is to be danger, we are much better off behind the front lines. Once we are south of Malakand, whatever the tribes of Upper Swat Valley decide will be of little importance to us."

"That is assuming we can make it behind the front lines in time. It would be safer to remain in a neutral territory, rather than risk being caught in the crossfire."

"If there is to be such a thing as a crossfire, as the officers at Malakand evidently do not believe, I'm hardly confident of Dir's neutrality."

"The Khan of Dir receives sixty thousand rupees a year from us. He would be a fool to take part in any sort of sedition that might impoverish his treasury so much."

"I don't doubt that the Khan, in his infinite wisdom, thinks first and foremost of his treasury.

But the fakir aims only to fan the passions of the common man. Who is to say that in staying here, we wouldn't make ourselves an easy target for hot-headed young men from nearby villages?"

He cursed the unfortunate timing of things. "If this is about last night," he said wearily, "then I take back everything I said. At this moment there is nothing more important to me than your safety. Stay and you can have whatever you want with me."

As soon as he said it he knew it was the wrong thing to say. She flushed, turned even paler than before, and took a step back from the window. "How noble of you, to sacrifice your virtue to my unforgiving rapacity. No, thank you, I don't want anything to do with you. And you are wrong. There is no more danger ahead of us than behind us or all around us."

He sighed. Further arguments served no purpose— her mind was already made up. He had two choices: Either he could take the autocratic route and remind her that she could not advance a step without him, or somehow he must find a way to massage her into compliance without stripping away all her dignity in the matter.

If only he'd kept his mouth shut before offering to prostitute himself for her acquiescence, he could have used seduction as a tool. Now the only thing he could think of was firearms.

"All right, let's settle this at twenty paces."

❧

She blinked. "What do you mean?"

But he'd already walked away. A moment later, she heard him coming into the dak bungalow. She stepped into the vestibule. "What did you say again?"

He didn't answer. He went into his room and came out with a rifle slung over one shoulder, a steel mug in his hand, and the handle of a pistol sticking out of his coat pocket. "Come with me."

They walked out of the dak bungalow, to curious looks from the coolies, and marched for nearly a quarter of a mile before he stopped and tied the steel mug from the branch of a small tree. Then he walked away from it.

"That's more than twenty paces," she said when he stopped.

"Forty, since the tree can't move twenty paces on its own," he said.

With that, he loaded the rifle from the breech, raised it, fired, and hit the mug with a loud metalic clang.

"Your turn."

"I beg your pardon?"

"If you insist on meeting danger head-on, show me you can protect yourself. I'll give you three chances. You hit the mug, I'll make arrangements to get us to Malakand as swiftly as possible. You fail, we venture no further south until either the trouble clears or it becomes evident that there will be no trouble. Choose your weapon, rifle or pistol."

"This is ridiculous. I'm not a crack shot."

"No, what is ridiculous is that I'm giving you a chance—any chance—to dictate the course of our action. If I'm wrong and nothing happens in Swat Valley, we lose a week of our life to boredom. If you are wrong and things go awry, we lose our lives. Full stop."

"Balderdash. Our soldiers in the Swat Valley were there for the previous campaign. They know the local population far better than we do. It is their professional judgment that they have nothing to fear. I prefer to put my stock in their expertise, rather than your intuition."

"Then let's shoot for it. Here's your pistol."

And it *was* her pistol, a double-barrel Remington derringer. She'd forgotten altogether that she had one. He must have kept it with him when he and the coolies packed her things before they left Rumbur Valley.

She grabbed the pistol. In a righteous huff, she

took aim and pulled the trigger. The pistol jumped in her grip, the noise startling her, but there was no echoing clank against the steel mug, only a dull thud somewhere.

She fired again. Again, nothing.

As she extended her hand for one more cartridge, he said, "May I remind you that this is binding? You accepted the challenge, you accepted the terms."

She pivoted the barrels upward and reloaded. "Is it as binding on you as it is on me?"

"Of course," he said.

Bastard. This was no contest. It was a trick to get her to accede to his wishes, while making it appear as if she'd been given a fair shake at *her* wishes.

No, I will not remain here with you.

It was hot. She perspired under the rear flap of her hat. She took it off and felt the sun beating down against her unprotected nape. The river was wide and swift here. A single rope hung over it. A man in a chair suspended from the rope was crossing the river toward their side. He stared at Bryony in astonishment.

She raised the pistol slowly and sighted the mug. She must succeed. And she would. She wanted to leave far more than he wanted to stay. If there was to be no new beginning for them, then their story had ended three years ago, and their epilogue ended the night before. It was time to close the book.

She pulled the trigger. And saw the jerky swing of the steel mug before she heard the jarring hit. She dropped her arm to her side and stood a moment, breathing hard.

Deliverance.

She turned toward him. He was still staring at the mug in disbelief.

"Did you say 'as swiftly as possible'?" she asked brightly.

&

She thought they would depart immediately. Instead, Leo huddled for a while with the guides, who then left by themselves.

"Where have they gone?"

"To set up a rudimentary stage system for us," he said curtly. "We will leave at first light tomorrow and make for Malakand."

"In one day?"

"I can't in good conscience caravan on as if nothing is the matter. Since you want to get behind the front line, I will get you there as fast as I can."

"How far are we from Malakand?"

"Seventy miles or thereabout."

"And how many changes of horses will we have?"

"Two."

On the road into Kashmir, ponies were changed every six miles. Here they would have to use the same horses for twenty-five miles.

"What about the coolies?"

"They will remain here until the guides return for them and then head south. I will wait for them at Malakand. Don't worry about your things. I'll have them shipped to London."

She nodded. "Very good."

"Prepare for a long day. The horses are not bred for speed; we'll be lucky if we can manage seven miles an hour on average."

"Understood."

He sighed and put his hands on her arms.

"You can still change your mind, Bryony," he said. "Let us wait here in safety rather than going forward to tempt Fate."

"Nothing will happen. We will arrive in Malakand tomorrow night sore but well."

"And if not?"

A chill ran down her back. Until this moment she'd been immune from any and all fear with regard to the Mad Fakir and his doings—but that was because Leo had shouldered all the responsibilities for their safety. Now the onus had shifted. Should anything go wrong, all the blame rested squarely with her.

"I believe I've already proved that my marksmanship is up to the task," she said. "The die is cast. Let's have no more doubts or demurrals."

He moved away from her. "I hope you are right," he answered. "I hope to God you are right."

Chapter Thirteen

By eleven o'clock the next morning they finally came across a blue scarf tied on a tree, signaling the end of their first stage. They were running late. Even under perfect conditions, with the narrowness of the road and its tendency to shift, twist, and drop unexpectedly, they would not have been able to gallop at any appreciable speed. But the storm from two nights ago had slowed their progress even further. At quite a few stretches, the rain had washed mud, rocks, and broken tree limbs onto the road, forcing them to pick their way through the debris.

Hamid had two new horses ready for them and food he'd procured at a nearby village. He also had encouraging news. The Khan of Dir had expressly forbidden his people from participating in the Mad

Fakir's schemes. Their safety should be assured for as long as they traveled in Dir.

And as soon as they left Dir, they'd be within view of a British installation. Bryony unwound somewhat—she hadn't realized how tense she had been, how anxious, as the road stubbornly refused to allow them a rapid progress.

By mid-afternoon they reached Sado, a village that had no significance whatsoever, except that it marked the point where their road would leave the Panjkora Valley and take a sharp turn east-southeast.

From Sado it was thirty-five miles to Chakdarra, and another eight miles to Malakand. She estimated that they had perhaps four hours of daylight left. They'd have to slow down once night fell, so it was likely they'd only manage to get to Chakdarra at the end of the day. But that was fine. At Chakdarra they'd still be completely out of danger and from Chakdarra she could still reach Nowshera in less than a day.

"Are you all right?" Leo asked.

They'd stopped to rest and water their horses by a stream that fed the Panjkora. She was crouched by the water, soaking a handkerchief. *Horses sweat; men perspire; ladies merely glow*. In damp, cool England perhaps. In India ladies too sweated like horses, especially ladies who rode in the middle of the day under an unsympathetic sun at an altitude of less than three thousand feet.

She looked up at him. He usually shaved in the evenings, but he hadn't the night before. She wanted to stare at the stubbles on his face—the shadow of growth that kissed the firm set of his jaw and the leanness of his features. She turned her face back to her handkerchief. "I'm fine, thank you. And you?"

"I'm used to this," he said. "Is the sun getting too harsh?"

He'd been quite lovely to her. Were she to judge him solely by his demeanor, she'd never have guessed that they'd fought heatedly the day before and that he was staunchly opposed to this southward venture.

She wrung the handkerchief dry and patted her face with it. "The sun is tolerable."

As she rose, he handed her a canteen of water. "You can open a button or two on your jacket if it gets warmer. You are a man today. Enjoy your freedom."

He'd decided that it was safer for them to appear as two men traveling, rather than a man and a woman. He'd have preferred for them to be in native dress, but neither of them could keep a turban from unraveling, so two *sahibs* they remained. She was dressed in his spare clothes. His shirt and jacket were loose on her but his trousers had braces and stayed loyally above her waist.

She sipped just enough water to moisten the inside of her mouth—relieving herself was even more of a problem in men's clothes than in women's; best to have as little need of it as possible. Capping the canteen, she gave it back to him.

He helped her into the saddle and handed her the reins. "This is not how I would have us part ways, Bryony."

"Yes, it is," she said. "So let us get on with it."

❦

The storm seemed to have bypassed Lower Dir altogether. Southeast of Sado, the road improved nicely, wide and smooth enough for wheeled vehicles. The terrain continued to slope lower; their horses picked up speed.

Along the road there were more travelers than Bryony was accustomed to seeing—she attributed it to the better condition of the road and greater proximity to the more populous Swat Valley. Her mind still clouded with the events of the two previous days, it took her a while to see that for every traveler going northwest, there were ten going southeast.

They were all men—no surprises there—traveling on foot. They were armed—again not surprising, in a land where blood feuds were common and disputes frequent. She considered for a moment whether they were the Mad Fakir's followers, then dismissed the thought out of hand—Upper Swat Valley lay quite in the opposite direction of where these men were coming from. Far more likely that they were on their way to a wedding or some other such communal celebration.

They were two miles past Sado when they passed a group at least a hundred strong at prayer, their weapons by their sides. Another mile later, under the shade of an enormous banyon tree, some fifty men sat drinking tea and chatting. This latter group looked up as Leo and Bryony rode past, but otherwise ignored them.

Half an hour later, however, they came to a third large group of men. The men were about sixty in number and took up almost the entire width of the road. At the sound of riders approaching, the men stopped and turned around. They looked at Leo and Bryony. To Bryony's dismay, almost half of the men, particularly the younger ones, reached for the hilts of their swords.

She opened her mouth to call to Leo, but no sounds emerged from her suddenly numb throat.

But as if he heard her silent entreaty, Leo slowed his horse somewhat and motioned Bryony to draw up to his left.

"We will pass them on the left. You stay exactly abreast of me and you do not stop no matter what, do you understand?"

She nodded, her heart not quite beating.

"Now ride as fast as you can."

They urged the horses into as much of a gallop as these sturdy beasts of burden were capable of. The men continued to stare at them, as they drew near, as they veered up the slope beyond the edge of the road, Leo passing just out of reach of the men at the periphery of the group.

And the men were behind them. But before Bryony could breathe again, a series of soft metallic hisses made her peer over her shoulder. A good three dozen swords had been pulled out of their sheaths and held overhead, their blades gleaming in the afternoon sun.

Leo beheld that same display of power and belligerence. His face turned to hers. There was no fear in his eyes, but his hand clutched tightly around his revolver.

"They were all wearing white," she said, her heart now beating like a war drum. "In every group we've passed, the men were all wearing white."

He returned the revolver to its holster under his jacket. "So they were."

He needed to say nothing more. The men were headed toward a common purpose, and it wasn't a Pan-Swati game of cricket.

"I don't—I don't suppose we can turn back now?"

"No, can't turn back now," he said. "Ride faster."

❧

Bryony was petrified. So much so that when they came to the rendezvous point with Imran, the elder guide, Leo had to pull her off her horse and then pry her fingers one by one from the reins.

She stood with her back against an apricot tree. They were at the edge of a quiet village. The sun had slid behind the top of the slopes. The air, smelling of hoof-trampled oregano, cool with the arrival of early evening, would have been hugely welcome at their previous stop; but now the breeze made her shiver—or perhaps it only made her shiver *worse*. And the village itself further fueled her fear: It was fortified, with silent, watchful presences behind narrow slits in the high earthen walls.

Beside her, Leo and Imran conferred in whispers.

"I thought the Khan of Dir had forbidden his men to rally to the Mad Fakir," Leo said.

"These are not Dir men. They come from Bajaur."

Imran's leathery face was troubled. "They even invited me to join them, an old man like me. You must get away from here as soon as possible."

Leo did not ask whether there was still time to get away, and Bryony did not dare. The men saddled the new horses and transferred saddlebags that held bare essentials. When they were done, Leo told Imran to be mindful of his own safety and sent the guide on his way back north.

He turned back, looked at Bryony, and frowned. "Did you drink?"

Bryony looked down at the canteen he'd given her after he helped her off her horse. Did she drink? She had no recollection. She'd forgotten altogether that she had the canteen.

He took the canteen, unscrewed its cap, and put it back in her hand again. "Drink. And take more than a sip. It will be dark soon enough and no one will see you if you must relieve yourself."

She did as she was told with a dumb obedience.

"And eat this." He pressed a biscuit into her palm.

"I'm not hungry." Her stomach felt as if it had been stepped on, repeatedly.

"Your nerves may not want food. But your body does. We've still hours of riding ahead of us. You must keep up your strength."

She could not suppress a whimper of panic.

Hours. How many more armed men would they come across? The region was crisscrossed with valleys rich in alluvial deposits. Crops pushed eagerly through the soil and grew with a lust that would have amazed peasants who had to eke out their living on less blessed dirt. She could only guess at the size of population this ease of cultivation supported.

"Oh God, Leo, I'm sorry," she blurted. "I'm so sorry!"

"It's all right, Bryony."

It was not all right. Things were going dreadfully wrong. "I really, *really* am sorry."

He reached up and cupped her face. "Listen, nothing has happened to us. And nothing might yet."

Or everything could happen to them. He was so beautiful, his eyes the color of tide pools, she could not bear to think, God, to think that—

"I love you," she said hopelessly. "I love you. I love you. I—"

He took her by the collar and yanked her toward him until their noses almost touched. For a lightning-bright moment, she thought he would kiss her. But he only said, very clearly and firmly, "Shut up, Bryony."

She blinked in confusion and shock.

"We are not dying—not yet, in any case. So save your farewells for when we actually are. Now pull yourself together."

She stared at him a second longer—she would not have believed it of herself, but it would seem he'd just snapped her out of a case of mild hysterics. "Right," she said, her voice hoarse. "Right."

She ate the biscuit while he loaded her derringer and stuffed it into her pocket. She managed to not moan again in panic as he emptied a case of spare cartridges into her other pocket. And she listened to him with actual attention as he said, "The next time there are men blocking the road, it doesn't matter which side of the road I veer toward, ride to my outside. Understand?"

She nodded.

"Good. Let's go."

❧

The road climbed before it descended again. Bryony's arms hurt from holding the reins since dawn. Her seat and thighs ached in acute, unhappy ways. But the discomforts she forgot in an instant each time she caught sight of white-clad men. Fortunately, they usually traveled in threes and fives rather than groups of fifty or a hundred. The one sizable group they passed stood to the side of the road, talking animatedly among themselves.

Their road took them in a steady east-southeast direction. At twilight, they entered a wider valley with a river flowing through its center, and the road, wending between fields of rice and maize, turned due south. Where this particular tributary met the Swat River stood the fort at Chakdarra. It was not too far now.

Ahead, in the thickening gray-blue dusk, a turbaned man appeared, riding across the valley. His path would intersect theirs in minutes. Leo drew his revolver. Bryony swallowed and drew the pistol from her pocket also.

But as they closed the distance, she realized that not only was the man not dressed in white, he was in uniform—a sowar, a cavalry soldier of Indian descent serving under British authority.

Leo had already put away his revolver and hailed the sowar. They all reined to a halt.

"Are you from the garrison at Malakand?" Leo asked.

"The fort at Chakdarra, *sahib*. Eleventh Bengal Lancers," said the sowar. His English was spoken at the speed of Italian and singsongy, but perfectly comprehensible. He pointed west. "I was sketching at the foot of the hills."

Since Bryony didn't think his commanding officer would provide him a mount and an afternoon off for his personal enjoyment, she assumed by sketching he meant some sort of land survey.

"I was starting back for the fort when I was set upon," continued the sowar. "There were men, at least a hundred of them. They took my compass, my field glass, and one rupee and six annas from me. I must return to the fort immediately to warn everyone."

Bryony looked anxiously toward the direction the sowar had pointed. But she could not see anything except the air and the slopes fading together into a smudged indigo. At the top of the hills, a lone pine thrust into an unseen sky, lit by the last scattered rays of a distant sunset.

The sowar galloped away on his fresher, faster horse. The first stars were already out in the eastern sky, tiny and isolated, as if they were lonely outposts in a galactic wilderness.

"Scared?" Leo asked.

"Witless."

He handed her his silver flask. She took a large gulp, almost finishing what remained of Mr. Braeburn's special whiskey.

When she gave the flask back to him, he took hold of her hand. They both wore riding gloves, yet she felt his warmth solidly.

"Do you trust me?" he asked.

His features were shadowed by the coming of night, beginning to become indistinct. But his eyes were clear and lucent—and calm, when she was all cold sweat and dread.

"Yes," she said.

He smiled, a smile that went straight to her heart. "Then trust me when I say we will be all right."

&

It was strange to lay his hand on the waist of a fully dressed woman and feel, instead of ruffles and bows, the pocket of his coat, with the button just slightly loose on the flap. But this adoption of masculine attire was only a surface affair. Beneath his jacket and his shirt, she still wore her corset, a smooth, hard impediment against the pressure of his hand. He was certain that if it had been at all possible, she'd have worn her petticoats too beneath the trousers.

Ten minutes after their encounter with the sowar, Leo's horse had thrown a shoe, and they were forced to share Bryony's horse, a sturdy, cheerful mare which did not seem to mind too much the additional weight. But their speed, already less than impressive—this particular mountain breed was more durable than swift—suffered even further.

They did not speak. The sliver moon and the stars were mere decorations in the firmament, their light too diffuse to be of any use at all. In the near complete darkness, she needed all her attention on the road.

The night smelled of cool water, ripening orchards, and more faintly, turned manure. And there sitting behind her, not doing much except keeping his eyes and ears open and holding on, Leo was strangely optimistic.

He could attribute his optimism to the reassuring ordinariness of the manure, surely the very odor of rustic peace. He could further attribute it to the distance they'd already covered; by his calculation, they'd sight Chakdarra any minute now. But he suspected that in truth, his sanguinity had more to do with the back-to-chest closeness between Bryony and himself than anything else.

The warmth of her body, the expansion and contraction of her diaphragm with her breaths, which he felt only barely through the constriction of her corset, the lithe tension in her torso as she moved as one with the horse—it was easy, or at least easier, to believe that they would be all right in the end, when he held her so.

❧

"Look ahead!" Leo whispered.

Bryony did and just barely made out the horizontal glimmer in the distance. "Is that the Swat River?!"

"I think so."

A huge weight lifted from her chest. *Yes.*

"Thank goodness! I hope they don't mind putting us up for th—"

"Shh."

Something in his voice throttled her incipient euphoria. "What is it?"

"Stop."

She reined in the horses and listened, not sure what she was supposed to hear above the sound of the tributary hurrying toward the Swat.

"Do you hear that?"

She didn't. Then she suddenly did. People on the move. A very large number of people on the move, coming down the slopes to either side of the river.

"Run for it."

She dug her knees into the mare's flank. She'd slowed nearly to a walk because she could hardly see. But now she must gallop. She stared fiercely ahead, determined to distinguish the road from the nearly uniform darkness of the ground.

"Faster!" he hissed in her ear.

She saw the cause of his urgency. A particular spur of the human tide coming down the hills had almost reached the road—all clad in white, silent, swift, and purposeful.

The pony seemed to sense her fright. Or perhaps the road had assumed a greater downward grade. It ran more swiftly despite its weariness and heavy load.

They dashed past the vanguard of the rebellion—for certain it was going to be an uprising now—with only a few yards to spare. The air hissed. Bryony shrank instinctively down in the saddle. A rock sailed over her head. Another fell short and thudded against the road behind them. Yet another hit something. The other pony, which they kept on a lead, neighed in pain—it had been struck on the flank, but it too kept running.

She had a vague impression that the hills on either side of the valley were receding: The valley was widening.

"Are we getting close?"

"Closer," was all the answer Leo gave.

The thundering hoof falls of the horses rendered her deaf to the rest of the world. But she imagined she heard things, a crowd closing in on them, so dense that thousands of sleeves brushed against one another in a persistent shushing.

She became aware of the Swat River again, wide and black. They were nearly at the confluence of the two rivers. But where was the fort?

"There!"

There, further to the right, she could just make out the fort's outline, atop a knoll that rose over the edge of the river. It was rather smaller than she'd hoped for, but a fort nevertheless by its shape and height.

"How do we approach?"

"I have no idea. It's connected to the bridge, so there has to be a southern entrance."

That would require her to ride around the edge of the knoll until she found the bridge. She did not think. She gave over her fate to the stalwartness of the mare and to the accuracy of Leo's direction. More to the right. Straight. Watch out for a slight curve to the south.

The knoll loomed just ahead. Safety was within reach.

Then Leo said something she'd only ever heard men utter in extreme pain. Men sprinted at them, those in the very front actually fleet enough to intersect them. And were those swords glinting in the starlight? Her heart froze.

"Give me the stirrups and pay no attention."

She vacated the stirrups and pushed away all thoughts of impending doom—of half-successful decapitation, fully successful evisceration, and the two quarts of blood loss she could sustain before she was no good to anyone anymore. She only rode, murmuring meaningless syllables to soothe and encourage the brave filly who'd faithfully carried two strangers who had yet to feed her an apple or a sugar cube.

Leo asked for the lead rope of the horse and gave it a hard thwack on the hindquarter. It neighed and shot forward—he was using it to disperse the crowd ahead of them. She followed closely in its wake, praying for the best.

Behind her Leo's weight shifted: He'd stood up on the stirrups. Her jacket pulled up abruptly at the right shoulder—he used her for a ballast. She ignored everything and focused only on the road.

There was the clang of metal right by her ear: the barrel of his rifle clashing against a sword. And then it was the butt of the rifle on the side of someone's head—she knew a concussion when she heard one. The rifle swung—with an acute swoosh—this time it sounded like a clavicle giving away.

His grip on her jacket pulled the collar into a choke hold around her throat. She could barely breathe even with her lips parted wide, panting for all she was worth. Were those stars she was seeing at the edge of her vision? No, she must not do anything so useless as submitting to the vapors. She would not permit it. She would never forgive herself.

He let go of her jacket. She panted, thankful for the reprieve. Now he was fighting with both hands.

His weight leaned hard to the right—too much. He would topple from the horse. But he didn't. The strength of his legs held him mounted.

He parried. He smashed. He shoved. Good Lord, how many more of them were there? Had she ever known a time when her hearing wasn't saturated with grunts of effort, grunts of pain, and the creaks and snaps of miscellaneous bones under assault?

Then suddenly they were in the clear. Leo slumped back into the saddle, breathing heavily.

There was the smell of blood in the air. "Are you all right? Are you hurt?" Bryony called anxiously. She turned around to look at him, but could see little beyond his form.

"Pay attention to the road and don't slow down."

He *was* injured. "Where are you hurt and how badly?"

"Just ride!"

The hoarseness of his voice frightened her. She pushed the mare the last half mile to the river and maneuvered it up the hillock, barely turning in time to avoid a thicket of barbed wires, which she'd first taken to be badly maintained shrubbery.

The gate of the fort was in the shadow of the suspension bridge that spanned the Swat River. At their approach, it opened silently from inside, revealing a quietly lit bailey. Bryony urged the pony across the last few yards of open space.

Safety, at last.

❧

Leo did not even realize he'd been injured until not one but two sepoys sprang forward to help him dismount. Only then did he look down at himself and see blood everywhere. Bryony took one look at him, swayed, and gripped the saddle for support.

He smiled weakly at her. "Don't tell me you faint at the sight of blood."

"Of course not," she said. "I only faint at the sight of *your* blood. You idiot, why didn't you shoot at them?"

"I didn't want them shooting back at us." He could protect her from swords better than he could from bullets.

"Gentlemen," said a young English lieutenant. "What happened?"

Bryony turned and extended her hand. "Mrs. Quentin Marsden, sir. My husband is injured. Please take us to your surgery immediately."

"Lieutenant Wesley," said the subaltern, once he got over his surprise at speaking to a woman. "Please follow me. I'm sorry to say our surgeon-captain is at the south camp in Malakand—filling in for the surgeon-major who is ill. I hope our hospital assistant would be equal to the task of mending your husband."

"Not to worry, sir," Leo said, as Lieutenant Wesley shook hands with him. "My wounds are superficial. Mrs. Marsden can take care of them."

The walk to the surgery in the rear of the fort, however, let him know that his wounds weren't quite as superficial as he'd hoped. Now that their lives were no longer in immediate danger, his left side burned, and every step, even leaning on a helpful sepoy, sent a jagged pain through his right leg.

The hospital assistant, a small, quiet Sikh named Ranjit Singh, was already waiting for them. Leo was instructed to lie down on the operating table. Bryony, in her element in a place full of jars and drawers and the smell of disinfectant, asked for a pair of scissors and cut away at his clothes.

He was injured in two places on his left, one a long but relatively shallow cut down the length of his upper arm, the other a more serious cut along his rib cage. The worst, however, was on his right thigh. As she peeled away the blood-soaked wool of his trousers, she sucked in a breath at the nasty slash she revealed.

"It just missed the aorta," she said, her voice on the verge of shaking. She turned to Ranjit Singh. "I need a beta-eucaine solution for infiltration anesthesia. I also need a sterilized needle and thread and a pair of sterilized gloves."

As she washed her hands in a corner of the room, the hospital assistant looked to Lieutenant Wesley. Lieutenant Wesley in turn looked to Leo. "Mrs. Marsden is a surgeon by profession. She knows what needs to be done," Leo said impatiently.

That settled it. While Bryony pushed her hair under a cap the hospital assistant provided for her, Ranjit Singh set himself to prepare everything else she needed.

"One part beta-eucaine to one thousand parts water, *memsahib*?"

"Also eight parts chloride of sodium, to prevent irritating the tissues."

She donned the gloves and cleaned Leo's wounds, first with sterilized water, then with carbolic acid. He gritted his teeth against the harsh stinging. Once his wounds had been disinfected, she tapped lightly on a syringe Ranjit Singh handed her and injected the beta-eucaine solution into the tissue beneath his thigh wound.

"That's it?" Leo asked as she reached for the needle.

"That's it. Infiltration anesthesia takes effect instantly."

She was right. As her needle stuck into him, he felt absolutely nothing. He watched in fascination as she began to close his flesh as if it were but a torn sleeve.

A man in a polo kit hurtled into the surgery. "Captain Bartlett," said Lieutenant Wesley. "You are back! I was beginning to wonder whether my message reached you."

So it really was true that the officers still played polo, even to this very day.

"I received your message and started back right away," said Captain Bartlett, sounding completely out of breath. He was of medium height, a somewhat portly build, and a ruddy complexion. "Surgeon-Captain Gibbs, good to see you back too. And, sir, I see you have survived your initial encounter with the Pathans. Captain Bartlett of the Forty-fifth Sikhs, at your service, Mr.—"

"Marsden," replied Leo. "And the good doctor here is Mrs. Marsden, rather than Surgeon-Captain Gibbs."

The captain's eyes widened. He looked at Bryony again. His already pink face reddened further.

"I apologize, madam. I don't know how I made the mistake."

"It would be the men's clothes and the men's profession, I imagine, Captain," Bryony said dryly.

Captain Bartlett chuckled. "Quite true. Quite true."

"We seem to have picked a most inconvenient time to tour the North-West Frontier," said Leo.

"I apologize for that too, sir," said Captain Bartlett. "It has been so singularly peaceful since ninety-five that I'm at a loss to explain these extraordinary events. Now, sir, if you don't mind, what do you estimate to be the strength of the gathering tribals?"

"Thousands. I should be astonished there isn't a contingent at least two thousand strong."

Lieutenant Wesley drew in a dismayed breath. "My God. We have only two hundred men in the fort."

For a moment nobody spoke. Then Captain Bartlett turned to Lieutenant Wesley. "Quick, send a cable to the main camp to let them know. A large mob is marching on the fort."

"Captain, I will be glad to remain and assist you and your men in any capacity I may," said Leo. "But I should like to see my wife escorted south to safety."

Bryony looked at him and mouthed "No!" He ignored her.

"That is not advisable," replied Captain Bartlett. "Coming back from the polo field, I passed a very large crowd of Pathans south of the river. Fortunately they took no notice of me—just then I believed it was to be my last hour on earth."

For a moment Leo thought he must have lost too much blood, because he couldn't think. But no, it was not that. Judging by the blood on his clothes, which looked worse than it was, he'd lost about a pint and no more. The reason he couldn't think was because he couldn't think. The situation had become such that it was impossible for one man to think his way out of it.

"I wouldn't worry, Mr. Marsden," said Captain Bartlett gallantly. "We hold the advantage in weaponry and position. My men are well practiced. And we have all the might of the government of India, and ultimately that of the entire British Empire, behind us."

Leo supposed Captain Bartlett was right. He would have preferred not being anywhere near the Swat Valley tonight. But since he was here, the fort of Chakdarra was not the worst place to be, with its well-practiced men and its advantage in weaponry and position. He nodded. "Let's hope it will be no more than a minor skirmish."

"Once you've been patched up, sir, you can recuperate in Surgeon-Captain Gibbs's quarters," said the captain. "And if you feel up to it, the officers and I would be glad to have you and Mrs. Marsden join us for dinner and—"

"Captain!" Lieutenant Wesley returned, running. "The telegraph line! The line has been cut."

"Bloody hell. Beg your pardon, Mrs. Marsden," Captain Bartlett said hastily. "Did our warning go through to Malakand, Lieutenant?"

"It did. And the line was cut as they were wiring the beginning of a return message."

"Intolerably rude," huffed Captain Bartlett. "You'd think since the Pathans have no plan to open the first salvo til morning, they'd at least have the courtesy to let us keep telegraph service for the night."

"Perhaps they intend to attack sooner?" asked Leo. "The men we passed along the way were primed for a fight, not for a nighttime vigil."

"Unlikely," Captain Bartlett said decisively. "The Pathans always attack at first light—these men of the hills are completely beholden to their outmoded ways."

Almost before he'd finished speaking, a collective shout went up around the fort, the kind of shout that Leo imagined greeted the sighting of a pirate ship. The two officers sprinted out of the surgery, Ranjit Singh in their wake.

The hospital assistant came back a minute later. "The flare has been lit."

"What flare?" Leo and Bryony asked in unison.

"The Khan of Dir's men promised to light a flare from their position in the hills to warn us of an attack."

And now the flare had been lit.

"I need you to lie with your head where your feet are now, so I can stitch the cut on your side," Bryony instructed, white-faced.

He looked down at his leg, which he'd forgotten about entirely. Not only had she finished stitching the wound, she'd dressed it too. She helped him turn around, injected him with more local anesthesia, and set to work.

"Do you keep any crutches around here?" he asked Ranjit Singh.

"In storage, I think. I will look, *sahib*."

"Are you all right, Bryony?" Leo asked, when the hospital assistant had gone.

She did not look at him. "Would you let me apologize now?"

He sighed. "No. We are safe."

"We are going to be attacked."

"The *fort* is going to be attacked. *We* will be fine."

"*You* are *not* fine. You could be fighting for your life now, had the cut on your leg gone any deeper."

"But it didn't go any deeper. And I'll be able to get around with a crutch as soon as you are done."

She set down the needle and thread, lifted him very gently to a sitting position, and bandaged his side and his arm. "Don't move. I'm not done yet."

She took off the rubber gloves and wetted a towel. There was still much dried blood on him, in patches, rivulets, and smears along his arm, his side, and his leg. She cleaned him carefully, thoroughly.

"Listen," he said. "It's not your fault. I thought staying behind was more prudent, but I didn't believe for a moment that by going forward we'd end up in the middle of an uprising. So it wasn't as if you coerced me into this."

"I did coerce you into this."

"But I was responsible for our safety. I should have known better."

She sighed, a long, unsteady exhalation. "If anything happens to you, I am going to kill Callista with my bare hands."

"I think the headline would be far more interesting if it read 'Lady surgeon attacks sister with scalpel.'"

She laughed, startled.

He placed a hand on her cheek. "Do you still trust me?"

"Yes."

"Then trust me when I say that nothing will

happen to me and nothing will happen to you." He kissed her lightly on her forehead. "This too shall pass."

৵

Surgeon-Captain Gibbs's quarters was as neat as his surgery, with a bed, wardrobe, desk, chair, and two laden bookshelves. There was also an attached bathroom with a flat tub and a bath stool inside, to stand on while washing.

Their few things had been brought in already and laid in a corner of the room. Leo's rifle was there, looking as if it had been gnawed by an iron-jawed beast, full of nicks, cuts, and gouges both on the stock and along the barrel.

Leo leaned against the edge of the desk. "Could you help me with my boots?"

"Of course." She carefully pulled them off.

"I need to change clothes."

He did. His jacket and shirt were both missing the left sleeve and the left side, his trousers missing the right leg. She checked his saddlebag and brought out the kurta pyjama.

"No, I only wear those to sleep."

"Which is exactly what you are going to do now, aren't you?" she asked suspiciously. "Right after I find us some food."

He shook his head. "I'm not injured so severely that I can take to my bed with a clear conscience while the men of this fort are outnumbered ten to one."

Her jaw went slack when she realized he wasn't speaking in jest. "Absolutely not. You will not leave this room."

"I must. It's a matter of duty."

"You've no duty to anyone here. You are a passerby and you are injured, while this fort is full of able-bodied men, trained and paid to fight. Let them fight. You rest."

"The officers and soldiers of this fort have offered us shelter in our most desperate hour. I will not rest easy if I don't do something for them in return."

She sighed, knowing a lost cause when she saw one. "Wait here. Let me change out of your clothes and I'll help you dress."

She did her changing in the bath and returned in her blouse and skirt. With great care she disengaged him from his ruined garments, eased him into clothes yanked off her back, and pulled on his boots for him.

"Promise you will be careful about the stitches?"

"I will. I will sit in a corner and load rifles, which is all I can do now."

"And you will be careful otherwise too?"

"Of course. I plan to live a long and much-laureled life yet. You stay here. Some of the men marching on the fort have firearms. There will be loose bullets flying about."

She handed him his crutch and his rifle and walked ahead to open the door for him.

As he passed under the lintel, he stopped and turned toward her. "About what I said night before last, I'm sorry. It's because I cannot forgive myself that I think you too cannot possibly forgive me."

Tears stung the back of her eyes. She rose to her tiptoes and kissed him on his chin. "Just come back."

Chapter Fourteen

Such was the fort's need for men that Leo, despite his crutch and his fresh wounds, was immediately assigned a place on the eastern rampart, next to another civilian, Mr. Richmond, Chakdarra's resident political officer. They'd barely shaken hands and introduced themselves before the first shots rang out.

Leo had never been in a war: The closest he'd ever come to a battle had been when he played Henry V in an Eton production and gave a rather stirring recital of the St. Crispin's Day speech. A nodding acquaintance with Shakespeare, as it turned out, was hardly adequate preparation for the overwhelming cacophony of modern warfare.

Machine guns—two mounted on the rampart, two in the guardhouse over the bridge—thudded loud and staccato. Hundreds, perhaps thousands, of rifles discharged continually in a messy, deafening percussion. Outside the walls, war cries rose like successive waves of a swelling tide, passion begetting passion, fever breeding fever. And cutting through everything else, the deep rumble of war drums, *ba-boom, ba-boom, ba-boom-boom-boom*—the pulsating heart of the Swat Valley Uprising.

Within minutes, the air was heavy with the smell of black powder—most of the cartridges used by the Indian army employed smokeless powder, but the ammunition of those laying siege to the fort was more old-fashioned. The officers sprinted from corner to corner on the rampart, directing the placement of the sepoys, as the Pathans attacked the west wall, the northeast corner of the fort, and the cavalry enclosure in succession.

There was no time to be afraid. Leo sat with his back against the loopholed wall of the rampart and loaded rifles for the bespectacled Mr. Richmond, who would mutter, "God, I can see their faces" every so often.

During a short lull in the fighting, coffee was brought up to the rampart. Mr. Richmond shared his mug with Leo.

"They certainly caught us with our britches

down," said the political officer. "I never thought it would really come to pass. Or that it would amount to anything more than a skirmish."

"You were hardly alone in that opinion."

"Well, at least it won't last much longer. By morning the Swatis will take a look at their fallen and decide it's not worth the fight."

"You think so?" Leo asked, half incredulous, half hopeful.

"The Swatis don't have much of a reputation as fighters—the other Pathans look down on them. And the clans up and down the river squabble with one another constantly—they are about as organized as a bag of sand."

Leo thought about the silent crowd trying to retain Bryony and him, so as not to have their ambush revealed—that seemed to speak of some organization. And the other Pathans might look down on the Swatis, but they were joining them in droves, coming from as far as Bajaur, if Imran had it right.

He kept his thoughts to himself. As a mere traveler, he could not hope to convince Mr. Richmond otherwise on his say-so. They'd learn soon enough whether the Swatis and their fellow Pathans were cohesive and united.

And soon, as it were, came at the end of that very night.

❧

"Twenty lancers, one hundred and eighty rifles, three officers, the surgeon-captain's assistant, myself, and the usual camp followers," Mr. Richmond said with regard to Leo's question concerning the precise head count inside the fort. The political officer leaned against the wall, his drowsiness barely held at bay by the quart of coffee he'd consumed. "And see, we made it through a whole night with hardly any casualty."

The sun was rising, the mantle of darkness quietly dissolving. Leo thought with some longing to the sunrise over the Swat River that he'd have enjoyed in times of peace, long ripples of flame and copper on wide, swift water, beneath a sky still streaked with purple.

Before he could reply to Mr. Richmond, gasps went up around the rampart. Sepoys and sowars pointed to the north of the fort.

In the hills that overhung the knoll on which the fort stood, hundreds of colorful standards fluttered in the morning breeze. Men, not in thousands, but in untold tens of thousands stood shoulder to shoulder, their ranks stretching as far as the eye could see east and west, the white of their tunics glinting like new snow in the first light of day.

"God have mercy," said Mr. Richmond, staring at

the banners. "All of Swat is here. And the Bajaur tribes. And the Bunerwals and the Utman Khels."

To cries of alarm and dismay, bullets rained *into* the fort. The fort, seemingly impregnable when viewed in isolation, strong and splendid upon its fortified knoll, was actually dwarfed by the cliffs to the north of it, which now abounded with sharp-shooters seeking to pick off the fort's defenders.

The officers organized a group of sepoys to carry sandbags and stones to pile on top of the walls for additional protection against the snipers. Mr. Richmond rushed off to help. Leo stared at the chaotic scene.

He'd failed Bryony. He was to see her to safety. Instead, he'd delivered her to the very battlefield of the worst uprising in decades. It didn't matter that this was what she'd wanted. He should have overridden her and he hadn't.

Now she was in mortal danger. Should the fort be overrun, it wouldn't matter that they were two hapless travelers caught in the wrong place at the wrong time. They'd share the fate of the rest.

He instinctively turned away from the images his mind generated. But fragments cut through. Her upturned hand on the ground. Her cheek, pale as marble. Her shirt, caked in blood.

He could not breathe. For the first time he understood what it meant not just to lose her, but to *lose* her.

And he was not strong enough for it.

☙

Bryony had thought she'd be kept awake all night by her worry and the constant barrage of gunfire. But instead, she fell asleep with her head on Surgeon-Captain Gibbs's desk, his field surgical manual on gunshot and other trauma wounds still open before her, and dreamed of circus cannons and the precise procedure for wiring a shattered knee.

The clamor of battle acted as a perverse lullaby. When the gunfire became more sporadic, she'd drifted closer to consciousness, only to sleep more deeply as the battle intensified, and the shots, the human cries, and the footsteps thumping on the rampart all fused into a uniform din.

She woke up shortly after dawn. The fort was almost quiet. She opened the shutters an inch and saw kitchen workers running toward the rampart with large pots of tea and baskets of foodstuff. At least Leo would be fed.

She brushed her teeth, rebraided her hair, and looked into Leo's saddlebag to see if he had anything for her to eat. He did, a few dried apricots, which tasted wonderfully sweet.

A knock came at her door. She rushed to open it. But it was not Leo, only Ranjit Singh, the hospital assistant. "*Memsahib,* we have a man who has been sh—"

"It's not Mr. Marsden, is it?"

"No, *memsahib.* It's a cook's assistant. Can you operate on him?"

She hesitated. She had very limited experience with the sort of surgical practice that was particular to battlefields. Her only encounter with a gunshot wound had been a hunting accident, when she'd last visited Thornwood Manor and the village doctor had been away on holiday.

"Yes, of course."

"Thank you, *memsahib. Memsahib* will please be very careful walking outside. The Pathans can get a shot clear into the fort from the top of the hills."

As if to underscore Ranjit Singh's point, two shots landed not fifteen feet behind him. They both jumped. Bryony swallowed. She had not believed the inside of the fort could be so vulnerable.

They ran for it. The cook's assistant had been shot in the shoulder. Bryony put him under general anesthesia. When she had extracted the bullet with a bullet probe, the hospital assistant found a laundry worker and the two of them carried the cook on a stretcher to the sick ward—now injury ward—next door.

Bryony washed her hands thoroughly. While the hospital assistant scrubbed down the operating table, she sterilized the rubber gloves and surgical implements she'd used and mixed more anesthetic solutions.

Another cook's assistant braved the rain of bullets to deliver a plate of breakfast to Bryony, which she gratefully accepted. But before she'd taken two bites, the door of the surgery opened to a pair of sodden sowars, one of whom bled profusely from his thigh.

She stopped the bleeding, extracted the bullet, sent the man to the injury ward, and returned to her breakfast. The door to the surgery opened again, and in came an officer, whose uniform, like the sowars', was drenched from the waist down.

"Are you the surgeon, ma'am?"

"Temporarily. May I help you?"

"Captain North of the Eleventh Bengal Lancers—I'm the commanding officer of Debesh Sen, on whom you just operated. I would like to know his prognosis."

The sowar would be *hors de combat* for a while. But provided that his wound did not become infected—she assured Captain North that all antiseptic measures had been taken—she did not foresee any long-term consequences.

Captain North shook hands with her. "Thank you, ma'am."

As he was about to leave the surgery, she could not suppress her curiosity any longer. "Captain, if you don't mind, why are you and your men all soaked?"

"We had to ford the Swat River, ma'am."

"Ford the Swat River? Why?"

"To get here, ma'am. We rode over from Malakand."

"Oh, that is wonderful!" She could jump for joy. The cavalry had come. The fort at Chakdarra was being rescued even as they spoke. "I assume you are the vanguard of the relief column?"

The captain shook his head grimly. "Unfortunately we *are* the relief column—forty sowars, another officer, and myself. The camp at Malakand was nearly overrun last night. The Pathans made off with almost all of the ammunition from one of our storehouses. It was decided this morning that we should still send some men to aid Chakdarra because we feared that it was badly surrounded. Could have been a fool's mission—the hills between Malakand and the river are packed full of more men than I've ever seen in my life. We barely made it through."

Bryony's heart sank. "So we can expect no more help from Malakand?"

"Not until Malakand itself is relieved by mobilization from Nowshera. And Nowshera is probably empty just now—the regiments sent on punitive expeditions to Tochi Valley haven't returned yet."

"I see," she said weakly.

"I'm sorry, ma'am. I suppose I should have said something more reassuring. I'm not accustomed to discussing such situations with ladies."

"It's quite all right, Captain," she said. "I assure you ladies prefer the truth to being kept in the dark."

Or perhaps not.

As long as help was just around the corner, she could pretend that her stupid mistake hadn't actually cost anyone anything. But now that Malakand itself was under siege, and no help was possible—

When I'm a wizened old professor at Cambridge, and can barely climb up to the podium to lecture, I will think back to the frontiers of India—and life's strange paths that had led me here—and remember that this was where the wanderings of my youth ended.

He would never become that wizened old professor at Cambridge. He would never leave the frontiers of India. And the wandering of his youth—his youth altogether—would end here when the fort fell.

Because she had no sense. Because she put her need to get away from him above their safety. Because she'd been so stupid as to believe that a week of heartache in peace and security would be worse than actual death.

It was all her fault.

❦

They were infinitely removed from the safety of the plains of India, but not so much geographically that the men on the rampart didn't swelter all day. The Pathans kept up their attacks on the fort. They seemed to have an endless supply of men and an endless supply of courage; their compatriots falling like dominoes at the base of the fort served only to harden their resolve. And any lull in the fighting was taken up with raising the height of the walls to provide better cover against the snipers in the hills.

At nine o'clock that night Captain Bartlett found Leo. "I've a message for you from Mrs. Marsden. She has informed me that if you, sir, do not go down to get your dressing changed and sleep a few hours, she will refuse to extract any more bullets from my men."

Leo shook his head. "Women and their wiles."

"My thoughts exactly, sir. I can't afford to be short a sawbones now, so you'd best do as she says."

But before he went to the surgery, Leo went to their quarters to wash: He didn't want to go to her grimy and malodorous. With his uninjured arm, he made unstinting use of Surgeon-Captain Gibbs's soap and probably squandered more water than he needed to rinse, just because it felt good to pour cool water over himself, after an entire day perspiring in both heat and fear.

She was waiting for him when he came out of the bathroom. They stood a moment, staring at each other. She looked pale and shaken, much the same as she'd looked after their first encounter with hostile Pathans. Except now he too was equally shaken, equally terrified of what might come to pass.

"Bryony," he said softly.

"You made your dressings wet," she said. "Good thing we are changing them."

She washed her hands, leaned him against the edge of the desk, and took off his bandaging. On one knee, she pushed aside the towel he'd wrapped around himself and cleaned the wound on his leg. He sucked in a breath at the stinging coolness of the carbolic acid solution.

He was tired—he hadn't slept in more than forty hours. The stitches, once the local anesthesia wore off, had hurt as if a rabid dog had sunk its teeth into him. And his head pounded from too much coffee and too little food. But as she knelt before him, her fingers brushing his upper thigh, the tiny little air fluffs of her breaths mercilessly teasing his skin, everything else faded into a dull ache against the increasing sharpness of his awareness of *her*.

Her white-streaked hair, smoothly coiled and obedient. The pretty lobe of her ear. The collar of her shirt, quite crumpled from the heat.

She rose to her feet, to work on the cut on his side. Her head tilted to the side to get a better look; the light from the lamp limned her slender neck, or what little of it that was exposed with her shirt buttoned resolutely to the edge of her chin. He wanted to open a few of those buttons, if only for humanitarian reasons—it had grown stuffy inside the quarters, with the shutters closed against ricocheting bullets, and the walls still releasing their embedded heat.

"Have you slept at all since we got here?"

"Nobody has, so I don't feel deprived. What about you? Were you able to sleep last night?"

Abruptly, the walls shook with the boom of the war drums. Gunfire, a minute ago desultory, intensified into the roar of a hailstorm. Shouts erupted as the Pathans charged the fort, always the shouts, single-minded and feral.

She stopped, listened for a while, then pressed on with her task, her teeth clenched. When she was done, she busied herself gathering the soiled bandaging. Only then did he see her hands shake, almost imperceptibly, but shaking nevertheless.

He took her hands in his, her fear a dagger in his heart. "Bryony."

"Sleep," she said, not looking at him. "You need your sleep."

He pulled her closer to him. "Bryony, listen to me. We are hardly at the end of our rope. The fort has plenty of store and ammunition. Our men are superior in discipline and musketry. We'll hold out until relief comes."

If only his words didn't sound so flaccid to his own ears.

He wasn't lying, but he'd certainly narrated only the most encouraging aspects of the situation. Not the sea of Pathans he'd seen in the morning, not the fatigue that was beginning to weary the defenders, and most certainly not the almost trance-like resolve on the faces of those who rushed at the front of the attacks. The Swatis and their neighbors wanted the British gone, and they were quite glad to die for it.

Her eyelashes lifted, her eyes moss green and wild. "If you want to put me at ease, it's really quite simple. Let me apologize. Let me grovel and rend my hair. Let me be abjectly, miserably sorry. Please. And let me do it now, before it's—before it's too late."

❧

"All right," he said. "Go ahead."

She looked at him uncertainly. "Go ahead?"

"Yes. Go ahead."

"I'm sorry," she said. "I was completely childish and irresponsible. Forgive me."

He kissed her lightly on her ear. "Forgiven."

A more beautiful word did not exist in the English language. She cupped his face and rained kisses upon his cheeks, his jaw, and his lips. Finally her mouth settled against his and she kissed him tenderly. He tasted of the roasted fennel seeds Indians chewed after meals to freshen breath. She wanted to savor him slowly, a connoisseur before the finest vintage of the century; she wanted to devour him, a drunk trembling for that first swallow of the day.

Her hands wandered down his arms. His skin was cool from the bath and smooth to the touch. The whole of him was tightly built, his musculature strong and spare. And he smelled, rather wonderfully, of Surgeon-Captain Gibbs's Pears soap.

She pulled back. "Let me put you to bed. You've only a few hours to sleep."

She put her arm about his middle, acted as his crutch as he crossed the room, and helped lower him to the edge of the bed. But as she straightened, he gripped the front of her shirt. She went utterly still. Outside the battle continued to escalate, but inside she could only hear her own tattered breaths and the hard thumps of her heart.

He kissed her on the tip of her chin, the tip of her nose, the corners of her eyes. Then, his teeth grazed the edge of her earlobe. She shuddered.

He released her. "Want more?"

She nodded.

He scooted back on the bed until his back was against the wall. "Then come here."

"What about your stitches?"

"We won't do anything to worry the stitches."

She sat down next to him, her back to the wall. He chuckled, put his uninjured arm about her waist, and swung her toward him. She squeaked, terrified that her weight would land the wrong way and pull on the stitches. But she came down on her knees, braced to either side of him.

She put her mouth to his again and kissed him, in ways that seemed rather pushy and improper. But he did not seem to mind. The soft sounds he made in his throat were those of pleasure and arousal. His hand skimmed along her arm, then along the outside of her thigh. He dragged her skirt and petticoat free from underneath her knee and lifted them out of the way. Underneath she had her combination.

Slowly, slowly, his hand ascended toward the open seam between her legs.

She whimpered. He stroked her there, almost-harmless little touches interspersed with the most unchaste caresses possible. The pleasure came like monsoon rain, hot and thick. She wanted to cling to him, to meld into him, but she dared only push her palms against the gritty surface of the wall, her fingers spread, seeking desperately to hold on to something. Anything.

The pleasure stretched her taut. It plucked and thrummed her. It made her thighs quake with the strain of holding herself upright.

All the while he kissed her, as if she were air, water, fire, everything he couldn't do without. As if she were as sweet on the tongue as the first snow melt high in the Himalayas. As if he'd meant to kiss her for years and years and must make up for the eternity of waiting.

And he kissed her as she gasped with the spikes of her climax. As she moaned and hissed with the intensity of it. As she called his name, again and again, a prayer for things beyond hope.

❧

"May I do that for you also?" she asked, her breaths not at all even.

He shivered. "Well, one of us would have to."

She shifted her person so that she was next to him, rather than straddling him. Looping her left arm about his neck, she kissed him on the shoulder. The little drop-kisses turned into moist nibbles. And then, openmouthed worship of his skin and flesh.

He grunted with the testes-jolting heat of it.

"I imagine I should take care to be very gentle about it?" she asked, the fingers of her right hand peeling apart the towel at his waist.

"I rather hope you will be very forceful about it. It's not a Ming vase."

"Goodness," she murmured. "Will you show me what to do?"

He took her hand and wrapped it about his length. "Grip it, as hard as you can."

"Are you sure?"

"It's what I always do."

She whimpered. And then, with a soft grunt of effort, her hand clamped over him, a hot, smooth vise. She was strong. And he was so aroused it would take barely a touch to undo him.

He guided her hand into a naughty motion. "Yes, that's it. Just—do that."

And she did just that. His heart pumped. His breaths quickened—to his own ears he sounded like a bellow operated by a madman. He seized a handful of her skirt.

Then she shifted her weight again and kissed him, her mouth warm, her tongue hungry. He lost all control. He kissed her back with the gentleness of an avalanche. His pelvis lifted from the bed despite all her exhortations to stay still. And he came hotly, endlessly, whispering incoherent words of relief and gratitude as he kissed and kissed her.

Chapter Fifteen

She scooted away from him to inspect his stitches, scolding him severely for not obeying her commandment. He wanted to tell her he wasn't quite that stupid, that he'd used solely his uninjured limb for leverage. But his exhaustion at last caught up with him, and he fell asleep with her admonishing words echoing sweetly in his ears.

He awoke three hours later, when the hospital assistant came to call her away to help an injured sowar. Within fifteen minutes he was back on the rampart and did not leave for the next thirty-six hours. She sent the hospital assistant after him one time. But Ranjit Singh took one look at the situation—the enemy inside the barbed wire enclosure, ladders raised against the walls of the fort—and concluded that it was no time to pull any man away from the battle.

When Leo did finally get away, he stopped by the surgery, but she was in the middle of an operation, her brows furrowed, her face pale, cursing in surprisingly vivid German. So he hobbled to their quarters, fell into bed and fell asleep instantly.

He dreamed that she was there with him, carefully nudging his trousers down to examine the stitches on his thigh and tsking in disapproval. Her fingers were cool and reassuring. He adored her touch.

Her fingers meandered away from the stitches and dipped down to the inside of his thigh. He was immediately aroused. *Put your hand on me. Give me some blessed relief. I have wanted you too long.*

Her hand moved away. His hopes plunged. But then something even better happened. She kissed him just above the dressing, a moist, lingering kiss. He groaned with the magnitude of his need. Inch by inch she nibbled and licked. He was dying—such pleasure, such torture.

And then she came to a most logical but no less shocking destination: She took him inside her mouth. He was instantly on the verge. It was *her* mouth, *her* lips, *her* tongue on him. Burning, exquisite, unbearable.

He shuddered and jerked, barely holding back at the edge. He tried to give her a warning: *I have to—I'm going to—* Too late. He lost all control. His emptied into her in hot convulsions, the pleasure fearsome, almost terrible in its blinding intensity. And she— good God—she swallowed everything.

In the aftermath he trembled and gasped, un- done. This had to be the best bloody dream he'd had in a long time. In real life, he would never even think to suggest to her that she pleasure him with her mouth, let alone that—

He opened his eyes. Judging by the light seeping in around the edges of the door, it was still the middle of the day. But as the shutters were kept shut—there were constant sniper shots during day- time—a kerosene lamp had been lit to dispel the dimness inside the room.

He had not lit the lamp.

He turned his head. Bryony knelt between his legs, panting slightly. At his look she quickly low- ered her head and pulled up his trousers.

It had not been a dream. For a moment he was paralyzed with dismay.

"I'm sorry," he mumbled. "I thought I was dream- ing. I didn't know—I wouldn't have—"

"Don't be silly," she said softly. "It had to go somewhere and it wasn't as if I didn't know what was coming."

Then she did something that amazed him: She

giggled at her own words. "That was a horrible pun, wasn't it? I'd better go make my rounds. You go back to sleep."

&

That night she woke up panting in arousal. It was pitch dark. He was in bed with her, his hand between her legs, playing her like a lyre.

"Move a little higher," he ordered.

He was on his back, she on her side. She wiggled toward the head of the bed, careful not to bump into his right thigh even by accident.

"Now come closer."

She did. In the next moment, his mouth captured her nipple, and warmly, kindly lavished it with attention. Desire ripped through her—he knew exactly how wildly she responded to the coddling of her nipples: A breath of air blown across the tips had them hard and quivering for touch; a gentle lick had her moaning and straining for more; a tug with just the right amount of force as she hovered on the edge of a paroxysm sent her over promptly.

When his lips retreated, she moaned in protest. He palmed her breast. "Patience, patience," he murmured.

His other hand still fiddled with her, gently, almost sleepily. She wanted more. She wanted more aggression from him, more urgency, more—

He pinched her nipple. As aggressive and urgent a pleasure as she ever knew jolted her. Suddenly she was there, her spine curving, her inside quaking.

He kissed her on the forehead. "I'd tell you to go back to sleep, but I'm not sure you are even properly awake."

"I am," she protested. And fell back asleep in the next second.

৵

When she woke up again, it was still night.

She stared at the ceiling, wondering what had pulled her out of her deep slumber. After a while she realized that it was the silence, the night as still as a thief. She sat up. Where was everyone? Was the battle over?

A match flared into life. Leo, seated at the edge of the table, his good leg propped up on a chair, lit the lamp. He discarded the match and lifted a half-eaten fig from the table. His clothes were hopelessly rumpled, his hair mussed, his face rough with a four-day growth of beard. He should appear haggard, but as he watched her, there was such a jauntiness to him— almost a swagger—that he merely looked at once battle-tested and virile.

Remembering the state she had been reduced to in her sleep—the front of her shirt open, her corset hanging loose, the top buttons of her combination undone, her skirt and petticoat up around her waist—she hastily reached for a blanket, only to realize that she was decently dressed, her skirts down at her ankles, her breasts perfectly contained.

"I didn't want to imperil anyone's chance of survival by keeping the surgeon in a state of undress," he said, smiling. "I also didn't want soldiers dying of bliss should you rush out of this room with your bosom in plain view."

She cleared her throat. "Thank you. Most kind of you."

"But *I* would like to see you," he said softly. "And perish of bliss."

She bit her lower lip, then set her face into an austere expression. "Not when I'm still upset with you."

He flushed. She stared at the abrupt and visible reddening of his complexion—she'd never seen him flush before.

"I'm sorry. I was dreaming and I—I—" he stammered.

She flushed too. "That's not what I'm upset about."

"No?"

She felt the warmth of her cheeks spread to her throat and bosom. It was a few seconds before she could speak. "You promised you would stay off your feet and only load rifles for others. But when Captain Bartlett came to tour the injury ward he couldn't say enough about your marksmanship."

He relaxed and tossed her a fig. "That is pure slander. I will have you know that I stayed calmly uninvolved as pandemonium erupted all about me."

"Captain Bartlett further said that when the sight on one of the machine guns malfunctioned, and their regular sharpshooter became injured, you were the one who held off the enemy while the sepoys repaired the sight."

"A momentary lapse. I blame it on the general panic among the men."

"A momentary lapse that lasted a day and a half?"

"Will you forgive me if I tell you that all throughout I was extremely, excessively careful with my stitches?"

"Your dressing was soaked in blood."

"Was it?" He looked genuinely surprised. "I didn't know."

"The stitches mainly held. But it took a while to clean and disinfect."

"I didn't know that either," he said sheepishly. "I thought you came, took a look at it, then . . ."

They both flushed again. She'd always viewed

such sexual acts as analogous to cliff-diving: surviv-able, and no doubt thrilling to a tiny portion of the population, but what was the point really? Yet as she'd knelt before him that afternoon, she'd remem-bered the searing pleasure he'd once given her in just such a manner. *One day you will return the favor,* he'd whispered in her ear that night. And she'd decided to return the favor then and there, because they might not live to see another day.

Perhaps she ought to rethink cliff-diving. Because she certainly enjoyed its analogous act more than she'd ever thought possible for anyone. Even the scramble at the end.

She cleared her throat. "I'm going to write a letter to the *Times*," she said, changing the subject com-pletely. "The last man I operated on was hit by friendly fire. The bullet shattered upon impact. And it was horrible—took me four hours to extract all the fragments. Ranjit Singh told me that these Dum-Dum bullets are designed to do that, to inflict maximum damage. I understand that bullets are supposed to be deadly, but surely it is against the spirit of the Geneva Convention to have bullets that maim so viciously when they don't kill."

He sighed. "This entire thing is mad. We spent untold amounts to maintain these forward posts, because we fear the Russians would come sweeping down the Pamirs any day. But I've seen photographs of the Pamirs taken from the air: It would be worse than Napoleon marching on St. Petersburg for the Russians to invade India via the Pamirs—they'd have a better chance sacrificing half their army in Afghanistan first."

She took a bite of the fig he'd given her. "I didn't know there were photographs of the Pamirs taken from the air."

"Remember my purpose for being in Gilgit, the balloon expedition? It wasn't to survey the Nanga Parbat, but to take aerial images of the Pamirs and study the routes the Russians could take."

Her eyes went wide. "You were on a *spy* mission?"

"It wasn't exactly spying since the Pamirs don't belong to either side. But I'd certainly gone to Gilgit in service to the empire. So I'm not quite as innocent a bystander in this uprising as you are."

It was her turn to speak sheepishly. "And here I thought you were merely following me around."

"I was." He finished his fig and wiped his fingers on a handkerchief. "I always had something legitimate to do, but I could have gone to Sweden and Italy instead of Germany and America. I chose to be closer to you."

She looked down into her lap. She still had trouble

thinking of him as devastated by their annulment—before she left for Germany, he'd entertained quite grandly at his hotel, leaving her to draw the very reasonable conclusion that he was more than happy to be rid of her as a spouse.

But then there had been that microscope. There had been the way he'd looked at her, hope and despair fused into one single, scalding emotion. What stupid children they had been, to cause each other such pain and then to hold on to their wounds so fiercely.

She got up, walked to him, and very carefully wrapped her arms about him.

He kissed the top of her head. "I wish we had more time."

But there was no more time to be squeezed from the all-consuming battle—he couldn't have had more than twelve hours of sleep in the five nights and days they'd been here. Sometimes it seemed to her that she'd lived her entire life in this fort, that there had never been anything in her years but this siege and this desperate struggle.

A knock came at the door. "Mr. Marsden, it's Richmond. We are due back on the rampart in two minutes."

"I'll be right there," Leo answered.

"Must you go?" she complained. "There is no fighting."

"But the enemy is still out there. Which is why I need to go, so that the next batch of sepoys can rest. I was just about to leave when you woke up."

"I wish you could stay," she murmured, as she kissed him just above his collar. "I am having an extraordinarily difficult time letting you out of my arms."

She was both surprised and not surprised to feel tears roll down her face. He kissed her tears. "It doesn't matter where I am; I'm yours."

❧

After a half day lull, all hell broke loose. Ranjit Singh informed Bryony in an unsteady voice that whereas they'd had two or three thousand attackers earlier, now they were surrounded by well over ten thousand Pathans, every last one of whom was dead set on storming the fort.

Bullets slammed into the fort as if they were some malicious god's idea of manna from heaven. The casualty rate rose sharply. A camp follower and two sepoys died not from battle but from the flying bullets while traversing the interior of the fort.

For some time Bryony existed in a state of abject fear. She was not ready to die. She was not ready for

Leo to die. Or for Ranjit Singh or Captain Bartlett or her patients or the brave cavalry soldiers who'd ridden from Malakand or anyone at all in this fort to be hacked to death.

Then the hours passed, the defenders still held, and her terror subsided to a grim apprehension. She went on with the work of the surgery, which was unfortunately all too plentiful. Leo sent her a hurriedly scratched note: *B., The stitches are fine. I changed the dressing—no infection as far as I can tell. Be sure you eat enough and sleep as much as you can. And walk in the open only under the most extreme caution. L.*

She barely ate and slept for two days, but when she finally returned to the quarters, she did proceed under extreme caution—Ranjit Singh had found a pair of spare shutters from somewhere and had accompanied her, the two of them each holding a shutter as a shield, running the gauntlet.

Leo came and lay down next to her at some point. She was so tired she couldn't even grunt to acknowledge him. But if it was possible to sleep with a smile on her face, then she must have—whether she had enough grace to die bravely she did not yet know, but at that moment at least she was strangely at peace and unspeakably happy.

He stirred when she got out of bed two hours later—she needed to make her rounds.

"Hullo," he said, his eyes still closed, his voice barely audible.

"Hullo," she said, sitting down again at the edge of the bed. "Since I'm here, let me take a look at you."

He obediently moved as she needed to help her. The wound on his arm had healed almost entirely. The cut on his side was also coming along nicely. Even the one on his thigh had made satisfactory progress, though the eventual scar promised to be much uglier than if he had been able to recover unmolested.

"You know what is tragic?" he murmured.

"What?" she said, smiling at his wry tone.

"That in what could be my final days on earth I spend all my waking hours killing men I've never laid eyes on before, and scant minutes making love to you."

"The very thought makes tears stream down my face."

He opened his eyes and touched the back of his hand to her cheek. The tenderness in his look was almost enough to make tears stream down her face in truth. "Bryony."

She placed her hand over his heart. "Is it as bad out there as Ranjit Singh says it is?"

"Worse."

She sighed. "I don't know why, but I have this

huge regret over having never seen Cambridge. I hear it's a lovely place."

"It is. You will like it."

"Do you really think I'll have a chance to visit it? And your house on the river with the cherry trees?"

"I do. You'll make it, Bryony. And one day you will be the first woman to be admitted to the Royal College of Surgeons," he said, his tone brooking no disagreement.

"Of course," she said, growing ever closer to tears.

"There are two letters in my bag, one to my brothers, one to my godfather. If something should happen to me, I want you to deliver those letters."

"Shh. Don't talk like that."

"I'm not talking like that. God willing, I am going to lecture at Cambridge until 1960, when I am so old that my students will ask if I'd met Newton in my youth. But bullets fly in war—a sepoy standing next to me was killed on the spot—and I want to prepare for all eventualities."

"No, you—"

"Listen, Bryony. In my letters, I wrote that we have married again."

"But that is not true."

"No. But should you survive Swat Valley and I do not—what if you should be with child?"

"You know how unlikely it is for me to conceive."

"Yes, I know. But the irregularity of your courses could also disguise a pregnancy for months. I won't have you ostracized." He brought her hand to his lips. "And don't worry, with Sir Robert and my brothers behind you, no one will dare ask to see a copy of our new marriage lines."

Her tears did come after all. He had thought of everything for her.

"I love you," she said, choking on her words, knowing that should things go ill, this was their farewell.

"You'll do it then, for me?"

She nodded. He closed his eyes. She rained kisses on his hand. When it seemed he'd fallen back asleep, she rose to leave.

"Almost forgot. There is something else I need to tell you," he murmured.

She sat down again. "What is it?"

"The day before our annulment was granted, your father came to see me at Claridge's."

"Did he?" She never knew.

"As soon as we were alone in my suite, he punched me so hard that I was on the floor, seeing stars."

"No, that can't be true." Her father was a scholar who never did anything more strenuous than raising a pen.

"Yes, it is true. And before I could get up he

punched me again. So there I was with a bleeding lip and a cut on my cheek, and he said, 'I trusted you to treat her right, you bastard.'"

"*My* father?"

He sighed. "Yes, your father. So there I was yelling that I treated you like a princess, that no woman in her right mind would act the way you did and why in the name of all that was good and sane would he choose to defend you when you hated his bloody guts."

She rested Leo's hand against her cheek, shocked and strangely exhilarated. "And what did he say?"

"He said that you hated him for damned good reasons. And so you must hate me for damned good reasons too. And with that he punched me again and left."

Her tears once again overwhelmed her control. "He never told me."

"Of course he wouldn't have." He rubbed away her tears with his palm. "When you see him again, do not think so harshly of him."

"I will try."

He smiled. "Good. Now go bother your patients and let me sleep."

Chapter Sixteen

The siege lifted as swiftly as it had begun. The cavalry literally came over the hill, the Amandara Ridge south of the river, the distant mobilization Captain Bartlett had promised at last galloping to their rescue. A loud, heartfelt cheer went up the rampart.

At the sight of cavalry—and the knowledge their brethren at Malakand had already been defeated—the Pathans, so fierce and dauntless for so long, lost their will to fight. They scattered before the cavalry, some running for the hills, others throwing aside their arms.

The men on the ramparts held their posts as Captain Bartlett rode out to meet the relief column. Even as the enemy retreated and capitulated, the sepoys dared not move freely: The walls of the rampart, piled high with logs, sandbags, rocks, and boxes of dirt, were a constant reminder of their imperilment from snipers in the cliffs above.

But eventually it dawned that they had done what they needed to do: They'd held an ill-placed fort against a much larger enemy for seven long nights and days. Even the snipers had fled. The valley, busy with horses, sowars, sepoys, and equipment on the move, was curiously devoid of further gunshots.

Leo found himself hugged by Mr. Richmond, whose face was badly sunburnt, and whose glasses had lost the left side lens. He found himself shaking hands with sepoys whose names he did not know, but with whom he'd fought side by side and in whose skill and courage he'd entrusted his and Bryony's lives. And he found himself, without his crutch, walking slowly along the rampart, looking out at this theater of war of which he'd only had the most limited view, hunkered down as he had been for fear of sniper fire, seeing the battlefield only through loopholes and narrow gaps in the crenellations.

In ancient times a Buddhist kingdom had flourished here, in the heart of the Swat Valley. The Chinese monk Fa-hien, passing through the country in the fifth century, had praised its forests and gardens. There were no forests or gardens to be found along the slopes of the wide valley in the present day, only rock and grass. But the valley itself was a robust green extending as far up- and downstream as the eye could see—paddy fields crowding either side of the river, pink and white begonias growing wild along the embankment.

It would have been beautiful were it not for the scene of carnage. The dead lay thick on the ground, too numerous for their comrades to remove. The defeated huddled with their heads bent, their spirits sapped. Already the air was beginning to turn slightly fetid, from corpses left in the heat. Leo was not a praying man, but he bowed his head and said a prayer for all the men who had perished in this brutal, yet ultimately senseless, battle.

In the distance field guns were on the move, dozens of them drawn by camels. Newly arrived officers surveyed the land and assessed the damages. Their sepoys organized the defeated to dig graves and bury the dead. The gears of the empire, once set into motion, would not stop so quickly. The fort would be repaired and made more secure. The officers would draw up plans. There would be retributive expeditions to Upper Swat Valley and Bajaur.

But his part was done.

He was going to live. And he would pass his days in the peace and fertile learning of Cambridge. And one day he would show Bryony his house on the river, with the cherry trees.

"Mr. Marsden!"

He looked down. It was Mr. Richmond. "The general would like to speak to you. He wants to know what you can tell him of the situation in Dir."

Leo sighed. It would seem his part in this war wasn't quite done yet.

❧

Bryony's last patient was none other than Captain Bartlett, who, after he led the charge, had been shot in the abdomen as he fought to retake the civil hospital outside the fort. As she operated on Captain Bartlett, she was dimly aware that another officer came into the surgery and watched her as she worked, but it did not occur to her to turn and look.

Only when she was done and Captain Bartlett moved to the injury ward did she remember the intruder.

"Surgeon-Captain Gibbs, ma'am," the man introduced himself.

That was the moment the war ended for Bryony. She shook the surgeon-captain's hand with quite a bit more enthusiasm than she normally greeted strangers with and all but shoved over the records of the recovering soldiers and camp followers and the death certificates she'd signed.

The surgeon-captain, an unsmiling man, toured the injury ward. At the end, he said solemnly, "Thank you, Mrs. Marsden. I will ask that the officers recommend you for a medal for your services."

"Thank you but please don't," said Bryony in all sincerity. "That would be setting the bar too low. I but did what every surgeon would have done."

They shook hands again. And she was free. She walked into the hot sun of an August day, feeling light as a dandelion puff, daring to loiter outside for the first time in a week and forever.

But the fort was crowded. Provisions and matériel rolled in the gates. The kitchen workers ran about in a frenzy, supplying everyone with tea and tiffin. And she was getting too many curious looks from all the men, Indian and British, for her comfort. So she abandoned her plan to stand in the open for as long as she could and removed to her quarters.

Leo was there, shrugging into his coat. She hurried to help him. "Your arm! Be careful."

"My arm is quite fine. I can even do this. See." He had her in a fierce embrace that quite crushed her breasts and squeezed every last molecule of air out of her. She could not get enough of it.

But eventually he let her go. "I have to go see the

general, or so I've been told—he wants to know about Dir. If it were any other man, I'd have told him to go bugger himself for keeping me from you. But since he and his troops rescued us, I am just going to ask him to hurry up with his questions instead."

"Well then go and come back fast."

He hugged her again and covered her face with kisses. "Take some rest, if you can in all this commotion. I'll see if I can get us out of here today itself."

She tried, but rest was out of the question. With every raised voice, alarm shot through her—and there were plenty of raised voices as the men inside the fort tried to make themselves heard above the din. Two times she ran to the door and had her hands on the knob before she realized that the war was finished, that there would be no more injured soldiers needing her attention.

So she packed instead—even if Leo couldn't secure transport for them today, Surgeon-Captain Gibbs would still want his quarters back. Not that there was much to pack—they had brought little beyond the clothes on their backs. She did find one stocking of hers under the bed and a pen engraved with Leo's name on the desk.

When she went to put the pen in his saddlebag, she noticed for the first time that it had been slashed through on one side. She shuddered, for a moment slipping back to the terror of their desperate ride. And then it passed and she placed the pen in an interior pouch of the saddlebag where he kept his other pens.

The inside of the bag was largely empty except for a few notebooks, and one of them too had been slashed halfway through. She picked up that particular notebook and opened it. Several sheets that had been torn from the notebook fell out.

Those would be the letters he'd told her about. The first one was to his godfather.

> *Dear Sir Robert,*
>
> *I write to inform you that I have married again. I beg that you would overlook the unusual circumstances and honor and protect Mrs. Marsden, née Bryony Asquith, with affection and esteem.*
> *My life has been immeasurably enriched by your presence. I regret this hasty adieu. I take with me nothing but the fondest of memories.*
>
> *Your friend and godson,*
Leo

The next letter, to his brothers, ran more or less along the same lines, with additional good-byes to numerous nieces and nephews and two postscripts.

P.S. Don't be surprised at the reading of my will. I did not change it after the annulment.

P.P.S. Will and Matthew, I apologize again for how long it took me to come around. In my affection for our father, I sided blindly with him. I cannot tell you how much it means to me that you have never taken me to task for it.

There was another sheet of paper. Bryony hesitated. He'd told her the content of the first two letters, so presumably he would not mind her reading them. But he'd said nothing about a third letter. She was about to put it back without reading when she saw that it was addressed to *her*.

Dear Bryony,

There are many things I wish I had time to tell you, so I will say just this: These past few days have been some of the best days of my life. Because of you.

My fervent hope is that you are safe and well as you read this letter. That you will have all the happiness I wish I could have shared with you. And that you will remember me not as a failed husband, but one who was still trying, til the very end.

Yours always,
Leo

Leo's voice drifted in from the shutters she'd left ajar. *Mrs. Marsden. As soon as possible. Thank you.*

She quickly put the letters back, came to her feet, and wiped the tears from her eyes.

"You are already done with the general?" she asked as he came in the door.

"No, I didn't meet him yet. But there is a cable from Callista."

"Callista? Here?"

"I think you'd better read it."

Somehow her heart sank at his expression. She took the cable from him.

> *Dear Bryony and Leo,*
>
> *I pray you are safe. I will never forgive myself if anything happened to either of you, since the bit about Father's health was a ruse.*
>
> *But it is no longer. Last night he had a massive stroke. Doctors say that he could have another stroke any time and that would be the end of him.*
>
> *If you receive this in good health, please hurry. And please let me know as soon as possible that you are all right.*
>
> *Callista*

"Did I say I was going to kill her with my bare hands if anything happened to you? I think I am going to do it anyway," Bryony said, grinding her teeth.

"No, I will not have you hang for her. I will see if I can have her committed to an asylum where she belongs," said Leo, shaking his head in exasperation. "She fooled me. When I cabled a friend in London and asked about your father's health, the response I got was that he was indeed housebound."

"So you did check. I was beginning to wonder if you'd become excessively gullible."

"I don't trust a word Callista says, at least not where you are concerned. When you were in Germany, she once told me that as a result of treating your own melancholia, you were severely addicted to cocaine and injected yourself at least three times a day."

"What?"

"And when you were in America, she reported that you fell in love with the husband of one of your colleagues and became so miserable that you attempted suicide."

"She's mad!"

"Mad to throw us together, that is for certain."

"Well, shall we believe her this time?"

"The cable was sent from Lord Elgin's office. So Charlie had to be involved. And for Charlie to be involved, she must have gone to either Jeremy or Will. I'm inclined to believe her."

The addition of shock to the mix of exhaustion and excitement was getting to be too much for Bryony. She sat down, the cable in hand, and tried to read it again. But the words only swam about.

She looked up at him. "I suppose I'll have to go right away."

"Yes. The road to Nowshera is crowded and the ponies for the tonga service are overworked. They say a trip now takes twenty hours. I have been promised an escort for you. Shall I help you get ready?"

"I'm ready," she said slowly. "I was already packing before you came back."

He pulled her out of her chair and hugged her close. "I'll miss you."

She hugged him back as fiercely as she dared. "Promise me you won't do anything brave."

"I will be the veriest coward. And I'll come to London as soon as I can get away from here. That is, if you haven't already left for San Francisco or Christchurch by the time I reach England."

She kissed him. "No, I'll be there. You were right. It's time I stopped running away."

Chapter Seventeen

It was always a shock to return to London, to the visibly sooty air, the grime-streaked houses, the poverty, and the sheer density of the population. But it was also the kind of shock that wore off fast. By the time the train pulled into the station Bryony had ceased to wonder how people managed to live in such collective squalor. And as the carriage drew up before her father's house, she no longer even smelled the pervasive stench of horse droppings along the thoroughfares.

It was much more difficult to look upon her father's face, the pale, papery skin, the thinning brows and lashes, the colorless and slack lips—especially slack on the side that had been paralyzed by the previous stroke—and realize that he was truly at death's door. He'd had a second stroke mere hours before

Bryony arrived. She conferred with his physician. Geoffrey Asquith was not expected to recover. He was not even expected to last more than a week. But he was still alive.

He had been very well cared for. Her stepmother, with years of experience looking after her fragile sons, had hired two competent nurses and directed them well. Both he and the room were clean as a whistle, and one could hardly tell that there was a bedpan in use.

"Tea?" Callista asked.

Bryony shook her head.

At twenty-five, Callista still retained the gamine face she'd had since she was a child, with the same wide eyes, same high cheekbones, same slightly pinched nose. She'd been there on the platform of the train station, waiting, a slender, sparkling young woman in a straw hat the green ribbons of which fluttered in the wind and the steam. And Bryony's heart had throbbed painfully: Such an uncanny resemblance she bore to her dead mother, as if Toddy had stepped out of the careful preserves of Bryony's memory.

They had not said much on the carriage ride home. They were not close. They had never been close, even though they had once been the only two children in a large, rambling house.

Bryony had tried. After Toddy's death, she'd poured all her love into Toddy's baby. She'd imagined them as fellow shipwrecked passengers in the same lifeboat: sisters and best friends who would make their way together to safety and a new life.

But whereas Bryony yearned for human contact, Callista shrank away from it. She did not want to be kissed or stroked or cuddled. She did not want to be sung to. And when Bryony tried to read to her, she hid under draped tables and bedsteads, her fingers stuffed into her ears.

Bryony could not get her to talk. She could not interest Callista in any of the games and recreations that she and Toddy had enjoyed so immensely. There had even been times when Callista had turned around and scurried in the opposite direction when she'd seen Bryony coming.

Eventually she'd learned to leave Callista alone. And accepted that there was no one else in the lifeboat with her, that she must row herself across the endless sea of her childhood, and that she would be alone too when she finally reached that far shore.

It almost didn't hurt very much when, at age five, Callista took instantly to both Mrs. Asquith and Mrs. Roundtree, their new governess, grew out of her shell, and became a happy, rambunctiously sociable girl.

"Are you going to leave again soon?" asked Callista.

"I don't have plans yet," Bryony answered, moving away from her father's bed.

"And Leo, is he coming back too?"

"Yes, he means to settle in Cambridge."

Nearly a month had passed since she kissed him good-bye, a separation that was already longer than the time they'd spent together in India and growing lengthier by the day. She'd had no news from him. She inferred that he was safe, that if something had happened then she would have heard of it. But still she fretted.

And not just about his safety.

He had not wanted a future with her. He'd doubted her capacity to love. In the heat of battle, with their lives on the line, it had not mattered. Death, whatever its faults, simplified life as nothing else did. But with the likelihood of decades upon decades of time before them, would not the potent intimacy that had shielded them from past wounds eventually lose its power and strength against the sheer monotony and ordinariness of daily life, against everything else that had held them apart?

She lifted a panel of the heavy curtain and looked down into the glistening street below. In India, the rain, when it came, was heavy and decisive. She'd forgotten how dithering and miserly English rain could be—a whole day of mist and drizzle and the actual precipitation might barely cover the bottom of a bucket.

And she'd forgotten how cool it was, fires lit at the very end of August, and still she felt the damp chill rising from the floorboards.

"Bryony," Callista called her name.

She turned around slowly.

"I'm sorry," said Callista. "I'm so sorry for everything."

Occasionally Bryony had nightmares, swords and darkness and Leo bleeding from a thousand cuts. She'd jerk awake, gasping, and not be able to go back to sleep for hours, her heart quaking with the knowledge of how close they'd come.

Times like that she'd get quite angry with Callista, for her reckless fabrications. Leo could have died from the Pathans' swords or been shot and felled, like that less fortunate sepoy standing next to him.

It was always easier to blame someone else.

She walked to the far side of the bed, where Callista stood with her back against the wall. She took Callista's hands in hers, touching her sister for the first time in years, perhaps decades.

"It's all right," she said.

Three common words, a common phrase, as ordinary as sparrows and moths. Yet, as the syllables left her lips, they felt like jewels, round and brilliant. And her heart was somehow more whole, more spacious.

She returned to her father's side, and sat down on the chair that had been placed by the bed. Only one lamp had been lit, but its light, the color of faded brass, caught every wrinkle and sag on Geoffrey Asquith's face. When had he become so old?

"You have changed," said Callista.

Bryony raised her head.

"When I was small, it was difficult for me to be around you," Callista continued. "All your emotions were so intense—your anger like daggers, your unhappiness a poisoned well. Even your love had such sharp corners and dark alleys.

"Then there were years when I thought you were sleepwalking through life, drugged with work, the way people who take too much laudanum feel nothing. But when you became engaged to Leo, the magnitude of your happiness frightened me. It felt like an overloaded apple cart—the least bump in the road might upset the whole thing."

Bryony almost chuckled at her description. It was quite apt, really, a cart overloaded with apples, a heart overloaded with hopes, both equally prone to overturning.

Callista smiled. "I guess what I'm really trying to say is that you used to shatter easily. But now you've become less brittle."

Bryony brought her hands to rest on the edge of the bed—the sheets were French, as fine and soft as spun cloud. In a way, Leo had been right. She'd shattered too easily because she hadn't known how to love anyone less perfect, thoughtful, and devoted than Toddy. But now, she thought, she was learning.

"I hope so," she said.

❧

Callista went to bed at eleven o'clock. Bryony remained by her father's side. A quarter hour later there were footsteps in the hall. She thought it was Callista coming back, but it was her stepmother.

Mrs. Asquith was in her mid-fifties, with the kind of finely wrought features that would still be finely wrought when she reached her seventies. She touched her husband's forehead and briefly fussed with the counterpane. They were perfect strangers, Bryony and Mrs. Asquith, even though Mrs. Asquith had been married to Geoffrey Asquith for twenty-four years.

By the time she came to live with Bryony and

Callista, she had been worn down by her sons' long years of illness and was herself in imperfect health. She had not made very many overtures to win over Bryony's affection. Bryony, with the memory of the execrable governess that had been Mrs. Asquith's hire very much fresh on her mind, had freely ignored Mrs. Asquith.

That distance, once established, took on its own air of immutability. Like a piece of furniture that pleased no one, yet offended no one enough to remove, it remained in place, year after year.

Mrs. Asquith straightened. She placed a thin hand against a bedpost and gazed down at her dying husband. She looked much older than Bryony remembered.

"Are you all right, ma'am?" Bryony asked.

"I'll be fine in time," said Mrs. Asquith. She lifted her eyes and looked at Bryony. "I don't know whether I shall see much of you after your father— I don't know how much I shall see of you in the future, so I thought I would speak to you now.

"I understood very well at the time your father proposed to me that he needed a mother for his children and I was prepared to assume that responsibility. But then both Paul's and Angus's health failed—"

She exhaled. "What I mean to say is that I did very

poorly by you and your sister in those years, but especially by you. I have no defense except to say that as my sons suffered and deteriorated, it seemed to me that you and Callista were blessed with everything children could ask for: good, robust health. By the time I realized the mistake in my assumption, years had passed and—and I was never there. I'm sorry."

"You couldn't have been everywhere at once, ma'am. You must not blame yourself for attending to Paul and Angus when they needed you."

"Yes, but you and Callista needed me too."

Bryony looked down at her father's inert figure. "We have a father, ma'am. He could have bestirred himself a little more when you had to be away."

"Yes, he could have. He should have," agreed Mrs. Asquith. "However, it did not occur to me to point out his failings to him, because I was so grateful that he did not take me to task for what *I* had failed to do."

She paused. "There was another occasion, however, when I did point out his failing to him. That was when he debated whether to allow you to go to medical school. I was adamantly against the idea. I thought—I'm sorry—I thought you were being headstrong and needlessly rebellious and I was aghast that he even gave the idea due consideration. I believed it would ruin your chance at a suitable marriage and reduce the prestige of the Asquith name all at once.

"He agonized over it. But in the end he said to me that he had not the moral authority to forbid you to go. That since he had given you so little in life, he owed you the freedom to choose your own path."

Mrs. Asquith bent and kissed her husband on the forehead. She did the same with Bryony.

"I thought you should know that," said Mrs. Asquith, before she left quietly in a swirl of trailing robes and lilac powder.

◆

Bryony thought she dreamed that someone was squeezing her hand. But as she lifted her head from the bed and blinked at the unfamiliar surroundings, her hand was again squeezed.

"Father!"

Geoffrey Asquith looked no different. His eyes remained stubbornly closed, his mouth disconcertingly slack on the side away from Bryony. She flung aside the counterpane and watched his hand.

"Can you hear me, Father? It's Bryony."

This time she saw it. His fingers, closing around hers.

SHERRY THOMAS

Her eyes filled with inexplicable tears. "I'm back. I came back from India."

He squeezed again, so she kept on talking. "It was quite an adventure. Mr. Marsden traveled a thousand miles to find me, so that I could come home to see you. Yes, that Mr. Marsden, the one who used to be your son-in-law. I would have arrived sooner, but Mr. Marsden suffered a malarial attack. And then we found ourselves in the middle of an actual war on the Indian frontier. But we are safe and I'm here now."

She raised his hand and held in tight. "Mr. Marsden is a staunch defender of yours, even though you once boxed him senseless over me—or perhaps because you once boxed him senseless over me. He likes your books. And he says that you love me."

Her father squeezed her hand hard. It was the strongest squeeze yet. She interlaced their fingers and rested the back of his hand against her cheek.

"I don't suppose"—she was suddenly choking a little. "I don't suppose I've ever thanked you for letting me go to medical school. Or for marrying Toddy—she was wonderful."

She touched her other hand to his bearded jaw. "Do you remember the summer when I was six? You came with Toddy and me on our walks a few times.

One time we went to the village. And you bought me a box of toffee. Another time we picked wild strawberries together and had them with fresh cream at home."

He squeezed her hand again, but it was a weaker squeeze.

"I don't think you cared for wild strawberries," she raised her voice, as if trying to make herself heard to someone who was moving further and further away. "But Toddy kept giving you looks, so you ate them anyway, because I picked them and I loved them."

The squeeze, when it came, was even more anemic. He was fading away. Something fierce gripped her heart. "I love you."

To that, Geoffrey Asquith gave one final squeeze.

She sat for a long time, his hand held in her lap. But he did not exhibit any more signs of consciousness.

At dawn, when she woke up again, he had already passed away.

❧

The house plunged into mourning. All the window blinds were pulled down—they would remain down until Geoffrey Asquith's body departed the house on the day of his funeral. Black crape was draped over the front door. Mourning clothes arrived by the boxful, in crape for Mrs. Asquith, in paramatta silk for Bryony and Callista.

As grieving family members were not expected to worry about funeral arrangements, her father's closest friends took care of them. Friends and acquaintances respected the privacy of the bereaved by not visiting, but Mrs. Asquith's relations did call on her to offer their condolences.

In their black dresses, Bryony and Callista worked in the study, sorting their father's papers. They were knee-deep in old invitations, cards, correspondences—her father had never thrown away anything addressed to him, it would seem. There were also boxes of manuscripts, newspaper clippings, and scraps of paper with various hastily scribbled fragments of thoughts on everything from Donne's wit to Johnson's hygiene.

"I wonder if they've gone yet," said Callista, looking up from where she sat on the carpet.

"Who?"

"Mrs. Bourne and Mrs. Lawrence." Mrs. Bourne and Mrs. Lawrence were Mrs. Asquith's sisters. "Mrs. Lawrence grates on Stepmama. I don't think she can take very much of Mrs. Lawrence just now."

"I'll go take a look and issue a medical opinion that she must have more rest."

"Would you?"

"Of course."

But before Bryony reached the entry hall, she heard footsteps descending the staircase and women's voices. And then her own name.

". . . never understood what Leo Marsden saw in Bryony Asquith. He could have had anyone. I tell you I wasn't the least bit surprised that he wanted the annulment."

"Oh, come, Letty, you don't know why they decided on an annulment. Marriages are like shoes; only those on the inside know."

"Well, everyone knew Leo Marsden was miserable married to her. What kind of happily married man would give dinner parties by himself and then go out and gamble all night?"

"Shhh, Letty. The servants."

They left. Bryony placed a hand over her heart. It throbbed in agitation. In her three years abroad she'd forgotten what it was like to be in London again, surrounded by so many reminders of her unhappy marriage.

"Bryony," said Callista behind her. "What are you doing here?"

"Nothing. Mrs. Bourne and Mrs. Lawrence just left."

"Good. Can't stand Mrs. Lawrence. Always babbling about things she knows nothing about. Stupid cow."

What did it say about Leo and herself that even a know-nothing woman like Mrs. Lawrence knew that Leo had been miserable married to her?

"Well, don't stand there, come with me," Callista walked backward toward the study, beckoning at Bryony with her hands. "Come and see what I've found."

What Callista had found was an eight-inch-by-ten-inch photograph of a group of picnickers, laid flat on the surface of the desk. Bryony gasped. It was the picnic of her sixth birthday. There she was, seated at the front and center of the group in her new frock, which in the photograph was an indistinct light medium brown, but which in real life had been a lovely shade of apple green. There was Will, looking as if he'd never heard of such a thing as running about in the nude—the photograph had been taken before the entire party piled into two charabancs for the chosen picnic site two miles away, and therefore, before his memorable incident. And there was Toddy, standing in the back row, looking so impossibly young that it broke Bryony's heart to realize that by the time the picture was taken, she had only one more year to live.

"It's your mother," she said softly.

"Yes, I know," Callista said wistfully. "I always recognize her, like looking at myself in costume."

Bryony fingered the edge of the photograph.

"This was one of the best days of my life."

Callista smiled. "I can imagine. And, look, there's Leo." She pointed at the picture.

She saw him the same moment as Callista pointed him out, the chubby child to her right. He wore a dark-colored dress, the occasion of her sixth birthday being long before he was breeched—given his first outfit with trousers.

"My goodness, he was so small."

"He should have been. He was two," said Callista, smiling fondly. "And already he couldn't stop looking at you."

Bryony wouldn't have described it that way. But in the photograph, Leo's face *was* turned curiously toward her, as if she were more interesting than the camera, more absorbing than anyone else around him.

It was a dizzying sensation, to see the two people she loved the most together in one frame. And there she was, basking in happiness, basking in life.

"May I have this?"

"Of course," said Callista. "The moment I saw it, I knew it belonged to you."

❧

The dark waters of the English Channel parted reluctantly before the bow of the ferry. The sea was choppy, fog-shrouded, and England, on a good day visible from Calais, seemed to be receding, rather than getting closer.

He'd been on the road forever.

Two days after Bryony left for Nowshera, Imran and the coolies arrived in Chakdarra. They'd been staying at a village three marches away, waiting for the fighting to subside.

Getting everything and everyone to Nowshera proved tricky. Travel had become impossible between Malakand and Nowshera. At several points along the dusty fifty miles, traffic degenerated into complete logjams with mules, pony carts, camels, and men unable to move two steps one way or another, broiling under a relentless sun.

Nowshera was in chaos, with regiments arriving from the south, regiments departing to the north, and all the pack animals and armaments that came and went with the regiments. Leo divested himself of everything he'd acquired for the trip. To each of the coolies and the ayah he gave a mule. All the horses he'd bought along the way he divided among Imran, Hamid, and Saif Khan, except the valiant mare that had carried him and Bryony safely to

Chakdarra: She was going to spend the rest of her carefree days in an English pasture.

It was a fight to get out of Nowshera with Udyana—he'd named the mare after the ancient Buddhist kingdom of Swat—and Bryony's things. He called in all the connections he had and shamelessly exploited his status as a hero of Chakdarra. The bamboozling paid off in the end. He got his way, boarded the train exhausted, and slept all the way to Bombay.

P&O steamers departed Bombay every Friday during the southwest monsoon. One had left three days before he arrived. But he was lucky: Austrian Lloyd's had an unscheduled extra steamer that departed the next day for Trieste. From Trieste he was again on the train, crossing the Alps from Italy into France, to Paris, where Matthew met him, and then on to Calais and the Channel crossing that would finally take him back to England.

To the rest of his life.

Sometimes he missed the war. Not the fear, not the exhaustion, and most certainly not the killing, but the almost blinding clarity of things. In that crucible, everything between him and Bryony had been distilled to the very essence: Only love had mattered, nothing else.

But as Chakdarra receded into the past, old fears

and doubts crept back. Once the exhilaration of their reunion wore off, once the newness of their lovemaking was no longer so new, how would she see him? No matter how careful he was, invariably someday he would do something to make her angry. What then? Would all the old unhappiness rush to the fore? Would she remember that he had once betrayed her and regret that she'd ever given him a second chance?

Or would she protect herself from the beginning by keeping a certain distance from him, so that their closeness would always fall short of true communion, always denying him that final forgiveness so that he could never hurt her again?

And he, was he strong enough to persist in the face of this lack of trust? It had been this very fear that had led him to reject her overture in the dak bungalow, unwilling to let the emotions of a moment dictate the rest of his life, afraid to be either an abject lackey at her side, or worse, a bitter mate resentful over being forever condemned for one mistake.

He looked down into the photograph in his hand, their wedding photograph. He used to think that she looked wooden. But no, she looked haunted, her eyes as bleak as the rains of January. How could anyone come back from that? How could she ever truly love him again?

He returned the photograph to his pocket at the sound of Matthew's footsteps.

"The fog is lifting," said Matthew. "We should see Dover soon."

They stood shoulder to shoulder on the bow. The fog dissipated, the sun shone, and even the opaque, unromantic waters of the English Channel glinted in the morning light.

When the white cliffs of Dover came into view, Leo did not have an epiphany; he made a choice.

Trust ran both ways. How could he ask her to trust him when he hardly trusted her? He *would* trust her, in her love, in her strength, in her decency and fortitude.

And when the time came, he *would* find the strength in himself.

Chapter Eighteen

Her father's body lay in repose in the drawing room of the town house for two days. On the third day, a black hearse, big as a rail carriage, drew up before the house and bore him to his funeral.

Women were often discouraged from attending the funeral, for fear that, overwhelmed by grief, they would cause a scene by breaking down in sobs or even fainting from a surfeit of feelings. But both Bryony and Callista chose to be present, to accompany their father on the last leg of his journey on this earth.

The service was solemn and moving. But Bryony spent it thinking more of the living than the dead. There was nothing more she could do for or about her father, but there was much she could do for Callista, for Mrs. Asquith, and for her stepbrothers. When she resumed work, she ought to try to be less of an automaton—a bit of compassion for her patients wouldn't hurt. And as for her future students at the medical college, she could smile once in a while so that they would not be too intimidated to ask questions.

The organist played "Now the Laborer's Task Is O'er." On the shoulders of his friends, her father's casket traveled slowly toward the door of the church, followed by his daughters.

Abruptly Callista poked Bryony in the side. Bryony turned toward her. Callista pointed with her chin. Bryony looked in the general direction her sister indicated and saw nothing but rows upon rows of mourners, some of whom looked vaguely recognizable, others she could not identify if her scalpel arm depended on it.

And then she saw them: Will Marsden, Matthew Marsden, and their eldest brother Jeremy, the Earl of Wyden. They were a striking trio, all blond curls and archangel faces. Only when she was about to look away did she see their taller, darker-haired baby brother, who actually stood closest to the nave of the church—closest to *her*.

Their time in India could roughly be divided between malaria and war, with Leo laid low on one end by the toxicity of quinine and on the other by his wounds and the fatigue of continuous battle. His clothes, by the time they'd met, had seen much service on the frontier, and were frayed and tired if not actually threadbare.

But there inside the church, surrounded by sunlight streaming in from the stained-glass windows, in perfect health and an immaculately tailored frock coat, he was something else altogether.

This was the young man who had felled her with one smile. He did not look like an archangel—if archangels looked as he did, there would be no women of virtue left in Paradise. Instead, he was an old-fashioned Adonis, fully human, yet so ravishing goddesses fell in love with him.

God, he was beautiful. And for the life of her, she did not know how she managed to keep walking.

She didn't register the black crape armband he wore until she'd walked past him.

He'd come in mourning, as a son of the family.

The interment was private. Bryony and Callista each tossed in a handful of white rose petals on their father's casket. Then Callista tossed in another handful for Mrs. Asquith, who had not felt equal to the funeral—it was understood that the bereaved sometimes preferred to grieve alone, rather than fall apart in public. Angus, the younger of their stepbrothers, dropped a handful of earth for himself, and another for Paul, whose withered limbs, as a result of his childhood poliomyelitis, made it difficult for him to leave the house.

As they made their way out of the cemetery, Callista was again the first person to spot Leo: He and Matthew waited for them by the Asquith carriage, poor Matthew practically invisible against Leo's luminosity.

A cauldron of emotions spilled over in Bryony. Tenderness. Longing. Pure bedazzled admiration. And happiness enough to float the entire Royal Navy.

Callista embraced both Leo and Matthew. "Leo, you ugly stoat, welcome home. Matthew, my goodness, you are more gorgeous every time I see you. And when are you going to offer for me? I'm not getting any younger."

Matthew chuckled softly.

"Soon, Callista, soon. Just now on the Channel crossing Matthew was moaning your name when he thought we were going down," said Leo, smiling. He shook hands with her stepbrother. "Angus, good to see you."

For Bryony, probably out of consideration of her elderly knees, he spared her a full smile, which would have sent her pitching forward into the side of the carriage. "Mrs. Marsden."

He really should have addressed her as Miss Asquith. An annulment meant that they'd never been legally married. But the way he said Mrs. Marsden, as if they were alone and he had every intention of stripping her naked, made her heart pound. As did the signal he sent via his mourning attire—besides the crape armband, he also wore a black hatband. She could already hear the gossips: *He came to the funeral dressed as if the deceased were still his father-in-law, as if he were still married to Bryony Asquith.*

"Messieurs Marsden," she answered. "Thank you for coming."

"We were wondering if you wouldn't care to come to our house for tea," said Matthew.

"I think that is a lovely idea," said Callista.

"I'm not sure," said Bryony. "We are not supposed to be moving in society so soon after our father's passing."

"You are not moving in society," Leo said firmly. "It's just family."

The only family connection the Asquiths and Marsdens had between them was Leo and Bryony's annulled marriage.

"You are absolutely right, Leo," said Callista. "Shall we?"

"What about Mrs. Asquith?" Bryony asked. "Only Paul is there with her and Paul took Father's passing rather hard himself."

"I will keep them company," Angus volunteered. "The two of you go."

"Still . . ."

"It's all right," said Callista. "We won't stay long."

Angus took the Asquith carriage home. Everyone else piled into the Wyden carriage. During the ride, Bryony learned that Matthew had left his holiday in Biarritz to meet Leo in Paris. And when he couldn't persuade Leo to go to Biarritz with him, had decided to accompany Leo to London instead.

They'd literally just detrained at Victoria Station when they learned that Geoffrey Asquith's funeral was being held that very afternoon. They had barely enough time to buy Leo his mourning crape and rush home to change out of their traveling clothes before driving to the service.

"Leo robbed me of my coat," said Matthew. "He had to look good."

"Liar." Leo smiled. "Matthew insisted that I take his coat, since I couldn't go to my father-in-law's funeral in a lounge suit, which was all I had at that point."

My father-in-law. Flustered, Bryony kept her face turned toward the window, so that she did not have to deal with the rampant curiosity in the carriage.

Callista pulled Bryony aside after they alit, before they entered the Wyden house. "Did the two of you marry again? Please tell me yes. If he is my brother-in-law again, he is less likely to kill me for what I did."

Bryony looked at her a moment, then leaned in and whispered in her ear. "He won't kill you. He just wants you committed to an asylum."

The Wyden house was full of men. Jeremy and Will had come up from Oxfordshire without their spouses and children: Matthew and Leo would shortly go down to the family seat to meet everyone.

"I can't tell you how glad we are you ladies could join us," said Will. "Jeremy was born mute, I am so quiet and retiring, Matthew never knows any good gossip, and Leo is the most boring person in the world."

"Just you wait," said Leo. "My wife never stops talking once she starts."

Jeremy choked on his whiskey and coughed. Leo slapped him between the shoulder blades. Bryony was glad she hadn't started on her tea yet. Or she would have joined Jeremy in the choking.

My wife.

"So, Callista, I understand you managed to pull off a fairly substantial confidence trick despite Leo's vigilance," said Matthew. "How did you do that?"

"No, Callista, don't confess. You know what will

happen afterward." Will imitated firing a gun. "Have you ever seen Leo with a firearm?"

"More to the point, have you ever seen my wife with a scalpel?" asked Leo. There was just enough menace in his voice to make Bryony feel like the veriest medical assassin.

Callista had the grace to blush. "My father was in on it. I figured Leo would check any claims I made, so Father stayed home for a week or so and we let it be known that he was not feeling well."

"How did you know I'd left Leh?" asked Bryony. She'd forgotten about that part.

"That was pure accident. Someone I knew turned out to be Mrs. Braeburn's niece. When she received a letter Mrs. Braeburn wrote her saying that they were departing Leh for the Kalash Valleys with a Mrs. Marsden who was a physician, she came to me and asked if that wasn't Bryony. I told her to say nothing to Mrs. Braeburn about it."

"So you knew she was in the Chitral region and you made me go all the way to Leh first?"

"Well, if I told you I knew where she was you'd have just told me to cable her myself and leave you alone. And please don't kill me. Are you glad you have your wife back?"

"Jeremy, do you still keep a pistol in the library?"

Leo was standing by Bryony's chair. She placed

her hand on his sleeve. "We are all safe now. And Callista is very sorry."

Leo looked at Bryony a long moment. His hand touched hers briefly and he smiled. "There is never a pistol in this house."

Bryony was uncomfortable with public displays of intimacy. But she let her hand remain under Leo's for another two seconds before pulling it back to her lap.

"Sorry, Leo," Callista said, shamefaced.

"Now what I want to know is what happened when you found Bryony, Leo," said Will. "Did you just say your sister sent me, pack up everything and come with me this moment?"

"More or less."

"And she came away with you?"

"More or less." Leo tossed Bryony a mischievous look. "Although there might have been laudanum, drugging, and a midnight abduction involved."

"Now that's a much better story," said Matthew. "I would pay to read that one."

"And for his knavery, Leo lost one of his—more important parts," said Bryony.

"No!" Matthew and Will shouted in unison.

"Bryony!" Callista squeaked.

"Kidney," Leo cried. "It was just a kidney. A man can live a perfectly vigorous life with one kidney."

"You can call it a kidney if you want," said Bryony.

Will hooted. Callista covered her eyes. Leo covered his entire face, his shoulders shaking with mirth. Bryony couldn't help it—she laughed, laughed so much that she had to dab at her eyes with a handkerchief.

This was what she'd once imagined marriage to him would be like, this festive normalcy, this sense of warmth and ease and belonging.

"So what really happened?" asked Jeremy.

Jeremy had the seriousness and authority of one who'd been groomed since birth for responsibilities. When he asked questions, people answered.

"Ah, the dreaded what-really-happened question," said Leo, still smiling. "Tell him, Bryony."

Now she knew what it had felt like for him when she asked him to tell the Braeburns why they had to leave right away. But she had not his talent for shaping words into a separate reality. She swallowed. "It was very simple, really. When Leo came, I wanted to go with him. I was—I was never so happy to see anyone in my life."

Leo leaned back in his chair, his head tilted. For a moment she thought he would mock her. He'd told such a beautiful—and ultimately true—version of their story to the Braeburns, and all she had to say to his brothers was these two plain lines. And then she noticed the shimmer of tears in his eyes.

He did not cry. But she almost did. It was a while before she was sufficiently herself again to rejoin the conversation.

And after that she could not stop smiling.

❧

She glowed. There was no other word for it, as if the walls around her heart had at last crumpled enough to reveal her hidden capacity for joy, for life. And what a radiant thing it was. Even her silence beamed softly, a mere absence of words rather than the dark void it had so often been.

They were asked about their ride to Chakdarra and the consequent siege. There was talk of Charlie and Charlie's motherless children. Callista flirted outrageously with Matthew. And throughout it all, Leo, drunk on hope, watched Bryony.

With every one of her smiles their past receded a little further; their future became not only more possible, but more secure. Suddenly he could think of such prosaic things as the size of writing desks, the weight of service china, the color of wallpapers and curtains—his head was full of them, the lovely, minute details of a new life together.

Bryony and Callista stayed for over an hour, until

Callista rose and said that they must go home to check on Mrs. Asquith. Bryony came to her feet rather slowly, as if she was having too much fun to wish to leave yet.

Matthew elbowed Leo. "Leo, why is your wife leaving with her sister?"

"Because our marriage is a secret, that's why," said Leo. He turned to Bryony. "Before you go, may I have a word, Mrs. Marsden?"

He only meant to give her Toddy's old letter, but as soon as they were out in the hall she grabbed him by the lapel and kissed him. He crushed her fiercely against himself.

"When will you ask for your post back?" he whispered in her ear. "I miss the smell of industrial-strength solvents."

She laughed softly. "Soon. And when will you have papers read at the mathematical society again? I rather like having my husband called a genius for reasons that are not clear to me."

My husband. The words rolled off her tongue, easy and beautiful. He kissed her fervently. "Soon. My brilliance quite overflowed on the way home. I have four notebooks to show for it."

"Good. We don't want people to think I love you for your looks alone."

"In that case we should also put you in some

rather revealing gowns once in a while, so that people don't think I married you for your accomplishments alone."

She laughed again—she probably had no idea how beautiful she was when she laughed, like the dawn of a new day. Her laughter quieted after a few seconds. There came a long moment of silence. She gazed up into his eyes.

"I know why you keep referring to me as your wife. But I'm not pregnant, Leo."

He hadn't truly hoped, but still it was not easy to hear. It would be wonderful to have a child together, to commit not just to each other, but to a growing life, a continuation and natural extension of their love.

"You don't need to be," he said. "Children are not essential to my life. Only you are. You have always been. And nothing has changed."

Her lashes lowered. "You will make me cry," she murmured.

"It's all right to cry," he whispered back, "when you get home, that is. Crying is not allowed in the Wyden house: It's the Marsden rule."

Her lips quivered. After a while, she looked up, her eyes still bright with unshed tears. "Did you say you wanted a word with me, sir?"

He'd forgotten entirely. He pulled the envelope

out of his pocket and pressed it into her hands. "For you. Something I promised. And tomorrow morning I'll call on you: We'll go to Cambridge."

❧

My Dear Lisbeth,

I love this season in the Cotswold. We go for walks every day, Bryony and I. Sometimes Mr. Asquith comes, when I can persuade him to be away from his books and manuscripts during the day. Yesterday— without Mr. Asquith, of course—his daughter and I lay down in a field of buttercups and rolled in that carpet of flowers.

The most exciting event in the next fortnight is going to be the picnic on dear Bryony's sixth birthday. She is quite involved and helps me with the lists and the games. There is something so very endearing about that lovely little girl as she writes down in her neat, round hand all the tasks still to be done, in the notebook I gave her—it makes me think how fortunate I am. My cousin Marianne is married to a widower too and moans constantly about his brood of hooligans, tricksters, and ruffians. And here I am, gifted with the most wonderful child in the world.

Sometimes Mr. Asquith complains about the amount of time I spend with her—he would emerge from his library looking for me and I would have gone off somewhere with her. I tease him that it is because she loves me more and in a way, it is true. Certainly she needs me more. I have scolded Mr. Asquith on not keeping her nearer to him in her motherless years. There is this fear in her, sometimes, and I know she still remembers the long months when she was alone in this house, looked after by only the servants.

I tell Mr. Asquith that before we know it she will be a beautiful girl of eighteen and some eager fellow will snatch her away from us, whereas I will always be his wife, for the rest of our days. And when I have no more children on whom to dote, does he think he'll be able to write in peace anymore? No, then it will be he whom I shall drag with me everywhere for company!

I enclose the recipe for ginger mulled wine that you requested, along with a book of pressed flowers Bryony and I made for you. Do please write me soon and let me know what this spring has been like for you in Derbyshire.

Love,
Toddy

Bryony wept. For sorrow. And pure, startling joy: Toddy had been happy.

She'd always imagined her father as a distant, neglectful husband. She'd believed Toddy lonely, a vibrant young woman married to a much older man who had little appreciation for her liveliness and spirit. But the letter alluded to a husband who treasured his bride, a Toddy who was indulgently fond of him, and an affectionate, comfortable marriage.

It was all she ever wanted for Toddy, that her days on earth had been filled with sunshine, and that she had known how much she'd been esteemed and loved.

When she'd read the letter a dozen times, she decided that it was enough for the night. Slipping the letter back into the envelope, she discovered that there was another sheet of paper inside.

Dear B.,

I cabled Lady Griswold from Bombay and asked if she could send the letter she'd once referred to in conversation with me to the Wyden town house. She has kindly granted my request.

I hope I will be able to give this to you after the funeral. I miss you terribly.

Love,
Leo

She kissed the note. *Tomorrow,* she thought. *Tomorrow, my love.*

Chapter Nineteen

The brothers Marsden spent the evening talking. Will had gained a seat in the House of Commons in the last election, bucking the Marsdens' tradition of support for the Tories by becoming a Liberal MP. He and the more conservative Jeremy argued good-naturedly about the policies of the government in South Africa and on the frontiers of India. Leo and Matthew, neither of whom had much interest in politics, spoke of the recent changes in Paris and London and occasionally heckled Will and Jeremy when the latter two's debate became bogged down in minutiae.

"Gentlemen, at least let us have some grandiloquence, if you are going to discuss the fate of nations," said Matthew.

"I'm saving my bombast for the House of

Commons," Will quipped. "The Wyden house isn't big enough for all the hot air I can unleash at a moment's notice."

Leo laughed. Of all the Marsden brothers, Will was the one who took himself the least seriously, who loved ribbing his brothers as much as he loved ribbing himself.

After that they went to Jeremy's club. It was while they dined at the club that Michael Robbins's name came up. Leo had met the young journalist briefly in Nowshera. Robbins, a correspondent for the *Pioneer* and the *Times,* had asked Leo some questions on the siege of Chakdarra.

Will immediately identified the young man as godson to Lady Vera Drake, the wife of his old employer Mr. Stuart Somerset. In the morning, Will telephoned Mr. Somerset to let him know that Leo had encountered Robbins, and Mr. Somerset said that his wife would be extremely pleased if Leo would call on her in person.

Will, having eloped with Mr. Somerset's onetime fiancée, could never say no to Mr. Somerset. And Leo could never say no to Will—or Matthew, for that matter. It didn't matter that he'd been only fourteen when their father threw out Will and Matthew; Leo had been so invested in proving that he was the earl's son that he'd forgotten, for some time, that he was also Will's and Matthew's brother.

And so it was that the first person on whom Leo paid a call on the first morning of the rest of his life was not Bryony, but Lady Vera, whose residence on 26 Cambury Lane was only a few doors down from his and Bryony's old house. As his carriage wheeled past the lifeless 41 Cambury Lane, even though he braced himself for it, he still shuddered somewhere inside.

At 26 Cambury Lane, Lady Vera received him most cordially. She was a lovely woman in her late thirties, attired in a stylish lavender morning gown. She spoke in such marvelously molded syllables, moved with such a delicate grace, and seemed to belong so overwhelmingly in her elegant green-and-white drawing room that it was impossible for Leo to imagine that she'd spent much of her adult life as a lowly cook.

They exchanged pleasantries. Lady Vera condoled with him on the passing of Mr. Asquith. Leo inquired into her recent stay in the country, where Will and Lizzy and their children had spent a week with the Somersets and their children.

"Will tells me that the little Marsdens and the little Somersets fight spectacularly," Leo said.

Lady Vera chuckled. "I'm afraid that is true. But they make up beautifully too."

"And are your children well?"

"Very well. When they are not fighting spectacularly with the little Marsdens, they fight spectacularly with each other. I'd always thought an elder sister and a younger brother would make a most tender pair. Alas, they are savages, the both of them."

She poured tea, and offered Leo possibly the best tea cake he'd ever tasted.

"I understand you met my godson in Nowshera, Mr. Marsden."

"Yes, at the time we met he'd just returned from Tochi Valley. I believe he'd been assigned to cover the punitive expeditions that General Blood would lead to Upper Swat."

"That has already happened. I follow his columns in the *Times* avidly, as you can imagine. He will go with the troops on the punitive expedition against the Mohmands next, that is, if he hasn't left already."

Leo wondered why Lady Vera needed to speak to him when she already had a good idea of her godson's movements by reading his reportage.

"But newspaper reporting is always whittled down to only dates and places and action," said Lady Vera. "It is not much use when I'm primarily interested in the reporter's frame of mind. Michael is a brilliant young man. I'd hoped that he would attend university. But he was eager to see the world and to leave his mark on it."

Will had told Leo that Michael Robbins was the adopted son of Mr. Somerset's gamekeeper in Yorkshire, but had been educated at Rugby, one of the most prestigious public schools in the country. That knowledge, along with what Leo had observed of the young man, gave him a certain insight into Lady Vera's unspoken concern.

"You are afraid his ambition might get the better of him, ma'am?"

Lady Vera smiled. "I see you are as astute as your brother, Mr. Marsden. Yes, I do worry about it. There are people in this world for whom nothing he ever does will ever overcome the irregularity of his birth. I worry that he should try too hard and that opinions of these hidebound idiots should come to matter too much for him."

The way she phrased things, Leo wondered if the opinion of a young lady was somehow involved. He did not ask it. "He is yet young, ma'am, and the world is an exciting place for an ambitious young man. When we met, he was eager to be closer to the action, to report firsthand rather than take accounts from those who had been there. Perhaps when he reaches his middle years, he would look upon his place in the world and wonder whether he'd been given a fair shake, but as of this moment, I'd say he is enjoying spreading his wings and testing his mettle."

Lady Vera took small sips of her tea. "You are right. I suppose I can ask for nothing more right now than that he should glory in his youth and the opportunities he's been given."

She had not been truly reassured.

"Toward the end of our conversation," said Leo, "Mr. Robbins let slip that he had not been sleeping well. He'd given up his room at the lodging house to a lady traveling by herself, who'd come into Nowshera too tired to stand, when Nowshera was overrun and beds impossible to find. When the lady left, the landlord had given the room to someone else, leaving Mr. Robbins to sleep in rather atrocious places."

"Dear me," said Lady Vera.

"He didn't know it, but that lady was Mrs. Marsden. And I, for one, will always be grateful that he helped her when there was absolutely nothing in it for him."

Lady Vera set down her tea. She reached forward and took Leo's hands. "Thank you, Mr. Marsden.

Sometimes I forget that beneath Michael's ambition, there is not a void, but much kindness. Thank you for reminding me."

🐋

Forty-one Cambury Lane made Bryony shiver. But it wasn't the air, musty and damp from the lack of occupation, nor was it the empty rooms, echoing with her footsteps. It was the memories, all the unhappiness that seemed embedded in the very walls, the failure of her marriage writ large in the cobwebs that dangled from ceilings and banisters.

She didn't know why she was here. In the morning there had been a letter from her solicitor, informing her that the house had been sold at last and the buyers would take possession within the week. Then there had been a note from Leo saying he would be slightly delayed as he had agreed to pay a call to Will's old employer. A few minutes later she'd found herself climbing into a carriage, the spare key to the house clutched tightly in her hand.

A complete mistake. What she wanted was to forever close the door on the past, the way one looked upon the deceased one last time before lowering the lid of the coffin. But here, the past hunted her, with clammy tendrils and cold arrows.

Here was the dining room in which they'd given

their last dinner together. Such had been his effervescence and charisma that those seated near her had strained mightily toward him, desperate to catch his bons mots and clever remarks. Her feeble attempts at conversation had not only gone unheeded, they'd gone unheard. She'd sat in a room full of people, completely ignored, completely alone—and had known in her heart that he had meant for it to happen precisely as it did.

Here was the bedchamber in which their lovemaking had gone from merely awful to disastrous. The last time he'd come to her while she was still awake, she'd shaken so much that in the middle of it he'd scrambled off the bed and left, throwing a lamp halfway across the room on his way out. There, that dent left by the shattered lamp, still there.

And here was the study in which she had had to sit and read the letter from Bettie Young, an actual written record of the day her happiness died.

This was the house in which her hair turned white from grief and despair.

She ran toward the front door, desperate to get out. And almost ran smack into the door itself, which suddenly opened. And in the doorway stood Leo.

"Bryony! What are you doing here?"

"I'm—I'm—What are *you* doing here?"

"I was at Mr. Somerset's house paying a call on his

wife—did you not get my note? They live right down the street. I had to stop when I saw an Asquith brougham on the curb." He took her into his arms. "Why are you here, of all places?"

"I received news that the house has been sold. So I had this daft idea to come and bury the past. Except . . ."

He kissed her temple. "Except what?"

"Except the past is not quite dead." She shook her head. "And I was literally running away from it."

"That bad, eh?"

"Worse."

He let go of her and walked past the foyer into the morning room. There he took a long, slow look. His path led him into the study next, with her trailing uncertainly behind, barely containing an urge to call out to him to be careful and venture no further into the house.

What must he be remembering? He'd bought everything for this house, from furniture and china to paintings and carvings to door stoppers and coal scuttles—things he must have planned to use and enjoy for the rest of his life. But when he'd left, he'd taken little more than his books and his clothes. The rest had been sold off in lots, the proceeds sent to him by her solicitor.

He climbed up the stairs. She could only lean on

the newel post and cry out silently, *No, no further, no higher.*

The next floor contained the dining room. There he had tried—for far longer than she had thought he would—to talk to her. Every day he'd asked her how was her day at the hospital, did she see any interesting cases, and was she perhaps interested in a new play at Drury Lane that they could attend together or a lecture at the Royal Zoological Society? And day after day, stewing in her bitterness, she'd returned nothing but monosyllables.

The floor above that contained their bedrooms. *Please don't. Don't go there.* But he did, his footsteps echoing across the bare floors.

What's the matter? Is there something I'm doing wrong? Please tell me what I can do for you. He'd asked and asked. And she'd refused to help him, refused to participate in any way that might make their marriage functional.

Suddenly she was running up the stairs, as if the house was on fire and she must drag him out of it.

"Leo! Leo!"

He met her on the stairs. "I'm here. I haven't gone anywhere."

"Let's go. Let's get out of here. I should never have come."

He draped an arm around her. "We can't disown

it, Bryony. This was us. This was our life together then."

"Then what are we to do? Carry it with us always?"

"We will carry it with us no matter what. The only thing we can do is not to let it have that sort of power over us, where we can't see the future for the past."

"And how do we do that?"

He looked at the bare stairwell—there once had been photographs of faraway places he'd visited going all the way up to the third floor. "You know what I remembered as I was walking through the house?"

She was afraid to ask. "What did you remember?"

"I remembered the last time I saw this house empty. You'd just bought it and I came to take a look by myself. I was surprised at how well I liked it. As I walked through the rooms, I could already see how they'd look when they'd been properly furnished.

"I also remembered how I'd felt the first few times I made love to you when you were asleep. I was so elated. I walked on clouds.

"And do you know what else I remembered?"

"What else did you remember?" she murmured.

"The microscope."

"On the day I asked for the annulment?" Her voice shook.

"It was a beautiful microscope. And I'd bought it

for you because my hope was undiminished." He tilted her chin up. "As long as we were together, there was always hope in my heart. And nothing that happened in this house could ever change that."

Now it was her heart that shook. "How do you do this? How do you find the grace to face the shadows?"

His lips grazed hers. "I made a choice before I reached England. I decided I would put my faith in you."

"In *me*?" her words echoed incredulously. "But I've done nothing to earn your trust."

"Trust is a choice. I choose to trust your love and your stalwartness. I trust that should there be a day when either the past or the present overwhelms me, you will be there to guide me past that dark moment."

She was without words. She could only cover his face with kisses as her heart broke into little pieces. A sweet and worthwhile heartbreak: Sometimes limbs must be rebroken to set properly; her heart too needed to shatter anew before it could truly heal.

❧

She was largely quiet on the train journey to Cambridge, even though Leo had tipped the guard to make sure that they had a first-class compartment to themselves. Halfway through to Cambridge, she came to sit next to him, and rested her cheek on his shoulder. For the rest of the trip, the fat plume at the back of her hat tickled his ear pleasantly.

He wanted to show her Cambridge, the Great Court of Trinity College, where he studied, the soaring Gothic facade of the chapel at King's College, and The Backs, a contiguous stretch of greenery along the banks of the river Cam, formed from the sweeping back lawns and gardens of half a dozen colleges. They'd come at the perfect time: Michaelmas term had not started yet; the sprawling acreage of the university would be quiet and uncrowded.

But she wanted to see his house first. So they went from one empty house to another. But the Cambridge house did not feel at all the same: It was merely empty, not neglected.

"It smells clean," she said.

"Will must have had people come in recently, since he knew I was coming back."

She walked to a window in the dim parlor, drew back the curtains, and opened the shutters. Bright clear autumn light flowed into the room, revealing butterscotch-colored parquet flooring and white-washed walls. In what little time he'd spent in Cambridge after the annulment, he'd ordered the house redone. He'd grown weary of the dark, somber tones of the London house—there hadn't been much of a choice, given the sooty qualities of the air—and he'd wanted something completely different.

"It feels like a cottage," she said.

"Do you like cottages?"

She flashed a smile at him. "I'm beginning to."

They went through all the rooms on the ground floor—another parlor, a study, and the dining room—Bryony drawing back all the curtains and unfastening all the shutters, until the house felt almost as bright and open as a sun-drenched bungalow on the Subcontinent.

In her black mourning dress, she was the dark focal point of the house. Quiet and beautiful, she stood in front of each window and looked over every square inch of the walls. At first he thought she might be looking for flaws in the construction. Then it suddenly occurred to him that she was seeing possibilities—a house that was no longer empty.

Sometimes it was impossible not to grow misty-eyed.

"Do you want to go out in the back and see the cherry trees?" he asked. "And the river?"

"May I see the rest of the house first?"

"Of course."

He showed her the upstairs, which had several bedrooms and another sitting room. And then, the shock. In the last bedroom, there was a bed, a large four-poster bedstead, handsome and sturdy, with crisp white linens over an enormous feather mattress.

He blinked his eyes to be sure it wasn't a mirage.

"I had nothing to do with this," he said.

She smiled, the first coy smile he had ever seen from her.

"No," he said slowly. *Bryony?*

"I asked Will to arrange it," she said, still smiling.

"*When?*"

"I telephoned him after I reached home last night. You were in your bath."

"Is that why he asked me to call on Lady Vera today? To have more time?"

"I don't know," she said. "Will works in mysterious ways."

She slipped past him into the room, let in the light, skimmed her hand across the bedsheet, then sat down close to the foot of the bed, her arm wrapped around a bedpost. The satisfied smile lingered around her mouth for a few seconds longer, but her expression eventually turned solemn.

"In our old house this morning—was it as terrible

for you as it was for me?" she asked, her voice subdued.

"I hope not." He did not want it to have been as terrible for her as it had been for him. "But probably so."

"I've been thinking about it ever since we left." She rubbed her thumb against the turned grooves on the bedpost. "I never understood what a coward I have been my entire life. Whenever things become too difficult, I've always run away—away from Toddy's memory, from my family, from our marriage. From you, when you wouldn't let me play chess with you by correspondence. And from our house, if you hadn't stopped me today.

"I despaired for a while during the rail journey—how did one deal with such ingrained cowardice? Then I realized that there is no such thing as courage in the absence of cowardice. Courage is also a choice: It's what happens when one refuses to give in to fear."

She rested her head against the bedpost and gazed at him. "Your trust gives me courage."

He understood her perfectly. "And your courage gives me faith."

She smiled a little. "Do you trust me?"

"Yes," he answered without any hesitation.

"Then trust me when I say that we will be all right."

He trusted her. And he knew then that they would be all right, the two of them. Together.

She undid her hat ribbons and removed the elaborate mourning hat from her head. Running her fingers along the curl of fat black plume atop the hat, she glanced at him. "Now, I don't suppose you still wish to see me naked, Mr. Marsden?"

His brow rose. "Have I ever expressed so ungentlemanly a desire in my life?"

She just restrained a smile. "In Chakdarra you did."

"Well, that. That was when I thought we were on the verge of giving up the ghost. Of course I wouldn't wish to harass you suchly now."

She felt her jaw slacken a little. "Are you sure?"

He laughed. In a fraction of a second, he was kissing her, with joy and abandon. Happiness flooded her. She'd missed him so, as a honeybee missed the spring, as a migratory bird missed its warm southern home when the breath of autumn chilled the air.

He took off her jacket and dropped it to the floor. The buttons of her shirt he opened one by one, kissed the skin he exposed as he went along, until he came to the scooped neck of her combination. Then he peeled off the shirt, kissing her shoulders and arms as he went.

Her corset fell next, followed by her skirt and petticoats. He knelt down on one knee to take off her city boots and her stockings. And bit her lightly at the back of her knee.

She gasped.

He straightened and kissed her again, holding her face in his hands. "Bryony," he murmured. "Bryony."

At the last hurdle, her combination, he slowed. He played with the slight ruffle that trimmed the neckline of the combination, kissed her at the rise of her breasts, and toyed with the buttons. She became so impatient that she swatted his hand aside and unbuttoned the combination herself, pushing it past her hips to fall into a puddle of merino wool at her feet.

Her breaths came rather hotly as she stood before him, without a stitch, without even her hair down for modesty. And he, with his starched collar, his necktie perfectly in place, and the fob of his watch just so, as if he'd just walked in from the street and caught her in a state of complete undress.

Lightly he ran his fingertips down her arms. Then, more provocatively, the back of his hand across her already excited nipples. Her breath quivered. He caught her by the shoulders and tumbled her into bed. When he kissed her again, the kiss was ravenous, his body pressed hard into hers, his weight at once exhilarating and terrifying.

He shed his own clothes. Now she could at last dig her palms into the smooth muscles of his back. Now she could at last kiss his throat and shoulders. Now she could at last have her heart beat next to his.

He had become as impatient as she. They forewent all other preliminaries for the joining. She did not need lovemaking. She needed only him. The physicality of him. The vitality of him. The strength and power and intensity of him.

They broke together like a summer storm, heat and motion and pent-up energy releasing in wild bursts and electrical torrents.

᪥

She checked on his scar. "Everything is fine?"

"Everything is fine. I can walk. I can ride. I'm going to postulate that I can even dance."

She lowered her head and nibbled the length of the scar. He held his breath. He was hard again already. She took him in her hand. He stared at her lovely breasts—God be praised, he was finally seeing her naked—and licked his lips.

Not Quite a Husband

"I know a great deal about the penis," she said. "I can name its every last component, from the fundiform ligament that anchors it to the pubic bone, to the fascia that covers and binds the entire structure."

"No," he said. "Not my wife. Never."

She laughed. "Now, the column of the penis is composed of three cylinders—a pair of corpora cavernosa and the corpus spongiosum, which is this ridge along the length of the penis."

She rubbed her finger along that ridge. His poor captive member jerked with the stimulation. "Blood comes down the aorta, flows into the internal iliac artery, passes under the pelvic bone via the pudendal artery, and finally enters the common penile artery for engorgement. Then, through the corporo-veno-occlusive mechanism, the veins are blocked and the influx of blood kept in the penis, thereby maintaining the firmness needed for penetration."

Ah, penetration.

She batted her eyelashes at him. "Don't you want to know how I know all this?"

"No."

She laughed again. "Anatomy classes. Muscle and blood vessel diagrams. And dissections."

Not dissections. He moaned. "I was afraid you'd say that."

She lovingly wrapped her other hand about him. "I used to think the penis very boring, tedious and of no consequence whatsoever."

"The ignorance of our educated women is absolutely shocking."

"But now I have been re-educated." She smiled, almost coquettishly. "Now I look upon it as a feat of flesh-and-blood engineering."

He pulled her in for a kiss. Then quickly flipped them around so that she was underneath him. "My turn."

"Your turn for what?"

"For doing what you just did to me, a scientific examination of a certain body part."

"No!"

It was his turn to laugh. He used one hand to push her knee down, preventing her from clamping her legs together. "You know what I think about when I'm alone and you are far away?" he murmured. "I think about you, naked, under the sun."

He licked her nipple. She whimpered.

"Not the English sun, mind you, because it is never adequate. But the sun over the Arabian sea. Or the sun of the south of France. Light brilliant enough to shatter mirrors. And you, naked, in that light, your thighs open this wide—"

He pushed her thighs apart so much she gasped

again. And then panted, the sounds of heightened arousal. Music to his ears.

He took off his hands and sat back. She trembled, but her thighs remained open as he'd arranged them.

She was truly beautiful all over.

He kissed her there, inhaling her hungrily. His kiss turned into an openmouthed possession. She moaned and undulated, her hips soft, her thighs even softer, and her mysterious center the most heart-poundingly soft place he'd ever encountered.

And she came so beautifully, at once almost bashful and with complete abandon. He could not hold back. He was inside her in a heartbeat and immediately towed under by those currents of pleasure.

❧

She traced her finger over his brow bone. "You know what I think?"

"What do you think?"

"I think your beauty is your great misfortune."

"It got me you."

She smiled half in embarrassment, half in delight at his understanding of her. "True. But I still think it's a shame that when people look at you, they see only this gorgeous exterior. I can't wait until you are wizened and toothless, then people who meet you will be struck by your inner beauty."

"You sure they won't just be struck by my tooth-lessness instead?"

She was very sure. "No, inner beauty."

He blushed. There was such an adorable shyness to him. She didn't think she'd ever seen him look shy before.

"Thank you," he said softly. "It means a great deal to me that you think so."

"I love you," she said.

"Hmmm," he said. "I love your hair. I love your eyes. I love your shoulders. I love your arms. I love your breasts. I love your hips. I love your thighs. I love your—"

She put her hand over his mouth.

He removed her hand. "I love you madly."

She snuggled closer into him. "I like Cambridge."

"You haven't even seen Cambridge."

"I want to live here, in this house."

"And give up your practice? Cambridge doesn't offer the same assortment of opportunities London does for a lady doctor."

"It's only an hour to London by train."

"Each way," he reminded her.

"Time for me to read all the medical journals in English, French, and German, which I need to do anyway—and I read slowly in German."

"Let's also have a place in London, then. That

way, I can live in London between terms and you don't need to spend so much time traveling."

She thought about it. "I like that. Then we'll have time to play chess too."

Their future settled, they celebrated by making love again, more leisurely and tenderly, until all leisure and tenderness became forgotten and there was only hunger and urgency and need. And then, only glowing satisfaction.

❧

He dressed himself then coaxed her out of bed.

"It's almost two o'clock in the afternoon. You haven't had anything for lunch. Come, let's go get you something to eat."

He laced her corset, buttoned her jacket, and adjusted her collar so that it sat properly. "Now you almost don't look as if you've been shagged three times in a row."

She hit him with her hat before setting it on her head. But just as she was about to push her hat pin through it, he removed the hat again and caressed her hair where it was white and fragile.

"I've been meaning to ask you. Did I do this to you? Callista said I did."

She shook her head. "It was a freak happenstance,

though at that time I took it as a sign. I asked for the annulment the next day."

He sighed and pressed his lips to her white hair.

"Should I dye it?" she asked. "I dyed it for a year or so. Then the effort didn't seem to make much sense."

"No, don't dye it. It might be imperfect, but it is still lovely beyond words." A reflection of their story: imperfect, but to him the most beautiful of stories.

She gazed at him, her green eyes deep and luminous.

"I think you are right," she said, pulling him into a tight embrace. "It *is* lovely beyond words."

Epilogue

In the course of his long and illustrious career, the Honorable Quentin Leonidas Marsden, Lucasian Professor of Mathematics at Cambridge University, was the subject of numerous newspaper and magazine articles. For introduction, the articles usually brought up the astonishing papers he published while he was still a student at Cambridge, one or two of his more daring globe-trotting adventures, and the Victoria Cross he'd received as a civilian fighting in the Swat Valley Uprising of '97.

Some of the articles would also mention that he was married to the medical pioneer Bryony Asquith Marsden, though only one article, which appeared in an American magazine, ever ventured to relate that he'd married Mrs. Marsden not once, but twice.

It was also only in America that Professor Marsden

ever commented on the subject of his marriage in public. Or rather, he wrote about it, at the end of the brief biography that Princeton University always requested to be included in the printed programs for the lectures that he was invited to give there every few years.

Over the decades, the body of the brief biography changed to reflect his accomplishments and accolades. But the last paragraph, however, never changed. It always read thusly:

During terms, Professor Marsden lives in Cambridge with his wife, chess player extraordinaire and distinguished physician and surgeon Bryony Asquith Marsden. His favorite time of day is half past six in the evening, when he meets Mrs. Marsden's train at the station, as the latter returns from her day in London. On Sunday afternoons, rain or shine, Professor and Mrs. Marsden take a walk along The Backs, and treasure growing old together.

Author's Note

Coolies carrying a bathtub over difficult terrains? Native cooks serving European desserts on mountain treks? Had I read it in a book of fiction, I'd have scoffed at the author for lazy research—and transparent scheming for the use of the bathtub. But such had indeed been the case, according to *A Sportswoman in India: Personal Adventures and Experiences of Travel in Known and Unknown India* by Isabel Savory, a fascinating glimpse into not only the common touring practices at the very end of the nineteenth century, but the fierce, opinionated independence of the woman who authored it.

In the April 27, 1901, issue of the *New York Medical Journal,* in an article documenting women physicians holding hospital appointments in the United

States and the British Empire, the following was said of the New Hospital for Women in London: "Staff consists of 41 physicians and surgeons, of whom 28 are women, holding the following appointments: 4 consulting staff, 5 physicians and surgeons for in-patients, 6 physicians and surgeons for out-patients, 6 clinical assistants, 2 ophthalmic surgeons, 3 anesthetists, 1 pathologist, 3 resident assistant medical officers." (The numbers don't add up to 28, as a select few physicians and surgeons probably held multiple appointments.)

In the second half of 1897 multiple uprisings broke out in the vast geographical area referred to as the North-West Frontier of India. Guess which ambitious young journalist got himself to the front as soon as possible to cover the uprising in the Swat Valley? None other than twenty-two-year-old Winston Churchill himself, who later published his account as *The Story of the Malakand Field Force*.

Will and Matthew Marsden first appeared in my book *Delicious*, with the irrepressible Will as the secondary hero. I'd given Will four brothers in order for his lady, who didn't know any of the younger Marsden sons, to plausibly mistake him for Matthew in some respects. Then, once *Not Quite a*

Not Quite a Husband

Husband reached the casting stage, I knew I needed a younger hero so I thought to myself, hey, why not the baby Marsden? And thus was born my first two interconnected books.

About the Author

Sherry Thomas burst onto the romance scene with *Private Arrangements,* one of the most anticipated historical romance debuts in recent history and a *Publishers Weekly* Best of the Year book. Lisa Kleypas calls her "the most powerfully original historical romance author working today." Her books have received stellar reviews from *Publishers Weekly, Library Journal, Chicago Tribune,* and *Romantic Times,* along with enthusiastic praise from many of the most highly trafficked romance review websites and blogs.

Her story is all the more interesting given that English is Sherry's second language—she has come a long way from the days when she made her laborious way through Rosemary Rogers's *Sweet Savage Love* with an English-Chinese dictionary. She enjoys creating stories. And when she is not writing, she thinks about the Zen and zaniness of her profession, plays computer games with her sons, and reads as many fabulous books as she can find.

www.sherrythomas.com

SHERRY THOMAS is
"the most powerfully original historical romance
author writing today!"—Lisa Kleypas

PRIVATE ARRANGEMENTS

To all of London society, Lord and Lady Tremaine had the perfect marriage—but that was because husband and wife resided on separate continents. Once upon a time, though, things were quite different for the Tremaines. When Gigi Rowland first laid eyes on Camden Saybrook, the attraction was immediate. But what began in a spark of passion ended in betrayal the morning after their wedding. Now Gigi wants to be free to marry again—but when Camden returns from America with an outrageous demand for her freedom, secrets will be exposed, desire rekindled . . . and one of London's most admired couples must fall in love all over again or let each other go forever.

DELICIOUS

Famous in Paris, infamous in London, Verity Durant is as well known for her mouthwatering cuisine as for her scandalous love life. But to rising political star Stuart Somerset, Verity is just a name and food is just food, until her first dish touches his lips. Only once before had he known such pure arousal—a dangerous night of passion with a stranger ten years earlier. But Verity's past has a secret that could devour them both even as they reach for the most delicious fruit of all. . . .

Available from Bantam Books